The Prettier Sister

Suzanne G. Rogers

...

Idunn Court Publishing

Idunn Court Publishing
7 Ramshorn Court
Savannah, GA 31411

First print edition, July 2022

ISBN: 978-1-947463-53-0

Published in the United States of America
Editor: Kathy Riley Miller
Cover Design: Suzanne G. Rogers

Printed in the United States of America

This book is dedicated to
Patrice & George B.

Suzanne G. Rogers

Chapter One
The Prettier Sister

Bromley, England • April 1886

Melanie emerged from the best milliner in town and turned to admire her reflection in the mullioned display window behind her. Her new hat framed her face beautifully, in her opinion, and the pastel colors of the lining and ribbons flattered her complexion. The spring morning was filled with possibilities, so anything could happen. Hopefully, the day would unfold with all manner of delightful events.

"Miss Starhope!"

The familiar voice came from across the street and Melanie felt a tingle of anticipation. Evidently, her hat had brought her luck more quickly than she could ever have imagined. When she waved at the handsome young man, he grinned in response and leaped into the street in a headlong fashion. His herculean efforts to dodge oncoming carriages and horses as he made his way across the thoroughfare sent a rush of pleasurable sensations down her spine, but she made every effort to compose herself.

When he joined her at last, he removed his hat and sketched a shallow bow. "I count myself fortunate to see you in town, Miss Starhope."

"Hello, Mr. Jones." She smiled." It's a beautiful day, is it not?"

"It's an incredibly fine spring we're having."

She glanced at him from underneath her lashes. "It gave me a turn to watch you brave the traffic."

"I would have braved a bull-run to speak with you." His eyes flickered toward the confection of feathers, flowers, and ribbons on her white straw hat. "You look unusually well, may I say."

Her heart seemed to skip a beat. "Thank you, sir. A new bonnet makes all the difference to a girl."

"Well, that particular one is certainly pretty enough to suit you." His dimples made her knees grow weak. "By any chance, is your younger sister with you today?"

Her smile froze. "Why, yes. Blanche is still in the milliner's shop."

The young man's gaze slid past Melanie as he peered through the window behind her. His expression brightened as he spotted the object of his search. "Ah, yes! She's leaving just now."

He hastened over to the door and wrenched it open. As a beautiful, dainty blonde swept past, his color rose. "Good morning, Miss Blanche."

She acknowledged the greeting with a flirtatious giggle. "Good morning, Mr. Jones." She turned a pirouette in front of the shop. "Do you like my new hat?"

"Oh, yes. No one in town has one quite so lovely, I imagine."

Despite Melanie's best efforts, her smile slipped.

Blanche's eyelashes fluttered. "I'm glad you think so, Mr. Jones. If you hadn't approved of it, I would have taken the hat straight back inside and exchanged it for another."

As the two exchanged more nonsensical pleasantries, Melanie felt like a fifth wheel. "If you two will excuse me, I have an errand at the bookshop."

She dipped into the briefest of curtsies before striding away. Although her head was held high, tears stung her eyelids. Mr. Jones was one of the best-looking gentlemen of her acquaintance and possessed an engaging personality as well. For a few long, breathless moments, she'd believed he might have developed an interest in her. As usual, however, her hopes had been cruelly extinguished.

Melanie entered the bookshop and headed for a shelf of gothic novels. Perhaps if she immersed herself in a lurid story, she could take her mind off her disappointment.

At length, Blanche appeared at her elbow and gave her a pout. "Why did you have to leave me alone with Mr. Jones? He's far too agreeable for my liking."

"You must be joking." Melanie leveled a glance at her sister. "You gave every indication of enjoying his conversation."

Blanche shrugged. "I was merely being polite."

Melanie made a noncommittal sound and returned to perusing her novel.

Her sister sighed. "That's right...I'd forgotten how much you liked Mr. Jones."

"Hush! Voices carry in here." Horrified, Melanie glanced around to see if anyone was within earshot. "At any rate, you're quite wrong. I've not formed an attachment to him."

"That's a relief. I wouldn't want to be accused of interfering." Blanche's violet eyes flickered toward the novel in Melanie's hand. "Vampires? Mama says books like that are decadent. Why do you read them?"

"You needn't turn up your nose. At least I read."

"You have a point. Nevertheless, I've always felt extensive reading is for bluestockings." Blanche tugged on Melanie's sleeve. "Buy your silly novel and let's go. Mrs. Hines is making chicken salad for lunch and I'm starving."

"I'll make my selection far more quickly if you are not pulling on me, dearest." Melanie eased her arm from Blanche's grip. "You can wait for me outside, if you prefer."

"I'll be in the scent shop next door, picking out a new bottle of eau de toilette."

As her younger sister flounced off, the white ostrich feathers on her hat swayed in an alluring fashion. Melanie brushed aside a wave of annoyance. After all, it was not Blanche's fault that every eligible gentleman in town was drawn to her. Even so, she could not help but find the situation increasingly tiresome.

As she approached the register with her book, she overheard two ladies in the reading corner, engaged in a whispered conversation.

"Did you see Miss Blanche leaving just now? That girl has the face of an angel."

"I pity her elder sister. She is a sweet young lady, but she can't hold a candle to Miss Blanche."

Melanie bit the inside of her cheek so hard, she tasted blood. Her hands trembled as she slid money across the counter along with the novel. "D-Don't bother to wrap it, Mrs. Orvis. I'm pressed for time."

The older woman cast a disapproving eye toward the gossips in the corner. "I'm sure they don't mean any harm," she murmured.

Melanie forced a smile to her lips. "I'm sure you're right."

She picked up the novel and left the shop, glad her new bonnet shielded her embarrassment somewhat. Her face felt hot from a painful blush and she was absolutely certain her cheeks were as red as a beet. The nasty remark she'd heard was humiliating, admittedly — but not untrue. Melanie did not consider herself unattractive, but she felt completely overshadowed whenever Blanche was nearby. Oh, why did she have the misfortune to be related to the prettiest girl in three counties?

When she entered the scent shop, her sister was just leaving.

"There you are!" Blanche beamed. "I thought you might stay in the bookshop longer."

"I found what I wanted, so there was no reason to linger."

As they made their way toward their gig, Blanche fished a small package from her carry-all and pressed it into Melanie's hands. "This bottle of eau de cologne is for you. I know how much you like gardenias."

Melanie peered at her. "That's very kind, but there's no occasion that calls for a gift."

"I know, but I feel a trifle guilty." Blanche lowered her voice. "Despite what you said, I know how much you like Mr. Jones."

"Then why did you flirt with him?"

"I know I shouldn't have, but I can't seem to help it. If someone is nice to me, I wish to be nice in return."

Although Melanie accepted the gift with a smile, she was in no way mollified. As long as Blanche remained unmarried, Melanie's future romantic prospects were likely to be riddled with similar events. Even after her sister was wed, however, Melanie would never be sure if any of her potential beaux were merely settling for second best.

"How ghastly," she murmured.

Melanie didn't intend to speak aloud, but apparently Blanche mistook her meaning.

"Don't I know it!" Her sister tossed her head. "Gentlemen are always so attentive and pleasant, I spend all my time reciprocating. I never seem to have enough time for myself!"

"I wouldn't talk that way if I were you." She gave Blanche a sidelong glance. "People might mistake you for someone who is vain."

••••

Three Weeks Later

Mr. Starhope glanced through the morning post and gasped, "Merciful heavens."

Both Melanie and Blanche glanced up from eating breakfast.

Mrs. Starhope put down her fork. "What is it, James?"

"I've had a letter from *Genevieve*." He said the name as if it were a shocking event.

Mrs. Starhope grimaced. "Oh, dear."

As Mr. Starhope opened the letter and began reading the contents, Melanie felt a warm furry body brush up against her ankle. She cut a piece of kipper on her plate and surreptitiously lowered it toward the floor. After she felt tiny teeth take the morsel of food from her fingertips, she wiped them on her napkin.

"You're not feeding that cat at the table again, are you?" Her mother's blue eyes met Melanie's. "You know I don't approve."

"I'm sorry, Mama."

Melanie pretended to be abashed, but when she heard the sound of her cat's purr, she couldn't suppress a smile. In short order, another piece of kipper found its way to Penguin's belly.

"I've never met Aunt Genevieve." Blanche wrinkled her nose. "Is she so very disagreeable?"

"I wouldn't say she's disagreeable." Mrs. Starhope stirred a teaspoon of sugar into her tea. "Genevieve can be quite pleasant — as long as she gets her way."

"I met Aunt Genevieve once when Grandpapa passed on and then again at her wedding to Mr. Hornsby." Melanie spooned a bit of fried apples onto her toast. "She was a beautiful bride." Penguin darted under her skirts and draped herself over her slipper-clad foot.

Blanche cocked her head. "I don't remember Grandpapa — or Grandmama, for that matter — and I don't recall attending Aunt Genevieve's wedding."

"You were an infant back then." Melanie focused her gaze on her father. "Is everything all right, Papa?"

"I'm not entirely certain." He tossed the letter to the table. "Your aunt has asked you to visit her over the summer."

Blanche groaned. "But I don't *want* to leave Bromley just now! All manner of entertaining things are planned for the summer and now that I'm of age, I'm finally old enough to attend. In fact, Mr. Jones offered to escort me to the Easter recital at church."

Had he, indeed? Annoyed, Melanie hid her pique behind her napkin.

"You needn't miss a thing." Her father chuckled. "Ginny has asked Melanie, not you."

Blanche recoiled. "What? How horribly rude of her! I have just as much right to visit Aunt Genevieve as Melly does."

He lifted an eyebrow. "Not if you aren't invited."

She tossed her head. "That's beside the point entirely. Aunt Genevieve should have invited both of us and then I could have politely declined — or not, whichever way I chose."

Melanie gave her a level glance. "You are quite impossible."

"Not really. I just don't like to be left out." Blanche paused. "Where does Aunt Genevieve live?"

Mr. Starhope cut into a sausage. "Ledbury."

"What?" Blanche burst out laughing. "Better Melanie should go than me, then. Ledbury is *hours* away from London by rail."

Mr. Starhope frowned. "Ledbury is quite a beautiful little town. Since you've never been there, I cannot imagine why you are sneering at it."

Blanche shrugged. "Nothing exciting ever happens in the country."

"We live an hour from London by train." Mrs. Starhope gave her younger daughter a pointed glance. "Some people would say we're in the country."

"There is no comparison." Blanche shook her head. "Ledbury is over three times the distance away from London as we are!"

Melanie glanced at her father. "Have I your permission to go, Papa?"

"I suppose so." He gave her a concerned smile. "The entire summer is a long time for a visit, especially when you'll be so far from home. Won't you be a trifled bored?"

"Not at all." Melanie smiled. "I daresay I'll make some new friends and have a jolly time." Penguin rolled over and stretched.

"Hmph!" Blanche crossed her arms and pouted. "I shall write Aunt Genevieve and ask if I may come along."

"That's not a bad idea, really." Mr. Starhope rubbed his chin. "Actually, it would be better if you go in Melanie's stead."

Melanie's eyes widened. "Why is that, Papa?"

"If my sister takes a liking to Blanche, she might be apt to sponsor her for a Season or two in London. I'm afraid I cannot manage it on my own."

"Why should Blanche have a Season in London, Papa?" Melanie shook her head. "I'm older, after all."

He shrugged. "Between the two of you, Blanche is apt to make the better match."

Stung, Melanie fixed her gaze on her plate.

"James!" Mrs. Starhope glared at her husband. "How could you say such a thing about Melanie?"

"Forgive me, but I'm merely being practical." He offered her a conciliatory smile. "Life has seen fit to give us two pretty daughters, but you must admit Blanche's looks are unusually fine. That, along with her youth, ought to tempt several wealthy gentlemen into making her an offer."

Blanche giggled. "Thank you, Papa."

Melanie struggled to keep her temper. "I think Blanche *should* go to Ledbury in my stead." She nodded at her sister. "You needn't worry about missing anything exciting here. After every party or gathering, I'll send you a letter with all the details. It will be almost as if you are in both places at once."

Her sister scoffed. "Thank you for offering to trade with me, but Aunt Genevieve invited *you*. You can write to me from Ledbury while I'm having fun in Bromley." Her eyes suddenly flashed with merriment. "I expect to hear from you about every milk stool that's kicked over by a cow."

Her sister's smug manner was infuriating but Melanie covered her irritation with a dismissive wave of her hand. "I would never bother to write about anything so mundane."

Either Blanche failed to hear the cool note in Melanie's reply or she chose to ignore it. Either way, she craned her neck toward the sideboard. "Have we any more sausages?"

"Your father ate the last one, I'm afraid, but we have plenty of bacon."

Mr. Starhope peered at Blanche. "Are you certain you wish to stay in Bromley?"

"Absolutely certain." Blanche rose. "I would refuse to leave, if it comes to that."

As she hastened toward the sideboard, he sighed. "As you wish."

Mrs. Starhope shook her head. "James, I don't know when you can make time to escort Melanie to Ledbury. Our social schedule is extraordinarily full these days."

"Ginny wrote to say she will come for Melanie at half past one o'clock on the first of June."

His wife's eyes widened. "She's to escort Melanie to Ledbury personally?"

"Unfortunately."

Mrs. Starhope gulped. "She doesn't mean to stay in Bromley for a few days, does she? Our home is comfortable, but Ginny is likely accustomed to grander accommodations."

"Her letter says no, but you should make up a room, just in case."

Mr. Starhope's trepidation at his sister's impending arrival piqued Melanie's curiosity. "If I may ask, what is the nature of your disagreement with Aunt Genevieve?"

"The less said about it, the better." Mr. Starhope tucked his napkin by his plate and rose from his chair. "If you'll excuse me, I should answer Ginny right away." He picked up the letter and strode from the room.

Blanche returned to the table with a plate full of bacon and began folding it into her mouth, two pieces at a time.

"Mama, tell me about Aunt Genevieve's husband." Melanie leaned forward. "I barely remember anything about Uncle Reginald except that he wore several rings on his fingers and he was extraordinarily good-looking. Is he affable?"

"Oh, he died years ago — in Greece."

"Died?" Melanie blinked. "Was it an accident?"

"Natural causes, the newspaper said." Mrs. Starhope frowned. "By then, our relationship with Ginny had become so strained, we only found out about it from reading the London *Times*."

Blanche wiped her fingers on her napkin. "Aunt Genevieve is far too young to be a widow."

"Yes, but at least she's an exceedingly wealthy widow. I believe she's..." Mrs. Starhope screwed up her face as she worked a sum out in her head, "...thirty-five."

Blanche looked dismayed. "That's ancient!"

Her mother laughed. "I'm sure to a girl who is barely eighteen, thirty-five seems ancient. Ginny is fully twelve years younger than your father."

Melanie's eyebrows drew together. "She has no children?"

"None."

"That's sad." A pang of pity brought a frown to Melanie's lips. "Aunt Genevieve must be very lonely."

Blanche wrinkled her nose. "I don't want to get any older than I am now. I want to be young and pretty, always, so my husband is always madly in love with me."

"Nobody can hold back the hands of time, dearest." Mrs. Starhope gave her a fond smile. "You'd best marry a man who admires who you are on the inside as well as on the outside."

"A man like that doesn't exist." She tossed her napkin on the table. "If you'll excuse me, I'm finished with breakfast. I'm going to pay Theodora Loomis a visit."

Blanche disappeared down the hall, leaving Melanie and her mother alone. Mrs. Starhope's expression was etched with concern. "Are you absolutely sure about accepting Genevieve's invitation? You'll mingle with far more gentlemen if you stay in Bromley."

"Quite sure, Mama." Melanie took a bite of breakfast cake, heartened by the prospect of a lengthy visit elsewhere. In a new town, no one would compare her to Blanche. Indeed, for the first time in a long while, she'd be judged on her own merits. She took another bite of breakfast cake and let the sweetness linger on her tongue. Surely, freedom would taste even sweeter.

●●●●

June 1, 1886

On the day of Aunt Genevieve's impending arrival, an atmosphere of nervous anticipation filled the

Starhope residence. Mrs. Starhope dropped her fork twice at breakfast, Mr. Starhope stared at the newspaper seemingly without reading it, the maid bustled about with a strained expression, and Penguin was nowhere to be found. Only Blanche was seemingly unaffected, although she chafed at being restricted to the house.

"Why can't I walk into town?" She pouted. "I'll be back before lunch, I promise!"

Her mother gave her youngest daughter a level glance. "If your aunt should happen to arrive early, you won't be here to welcome her."

"Why? It's not as if she gives a fig about me."

Mr. Starhope lowered his newspaper. "Blanche, everyone in this family must do their part today."

Blanche made a face. "It's only Aunt Genevieve who's coming, not Her Majesty!"

"You may be excused from the table." He jerked his head toward the door.

Her eyes widened. "But I haven't finished eating!"

"Now."

"Oh, all right." Blanche brought her napkin to the sideboard on her way out and scooped up a handful of bacon and several pieces of toast.

Mrs. Starhope gaped. "Blanche!"

Undeterred, Blanche merely scampered from the dining room with her booty wrapped in the napkin.

Melanie sighed. "I'm sorry everyone is on edge."

"Nobody is on edge." Her father rattled his paper. "Certainly not I."

Mrs. Starhope nodded at Melanie. "After breakfast, please check to make sure fresh flowers have been put in the spare room. We don't know if your aunt is planning to stay, but we'd best be prepared."

Melanie smiled her assent. "Yes, Mama."

After breakfast, Melanie made her way to the guest room, only to discover a vase of summer flowers and greenery had been set out on the dresser. As she turned to leave, Blanche joined her.

"I wish I had a pinecone to leave under Aunt Genevieve's pillow."

Melanie made a sound of disbelief. "I don't understand why everyone seems to feel so much acrimony toward a blood relative. For mercy's sake, you've never laid eyes on the woman."

"If Papa doesn't like her, that's good enough for me." Blanche dove onto the bed and kicked up her feet. "I feel quite sorry for you."

"You needn't bother. I'm glad to be going."

Her sister sat up and peered at her. "You are?"

"I am." Melanie gestured toward the bed. "Please smooth the coverlet before you leave."

She hastened to her room to check that she hadn't failed to pack something she might need. To her dismay, Blanche followed her inside and plopped down in a chair.

"Aren't you going to miss me, even a little?"

"Of course, but I should think you'd be glad to be the only Starhope daughter for a little while. You'll have the undivided attention of every eligible gentleman in Bromley." Melanie peeked inside her handbag. "Be sure to be nice to Penguin while I'm gone."

"I'm not sure the cat likes me, but I'll try." Blanche frowned. "You'll write to tell me of your adventures, won't you?"

"If I have any."

"You will, I just know it. Between the two of us, you've always been more intrepid."

Melanie laughed. "I'll take that as a compliment." The sound of a tinkling bell reached her ears. "Is that someone at the front door?"

"Oh, no. Mama was right and Aunt Genevieve has come early!" Blanche rushed over to the cheval mirror and swatted at the fabric on her bodice. "Ugh...I'm covered with toast crumbs!"

"That's your own fault."

Blanche met Melanie's gaze in the mirror. "Well, what was I to do when Papa sent me away from the table? I saw no reason to be hungry just because he's in a state."

The reply sent Melanie into a fit of giggles. "I needn't worry about you while I'm away. You always seem to be able to take care of yourself."

The maid appeared in the doorway. "Begging your pardon, but you're both wanted in the parlor. Mrs. Hornsby has come."

Blanche squealed and began smoothing her hair.

Melanie caught the maid's eye. "Velma, did Mrs. Hornsby arrive with any luggage?"

"No, Miss Starhope." The young woman curtsied before disappearing down the hall.

"Aunt Genevieve isn't staying, then. What good news!" In the next moment, Blanche's shoulders slumped. "I suppose this means you'll be leaving right away, then. I don't know what I'll do without you."

Melanie crossed over to pat her sister's cheek. "Take heart, dear. Consider that whatever clothes I've left behind in my room are yours to borrow."

Her sister brightened. "Really?" She darted toward the closet.

Melanie grabbed her by the elbow and tugged her toward the door. "You can look through my things later. Right now, come downstairs and greet Aunt Genevieve."

Blanche's eyebrows drew together. "Do I have crumbs?"

Melanie glanced over her sister's gown. "You are crumb-free."

They made their way to the stairs. As she descended alongside Blanche, Melanie heard her mother's voice in the entryway.

"Surely, you'd be more comfortable in the parlor?"

A female voice, rich and vibrant, replied. "I'm quite comfortable where I am, thank you."

Mr. Starhope cleared his throat. "Perhaps you'd like a cup of tea to clear the dust?"

"I won't have time for a cup of tea, James. I'll be leaving just as soon as Melanie's trunks are loaded into the cab."

After a few more steps, Melanie caught her first glimpse of her aunt. The woman was a stunning beauty by any measure, with an oval face, creamy complexion, and regular features. Although her hair was largely covered by her fashionable hat, the wavy fringe across her forehead was a lustrous chestnut color. Aunt Genevieve wore a travel suit in sober charcoal, but her waistline was impossible tiny and her feminine curves were enhanced by the bolero-style jacket. As the two sisters reached the bottom of the stairs, she gave them both an appraising glance.

"You're the elder daughter, Melanie." Her eyes focused on Blanche. "And you're the younger. I think I understand better now."

Blanche frowned. "I'm not sure to what you are referring, Aunt?"

"It's of little consequence, dear." Aunt Genevieve gestured toward Melanie. "Get your things and we'll be off."

The woman stood by with a passive expression as the Starhope family made their good-byes. After Melanie donned her hat and a lightweight travel cloak, she accompanied her aunt from the house and climbed into the waiting cab. Once they were settled and the cab was on its way, Aunt Genevieve's posture relaxed, and she gave Melanie a beaming smile.

"I'm so glad you wrote to ask me for a visit. We're going to have a great deal of fun together."

"Thank you for not giving me away to Mama and Papa just now. I'm not sure they would have approved had they known I'd written to you first."

Her aunt reached over to pat Melanie's hand. "What they don't know won't hurt them." Her eyes twinkled. "What would you say if we spent a week or so in London before traveling on to Ledbury? I have a home on Eaton Square and the staff is awaiting our arrival."

Melanie gasped with delight. "I would love a holiday in London, Aunt!"

"I was hoping you might." Ginny smiled. "I've already procured tickets to several performances this week. Since it's the height of the Season, we'll be surrounded by the *ton*."

"I-I hope I'm not expected to wear anything grand. I packed my best gowns but the standards in Bromley are quite a bit lower than London society might expect."

"You needn't worry about a thing, my dear. I've already made an appointment with the best modiste in town. Madame Montagna always has a few sample evening gowns available and I'm sure she will make you look your best."

Melanie's spirits soared... until she remembered her manners. "Aunt, your generosity is overwhelming. I'm terribly grateful for everything."

"We can't have you overshadowed by your sister, can we?" Aunt Genevieve gave her a sidelong glance. "From your letter, I'd expected your looks to be lackluster. I'm glad to be wrong."

"I don't think of myself as plain, but it is difficult to shine when I'm standing next to the sun."

"Blanche is terribly pretty, to be sure, but I suspect you have far more depth and imagination."

"To be fair, I *am* nearly four years older. Therefore, I've had time to mature."

"I'm in no mood to be fair." Aunt Genevieve tossed her head. "While we are in London, you and I shall fill our time with all manner of adventures. It's never too late or too early to live life to the fullest."

Melanie giggled. "Huzzah!"

••••

Three Days Later • Bromley

Blanche's eyebrows drew together as she read Melanie's letter at breakfast. "Blazes."

"Is anything amiss?" Her mother cocked her head. "Surely, your sister hasn't gotten into trouble so soon after leaving Bromley?"

"Ginny and I may not see eye to eye, but I'm convinced she's taking excellent care of our daughter." Mr. Starhope's interjection held a note of reproach.

Mrs. Starhope gave him a level glance. "I didn't mean to suggest otherwise, James, but Blanche seems exceedingly put out by Melanie's letter."

He peered at Blanche. "Why *are* you making such a face this early in the day?"

"Penguin scratched me this morning." Her lips turned down at the corners. "Furthermore, I feel neglected!"

Mrs. Starhope looked at her askance. "I can't imagine why."

"Melanie is to stay with Aunt Genevieve at her Eaton Square residence for a fortnight before they travel on to Ledbury. They are shopping for clothes, attending the theater, and going for carriage rides on Rotten Row. They even saw *The Mikado* at the Savoy Theatre." Blanche tossed the missive aside. "I *knew* I should have traded places with Melanie!"

Mrs. Starhope frowned. "Your attitude is not at all gracious. I'm glad Melanie is to have a wonderful holiday."

"Yes, but I'm stuck in Bromley!"

"Quite so." Mr. Starhope returned to his newspaper. "I suggest you make the most of it."

Blanche's face lit up. "Do you suppose we could travel to London for *The Mikado?*"

Mr. and Mrs. Starhope spoke at the same time. *"No."*

Suzanne G. Rogers

Chapter Two
Dazzling Spinsters

As Paddington Station came into view, Aunt Genevieve gave Melanie a glance. "Are you sorry to be leaving London?"

"A bit. I've never had a fortnight filled with such excitement before in my life." Melanie smiled. "Even so, I'm looking forward to seeing your home. Perhaps it will be nice to go somewhere more sedate for a while."

"Ledbury will fit the bill, I think."

Once the cab arrived at the station, Aunt Genevieve stepped onto the curb as if she were a general commanding a battlefield. She paid the driver and summoned a porter with such confidence and aplomb that Melanie stood back in admiration. The porter stacked a mountain of trunks, bags, hatboxes, and travel cases onto a trolly and followed Aunt Genevieve and Melanie into the station. Melanie's trunks had grown in number since leaving Bromley. Never before had she been allowed to shop to her heart's content, without regard to expense. Furthermore, guided by her aunt's expert advice, everything she bought was both flattering and fashionable. Melanie had donned one of her purchases for the journey to Ledbury, in fact, and she felt like a duchess.

After Aunt Genevieve bought their tickets, they continued on toward their platform along with the porter. Melanie noticed a particularly well-dressed group of travelers heading through the station. It was not their fine clothes that drew her notice as much as their air of general disdain and arrogant demeanor.

"Oh, my." Melanie spoke under her breath. "I'm not sure whether or not I should bow or scrape."

"Aristocrats, likely arriving in London to join the Season." Aunt Genevieve lifted her chin. "Never let anyone intimidate you, my dear."

"I'll try."

A group of dirty, raggedly dressed children mobbed the aristocrats, begging them for money. More than one pocket was picked in Melanie's presence, although the authorities hastened over to shoo the little criminals away.

Aunt Genevieve gestured toward a newsstand nearby. "Shall we buy something to read?" Her expression became mischievous. "I rather enjoy lurid novels."

Melanie nodded. "So do I — especially ones about vampires."

"Oh, yes. Vampire tales are the best ones." She beckoned to the porter and pressed money into his hand. "Please take our luggage to the platform and make sure it gets loaded onto the train. We'll be there momentarily."

The man touched the brim of his cap. "Yes, miss."

Melanie accompanied her aunt to the newsstand. A few minutes later, as she perused the sparse selection of penny dreadfuls available for purchase, she felt a tug on her skirt.

"Please, miss. Have you a spare penny?"

The thin, reedy voice came from a slender young girl whose eyes were too large for her face. Melanie reached into her handbag and gave the child a shilling.

The girl gasped with delight as she clutched the money in her hand. "All for me?"

"All for you." Melanie smiled. "I noticed a cart outside the station selling meat pasties. Perhaps you might get something to eat?"

"Yes, miss!" The thin creature darted off.

Aunt Genevieve glanced over and shook her head. "You have a good heart, dear, but that money won't really help much."

"Perhaps not, but at least the child knows someone cares."

After the two women purchased their reading materials, they continued on to the train platform.

Aunt Genevieve checked her pocket watch. "We're a trifle early." She sank down on a bench to wait.

As Melanie settled next to her aunt, she was unsettled. "It makes me feel terrible to know children must set to thieving and begging to survive. They deserve better."

"Yes, they do. Unfortunately, you could spend every penny you have and still make no difference. Many charitable people and institutions have tried to eradicate poverty, but no one has succeeded yet."

Melanie's shoulders moved up and down in a shrug. "I'm extraordinarily fortunate. I've never gone hungry or wanted for a pair of shoes."

Aunt Genevieve reached out to touch Melanie's hand. "And I'm fortunate to have such a kind niece who cares about something other than hair ribbons and baubles."

Melanie laughed. "I confess, I think about hair ribbons and baubles as well."

"It's good to have a broad range of interests." Aunt Genevieve winked.

A short while later, the train to Ledbury arrived and they took their First Class seats in a private car. When the train finally got underway, Melanie waited until London was behind them before fishing her new novel from her carryall. As she turned to the first page, however, a question popped into her mind.

"Aunt, did you ever have a London Season?"

Genevieve lifted her eyes from the pages of her penny dreadful. "I never had the pleasure, I'm afraid."

Melanie cocked her head. "If that's the case, how did you meet your husband?"

The woman focused on the scenery. "The match was arranged." She paused. "When I turned eighteen, your father insisted I marry Mr. Hornsby. Our parents had passed away by then and James was head of the household."

Melanie struggled for a response. "Forgive me, Aunt Ginny. I don't mean to pry."

"No, I'm glad you asked." Genevieve's lips tightened. "It's only natural you should be curious about the rift between James and I. To be fair, James might have believed he was doing the right thing. Reginald Hornsby was very wealthy and was expected to inherit a viscountcy."

"I didn't realize your husband was a peer."

"He died before he could inherit the title." Genevieve shrugged. "That unfortunate event was a great disappointment to my brother."

Melanie frowned. "I gather you never cared for Mr. Hornsby?"

"His interests lay elsewhere. I found out later that he married me to quiet certain rumors about his predilections." A note of bitterness crept into Genevieve's voice. "Reginald lived in Greece for most of our marriage and I was obliged to create a life for myself alone."

"I'm sorry."

Genevieve brightened. "Don't be. I've been rather happy, really."

"Yet, you cannot forgive Papa?"

"No." The woman's smile slipped. "The gentleman I had hoped to wed settled down with another bride. James knew I was in love and yet forced me into a marriage in name only. I've been waiting for years to hear an apology from him." Her laughter was soft. "I suppose I will never get any satisfaction in that regard."

Melanie averted her gaze. "It won't make you feel any better, but I apologize on his behalf."

"You're a sweet girl and I suspect you take after me." Genevieve beamed. "We shall be very jolly, you and I."

A wave of gratitude swept over Melanie. "You're very gracious. I shall endeavor to be the best company possible."

Her aunt's eyes danced with merriment. "I'm glad."

••••

They changed trains once more to begin the last leg of the journey and as they passed through the beautiful Malvern Hills, with its gentle peaks and serene green pastures, Melanie was increasingly glad she'd come.

Sooner than she had anticipated, the train arrived in Ledbury. As Melanie stepped onto the platform, she was taken aback by the tiny size of the railway station.

"Where is the rest of it?"

Genevieve laughed at her expression. "The station *is* a trifle small, especially when compared to Paddington or even Bromley."

"It's…" She cast about for something positive to say. "Well, the railway station isn't overly large, to be sure, but it *is* very attractive. I'm sure it serves the community very well."

"That it does."

After a porter brought around their luggage, Genevieve hired the only cab parked out front and gave the driver her address. As the cab lurched forward, Melanie focused her attention on the manicured hedgerows, lush trees, and bucolic pastures visible through the carriage window. The scenery was lovely, but not a single house came into view.

"Where is the town, Aunt?"

"In the opposite direction."

"Oh?" She swallowed. "I-I didn't realize you lived so far from Ledbury."

"Since it's summer, you'll have good weather for walking, at least." Genevieve winked. "I'm joking, of course. I have a full-size carriage as well as a pony trap."

Melanie's mood began to deflate, but she reminded herself to remain cheerful. She'd painted a picture in her mind's eye that had included an expansive, luxurious home with lovely grounds, a nearby town bustling with activity, and a life of ease and excitement. Compared to those fantastic notions, reality was bound to fall short of the mark.

"I'm glad Blanche isn't here." She sighed. "On closer inspection, I don't think Ledbury would have suited her at all."

"She is better off where she is."

When the cab turned into her aunt's drive, Melanie was dismayed at the sight of a modest Tudor dwelling up ahead. "Is that your home?"

Genevieve waved a dismissive hand. "That's the groundskeeper's cottage. It's very neat and tidy, don't you think?"

"Yes." Melanie tried to hide her relief. "It looks cozy."

The driveway continued to rise and once the cab passed a copse of trees, the main house came into view. Melanie gaped at the three-story red brick building dotted with mullioned windows and topped with numerous chimneys.

"Oh, my."

Genevieve's expression was one of pride. "While my husband lived, the estate was called Garden Manor. I thought the name rather dull, so once the property became mine, I renamed it Asphodel."

"I love it."

The cab drove through a decorative gatehouse and came to a stop in the courtyard in front of the residence. The front door was topped by an impressive triangular pediment, and two potted topiaries rested on either side. As the driver opened the cab door, several servants poured from the house and assembled in a line.

A butler approached. "Welcome home, Mrs. Hornsby."

"Thank you, Newman." Genevieve surveyed her staff as she gestured toward Melanie. "This is my niece, Miss Starhope. Please make her feel at home."

The housekeeper and maids curtsied, and the footmen bowed.

"Newman, put Miss Starhope's things in the pink room and inform Cook we'll be two for luncheon."

"Yes, Mrs. Hornsby."

"I'm glad you've come." Genevieve linked her arm with Melanie's. "Shall we go inside?"

"I'm looking forward to it, Aunt."

As Melanie stepped into the house, she discovered the imposing two-story entryway was both elegant and warm at the same time. She was struck by the many exquisite landscapes decorating the walls — some in oil and others in watercolor.

After Melanie gave her travel cloak, gloves, and hat to a maid, she focused on the artwork again. "These paintings are beautiful, I must say."

"Thank you." Genevieve gestured toward a watercolor of a mare and colt grazing in a field. "I finished this one just last month."

"You painted all of these?" Melanie gaped. "You're extraordinarily talented."

"You're too kind, I think, but painting has always relaxed me." She gave her things to the maid as well. "Shall we see the gardens first?"

Genevieve escorted Melanie down a long hallway which led to a brick patio. A neatly tended flower garden spread out across the grounds, lending the lovely view additional color and texture.

Genevieve gestured toward a white fenced area off to one side. "That's a vegetable garden." She pointed to a wing of the house. "I completed construction on that part of Asphodel about five years ago. I keep an art studio there and that glassed-in section at the end is a conservatory."

"You have a conservatory?"

Genevieve nodded. "I wanted to be able to grow things year-round."

"Our garden in Bromley is nothing compared to yours and we don't have room for a conservatory." Melanie shook her head. "I'm so impressed!"

"I'm glad you will have the opportunity to enjoy it."

"Asphodel is truly magnificent, Aunt." Melanie made no effort to conceal her admiration. "I can't wait to see the conservatory from the inside."

"We're to have our lunch there." Genevieve smiled. "I'll have one of the maids show you to your room so you can settle in."

••••

When Melanie entered her room, she was struck by the lovely color scheme and sheer prettiness of the bedchamber. The counterpane and canopy on the four-poster bed featured a pattern of pink rosebuds, the wallpaper was pale pink and white stripes, and the silk curtains were a pale blush pink.

"It looks like a princess lives here," she murmured.

The maid smiled. "Yes, Miss Starhope. Your aunt had the room completely redecorated when she learned you were to visit, from the wallpaper to the drapes. Everything used to be blue, and the room was terribly dark." She gestured toward a dainty writing desk in the corner. "You've stationery and ink in the drawer, and most of your clothes are hanging in the closet."

Melanie cocked her head. "Most?"

"Some of your gowns needed a press, so they are downstairs in the laundry room. My name is

Daisy and I'll be attending to your needs while you're here."

The maid helped Melanie shrug off her jacket, took her hat, and disappeared with them into the closet.

She emerged with a smile. "Lunch will be served in a half hour. Is there anything else you need right now?"

"Thank you, no." Melanie paused. "Er...does my aunt own any cats?"

"I'm afraid not, miss."

After Daisy left the room and closed the door behind her, Melanie took a few moments to admire her surroundings. The various shades of pink seemed to soothe her soul and the hothouse flowers on the chest of drawers lent the air an intoxicating scent. She felt so free, only a sense of decorum kept her from loosening her stays and letting her hair loose from its pins. With a little squeal, she threw herself on the bed and kicked up her heels with joy.

Aunt Ginny was certainly an extraordinarily independent woman. Not only was she beautiful and accomplished, but she had also forged a life for herself without a man. Although her husband had proven to be a dismal disappointment, she had not turned bitter as a result. Instead, she'd devoted herself to improving her home and her skills as an artist.

In the next moment, Melanie was seized by a daring notion. She'd never thought about it before now, but what if marriage need not be a goal for every woman? Although she'd been raised to think otherwise, securing a husband might not be the only way for her to be happy. If she *chose* to become a spinster, she would never have to fear the roaming eye of a spouse or worry about placing his needs above her own. Let Blanche be the Starhope daughter who married well, while her elder sister blazed a different and much braver trail. Together, she and her aunt could prove to the world that a lady did not need a man by her side to live a fulfilling and exciting life.

Only...she *would* miss having children.

Melanie pushed the thought away, rolled over on her back, and closed her eyes. How could she possibly miss something she had never known? She'd never been to Constantinople, Saint Petersburg, or Buenos Aires either, and she felt no dull ache at the thought of going elsewhere. Although motherhood had its allure, she could always substitute different experiences, couldn't she? Outings were forever being canceled due to rain, yet the time could be spent playing a good game of cards, reading a gripping novel, or practicing the piano. Life was always full of opportunity as well as compromise.

A happy sigh escaped her lips.

••••

"This space is so beautiful, and the light is amazing." Melanie marveled at the glass ceiling and windows in the conservatory. "It's almost as if you built your very own Crystal Palace!"

The two women sat at a small, round table situated next to a window with a view to the rose garden. The conservatory was filled with all manner of exotic flowers, fruit trees, and even a dainty fountain. A maid stood nearby with a rolling cart of covered dishes, and carafes of tea and water. After she lowered plates of food and a breadbasket onto the table, she stepped back a discreet distance and waited to be summoned.

Genevieve reached for her goblet of water. "The Crystal Palace was my inspiration."

"My bedroom is absolutely lovely, by the way. Daisy told me it had been redone, just for me."

Her aunt smiled. "If I had had a daughter, I would have decorated her room just like yours."

"It's perfect." Melanie picked up her fork and began to eat the tender cutlets and fragrant vegetables on her plate. "I've been thinking about my stay, Aunt. You devoted all your time to entertaining me in London and I couldn't be more grateful. Now that we're in Ledbury, however, I'm sure you yearn to get back to your routine."

"How thoughtful." As her aunt buttered a piece of freshly baked bread, the butter melted. "I do enjoy having my afternoons free to paint, to be honest." She took a bite of the bread and chewed.

"I thought as much." Melanie nodded. "Therefore, I feel it's important for me to establish a life of my own."

Genevieve put down her bread and blotted her lips with a linen napkin. "What did you have in mind?"

"I was rather involved with the church when I was at home, working on various projects to help the poor. I especially liked working with children." Melanie smiled. "Perhaps you could suggest something similar I could do here?"

Her aunt's eyebrows rose. "It's uncanny, how much you are like me. As a matter of fact, I gave art lessons at the local orphanage last summer. Have you any skills you could impart to the girls?"

"I play the piano very well, so I've been told." Melanie shrugged. "I also enjoy sewing and embroidery."

"I tell you what, let's drive over there this afternoon and speak with the matron, Mrs. Wheeler. She will be more intimately acquainted with the girl's needs than I am."

Melanie beamed. "I can't wait to see the place."

"Yes, the grounds of Ledbury Country Home for Children are exceptionally lovely, and I believe the staff are universally kind."

"I'm glad to hear that." Melanie remembered the urchins roaming through Paddington Station. "Children thrive when they receive attention from kind adults."

"I agree." Genevieve gestured toward a shelf of orchids nearby. "Children are a great deal like hothouse flowers, I imagine."

"Your independence is an inspiration to me." Melanie leaned forward. "Do you ever regret not having children of your own?"

Was it Melanie's imagination or did a wistful expression pass over her aunt's countenance?

"Not at all. Whenever I wish to spend time with children, I volunteer at the orphanage." When Genevieve smiled, the dimples in her cheeks deepened. "Then again, *you* are here. You may not be a little girl any longer, but since we've been together, I think of you almost like a daughter."

Melanie reached across the table to give her aunt's hand a squeeze. "That makes me very happy."

••••

The grandfather clock in the hallway had just struck two o'clock when a manservant brought a lightweight pony trap around to the courtyard. After Melanie left the house with her aunt, she gasped with pleasure at the dainty carriage.

Although most of the rig had been painted gleaming black, the spokes of the wheels were red. The pony was chestnut, although her socks were white. The polished brass hardware reflected the light as if illuminated from within and Melanie shook her head. "Aunt Ginny, you certainly have style."

"I should hope so." Genevieve laughed. "A woman with means who lacks style is like a gilded potato."

Melanie's subsequent fit of giggles was so contagious that even the servant bit back a grin.

A few moments later, Melanie and her aunt were making their way down the drive. Genevieve held the reins in her gloved hand, but the horse needed little encouragement to keep a fast clip. A breeze lifted the corners of Melanie's broad brimmed hat, and she was glad for the scarf that kept it firmly in place.

"The mare's name is Plaid, by the way."

Melanie gave Genevieve a sidelong glance. "That's...unusual, isn't it?"

"Yes, but it couldn't be helped. I *had* wanted to name her a color, but I couldn't decide which one." She shrugged. "That's where plaid came in."

"That has a twisted sort of logic, I suppose." Melanie began to giggle again. "I haven't laughed this much in ages."

"It's good to laugh." Genevieve beamed. "It keeps a woman pretty."

At the end of the drive, they took a left turn and Melanie sat up straighter. "Dare I hope we will be passing through town?"

"Indeed, we will be driving down the High Street and past Market House."

Melanie cocked her head. "Is that a local landmark?"

"Oh, yes." Genevieve nodded. "Market House dates back to the 1600s. Ledbury is a market town, you see, and that particular building was used to warehouse certain crops. It's raised on posts, and tradesmen sold their wares from stalls underneath."

"You paint a very picturesque image."

When they drove down High Street, Melanie spotted Market House right away, based on her aunt's description. Melanie was quite pleased at the tidy shops they passed, and she made notes on which ones she might like to visit.

"The architecture in Ledbury is very historic." She glanced at Genevieve. "I can almost imagine myself in Elizabethan England."

"When I first came here, I found it to be too sedate. London was a relatively short distance by train, however, so I bought a second residence. Whenever I craved excitement, I spent a few weeks there. Now, my life is in balance."

Genevieve reined Plaid to a stop when an older gentleman approached on a horse. "Mr. Halliwell, allow me to introduce my niece, Miss Starhope. She's to stay with me for a long visit."

The man doffed his hat. "I'm honored to make your acquaintance, Miss Starhope." His gaze lingered on Genevieve. "I hope you are well, Mrs. Hornsby?"

"Never better. Thank you for asking, sir." Genevieve loosened the reins and the trap started forward once more. She lowered her voice to murmur, "Mr. Halliwell owns a lovely manor home just outside of town. He made his money investing in railroads."

"He seemed to admire you a great deal." Melanie studied her aunt's profile a few moments. "Have you never thought about marrying again?"

"Heavens, no!" Genevieve made a scoffing sound. "My requirements are exceedingly stringent. Therefore, no suitable gentlemen exist."

"Do tell."

"Hmm." Her aunt's expression grew thoughtful. "My perfect gentleman will be irresistibly *stirring*. That is to say, my toes must curl and my knees must grow weak when I catch sight of him." She slid Melanie a wink. "Do you understand what I mean?"

A blush crept across Melanie's face. "I think so." She paused. "Is that all?"

"Of course not! He must also be wealthier than I am *and* be in possession of a title." Genevieve tossed her head and laughed. "Nothing less would tempt me, I'm afraid. So, I shall remain a dazzling spinster for the rest of my days."

"I like that — a dazzling spinster."

Genevieve gave her a sidelong glance. "What about your ideal fellow?"

"I've given up on romance."

"That's not how confidences work, Melanie. I confessed *my* standards and now it's your turn."

Melanie rolled her eyes. "All right." She sighed. "My ideal suitor could not be extraordinarily good-looking, I think."

Genevieve frowned. "Why is that?"

"I've come to dislike vanity quite passionately."

Her aunt nodded. "Lack of vanity is always commendable. What else?"

"Hmm." Melanie pondered the question. "He would have to possess the highest moral character, of course."

"Naturally."

"He must also prefer my looks over my sister's." Melanie averted her gaze. "Therein lies the problem. As you say, no suitable gentlemen exist and so I shall be a dazzling spinster as well."

"Ha! A million hearts just broke, I'm certain of it."

"I shan't be around to pick up the pieces." Melanie lifted her chin. "I'm too busy having fun."

Genevieve chuckled. "That's the spirit!"

Suzanne G. Rogers

Chapter Three
Disagreeable

When Melanie first caught sight of Ledbury Country Home for Children, she was struck by the beauty of the well-tended property. Three brick buildings were surrounded by several attractive trees, and the lawn spread out in an inviting carpet of green. A white fence surrounded what appeared to be a vegetable garden, a grove of apple trees, and a second grove of plum trees. A short distance away, Melanie spotted a hen house. "What a glorious place for children!"

"The building that's farthest away is the dormitory for boys, and the dormitory to the left of the main building is for girls." Genevieve drove the trap through the gates. "The main building is where the children and staff eat their meals. The orphans attend regular school during the year, but summertime is when they are allowed extra lessons. When I teach art, I use one of the rooms set aside for classes."

"It's too late for lunch." Melanie gave the premises a puzzled glance. "Where are the children?"

Genevieve frowned. "I don't know. It's such a fine day, they should be outside, playing."

She drove the trap under a shady tree and stopped next to a black stallion who was tied to a branch.

"What a pretty creature." Melanie gave the horse an admiring glance. "It seems we are not the only visitors this afternoon."

"I don't recognize this horse." Genevieve climbed down from the trap and ran a fingertip along the stallion's glossy neck. "He looks as if he cost a pretty penny, so perhaps it belongs to a wealthy donor."

Melanie blinked. "The orphanage isn't supported by the public?"

Genevieve shook her head. "The institution was established by a wealthy widow who has since passed away. Now, it's run by a Board of Governors, solely on private donations."

Melanie accompanied her aunt into the building. As soon as they passed inside, the sound of singing reached her ears — a man's smooth baritone sang a scale, followed by a chorus of children in repetition.

She exchanged a surprised glance with Genevieve. "You didn't tell me the orphanage had a singing teacher."

"I was unaware until now. I imagine he's a volunteer, like you." Her aunt gestured toward a nearby door. "Let me introduce you to the matron, Mrs. Wheeler."

When Melanie stepped into the office, an older woman was sitting at a desk with ledgers spread out in front of her. She was so busy adding columns, she didn't notice the newcomers until Genevieve cleared her throat.

"Mrs. Wheeler?"

The woman sat back with a start. "Oh...Mrs. Hornsby! Are you going to be offering art lessons again this summer?" She wiped her pen and capped her inkwell.

"No, but I'd like to introduce you to my niece, Miss Starhope." Genevieve turned toward Melanie.

"She's interested in giving lessons to the girls over the summer, if you can use the help."

"We can always use help." When Mrs. Wheeler rose from her desk, her plush figure was revealed. "Are you a student of art, Miss Starhope?"

"I leave that particular skill to my aunt." Melanie shook her head. "I *am* proficient as a pianist, however, and I'm also quite good at sewing. Would either of those talents be useful to your girls?"

The woman's pink lips parted as she gasped with delight. "Piano, did you say? That would be perfect! Over the last few weeks, we've been fortunate to have a lovely gentleman teaching the boys to sing. Our girls have been rather envious."

"I play the piano better than I sing, but I'm willing to give any sort of music lessons you wish."

"All we have is an upright piano, but it's serviceable." Mrs. Wheeler beamed. "Would you like to see it?"

Melanie returned the woman's smile with one of her own. "I would, thank you."

The three women left the office and headed down a long corridor. As they strolled along, the sound of singing grew louder. Apparently, the instructor had finished warming up the children and they were practicing, "Oh, better far to live and die."

"*Pirates of Penzance?*" Melanie peered at the matron, wide-eyed. "Your new singing instructor has a rather unorthodox choice of music, I must say."

Mrs. Wheeler chuckled. "A fortnight ago, it was *The Mikado*. Lord Cedric Peyton understands boys can be unruly. He thought he might have more success if they learned music that was unconventional."

Genevieve peered at her. "An aristocrat volunteered his time to help the boys?"

"His elder brother is a marquess with a son and so Lord Peyton's title is merely a courtesy." Mrs. Wheeler patted her hair. "Nevertheless, we are very fortunate to have his assistance. The gentleman is very popular with all the children."

"For I am a Pirate King..."

The lyrics from the comic opera reached Melanie's ears and she bit back a smile. "I can very well imagine how that would be so."

"Lord Peyton uses the dining hall up ahead for his lessons. We'll be passing right by."

They reached the end of the corridor and turned a corner, where a group of girls were clustered around a door with a window. Their faces were rapt as they were seemingly transfixed by the activity within.

Mrs. Wheeler made shooing gestures with her hands. "Clear a path, girls! We must get through."

The plump woman had to raise her arms to squeeze past the girls, who seemed disinclined to pry themselves away from the window. As Melanie passed by, she caught a glimpse of the room. Unfortunately, Lord Peyton was turned away from her and all she could see was the back of his head.

She and Genevieve joined Mrs. Wheeler a few moments later and made their way to a doorway at the end of the hall.

The matron escorted them inside the spacious room. "We meet here for smaller assemblies and entertainments." She nodded toward the upright piano in the corner. "There is the instrument you would be using for your lessons."

Melanie crossed over to the piano and lifted the fall. "Doesn't Lord Peyton need the piano for his lessons?"

The sausage curls on Mrs. Wheeler's coiffure danced as she shook her head. "He uses tuning forks and a guitar."

"A guitar?" Melanie exchanged a startled glance with her aunt. "That's not an instrument you often see in drawing rooms."

Mrs. Wheeler giggled in an oddly girlish fashion for a woman of her years. "As I said before, Lord Peyton is unconventional."

Melanie caught her aunt's eye. "Do you know the gentleman, Aunt Ginny?"

"I'm afraid not." Genevieve shrugged. "Perhaps he moved to Ledbury while I've been away."

"Yes, Lord Peyton is new to the neighborhood," Mrs. Wheeler said. "He has taken the former Sebastian estate."

"Really? Part of that property abuts mine." Genevieve frowned. "I must invite Lord Peyton and his wife to tea."

"The gentleman is unmarried." Inexplicably, Mrs. Wheeler's face turned pink.

"If that's the case, Aunt, perhaps a note of welcome will suffice," Melanie murmured. "We wouldn't want to give Lord Peyton the wrong idea about our intentions."

"Yes, I think you are quite right." Genevieve gave a decisive nod. "It's better to do too little in these cases rather than too much."

"I'm so glad to discover you both exhibit exemplary behavior, especially toward a gentleman like Lord Peyton." Mrs. Wheeler's hands fluttered. "So many women are entirely too forward these days."

Melanie cocked her head. "Why him especially?"

Mrs. Wheeler's color deepened. "Oh...well, he's an eligible bachelor."

"I see." Melanie sat down at the piano and began to play the overture from *The Marriage of Figaro*. After a short while, she was satisfied as to what she heard. "I prefer to play on a baby grand, but this instrument will do nicely. It has a nice tone for an upright."

Her aunt smiled. "Your skill at the piano does you credit, Melanie."

"Thank you." Melanie rose. "Well, Mrs. Wheeler, do you think any of your girls would enjoy taking piano lessons over the summer?"

"Yes, indeed! I will make an announcement at dinner this evening and arrange a schedule. When would you like to begin?"

"I must pick up some sheet music, so let's start the day after tomorrow."

Melanie and Mrs. Wheeler settled on a few more details before the matron showed her and Genevieve out. On the way, girls still clustered in the corridor outside the dining hall as they tried to catch a glimpse of the choir practice inside.

As Melanie passed, she heard guitar music. "Lord Peyton is quite facile with that instrument, I must say."

Genevieve nodded. "I'm no expert, of course, but he seems exceedingly accomplished to me."

"Lord Peyton is a student of music," Mrs. Wheeler said. "He attended The Vienna

Conservatory as well as the Conservatory of Barcelona."

They said good-bye to Mrs. Wheeler and returned to Ledbury, where Genevieve pointed out the music shop. "You can purchase sheet music at Abernathy's Fine Instruments. Would you like me to stop?"

Melanie shook her head. "Let me drive into town by myself tomorrow morning, so you may paint in peace and quiet."

"That would be lovely. I've not picked up a paintbrush in weeks and I'm beginning to feel the strain."

As they left the town behind, Melanie breathed in the fresh clean country air and let it out in a gust. "Lord Peyton has certainly made an impression at the orphanage."

Genevieve laughed. "Yes, Mrs. Wheeler was quite transported. I've never seen her behave in such a distracted manner before."

"Perhaps she's exceedingly fond of Gilbert and Sullivan." Melanie shrugged. "I'd planned to teach the girls how to play using traditional music but perhaps I should select a few unconventional songs for the more advanced pupils."

"Take care you don't select anything too *forward*."

Melanie gave her aunt a startled glance, but when she realized the woman was joking, they both burst into laughter.

••••

Early the following morning, Melanie arose feeling restless. Dawn had broken, but the house was so quiet, she suspected most of the servants were still abed. Unwilling to rouse Daisy, she dragged a brush through her dark hair, plaited it over one shoulder, and climbed into an old pinafore dress she usually wore to work in the garden back home. She finished off her ensemble with a pair of sturdy shoes and then let herself out the front door to take a long walk.

As Melanie strolled across the grounds, she admired the view of the hills. Although she had found the Malvern Hills to be less exciting than London or even Bromley, she was beginning to see how its calm beauty could soothe the spirit. Undoubtedly, Blanche would have chafed at the lack of society and might have sneered at the small size of Ledbury, but Melanie was enjoying her surroundings. She could probably walk for hours and not get tired of the landscape.

After she had traversed the grounds, she headed down the driveway to walk along the lane for a while. As she marched, she could not get the music from *Pirates of Penzance* out of her head.

"*When I sally forth to seek my prey, I help myself in a royal way...*"

She stopped marching and gaped. Was that a small cherry orchard in the near distance? It was a trifle early in the season for the fruit to be ripe, but she dearly loved cherries. If she could take a peek, she could determine when the cherries would be ready to pick. Her mouth began to water.

"And if I'm very fortunate, I might find one or two cherries are ripe now."

She glanced around, but nobody was within view. With little chance of getting caught, Melanie left the lane, picked up her skirts, and leaped over a narrow ditch to gain access to the property. She was suddenly glad she'd donned her homeliest garment that morning. The abundant fabric in the skirt allowed her to throw her leg over the split-rail fence and climb into the meadow beyond. She giggled as she sped toward the rows of cherry trees, just as a shaft of light broke through the clouds to light her way.

When she arrived at the small grove, she peered at the burgeoning fruit. As she had suspected, it would probably be another month before it was ready to pick. She sighed with disappointment — only to spot a gooseberry shrub nearby. Melanie gasped with delight and hastened over to pluck a handful of green berries. An abundance of sour flavor exploded on her tongue, and she wiggled with delight. She filled her mouth with as many berries as her cheeks could hold and then turned to scamper back to the lane.

A tall man stood in her way, his arms akimbo, and she froze.

His dark wavy hair fell loose about his face and shoulders, and he wore a linen shirt open to the waist. It appeared as if he'd paid as little attention to his attire that morning as had Melanie, but his state of dishabille lent him an air of danger whereas she looked like a ragamuffin.

He glowered. "You're too old to be scrumping, wouldn't you say?"

Since her mouth was full of fruit she could not respond. As she chewed and swallowed, a flush of embarrassment made her face feel as if it were on fire. Finally, she managed to clear her throat.

"Er...you should always pick the outside berries on a gooseberry shrub and prune the branches to gain the best crop."

He looked at her askance. "So you've done me a favor?"

The scathing note in his voice stiffened her spine. "No, of course not, but you needn't be so resentful. I've done little harm."

"You're a trespasser."

Her temper flared. "I apologize for treading upon your hallowed property, sir! I am utterly and completely in the wrong and it won't happen again."

Melanie stomped past the man in a fury, made her way back to the split-rail fence, and climbed over. When she glanced over her shoulder, she discovered the man had actually followed her, as if to make sure she left.

With gritted teeth, she leaped over the ditch once more, and made her way up the lane. As she turned into her aunt's drive, she refused to look back. If the nasty man wished to see where she lived, she could not stop him. No doubt he would complain about her to Aunt Ginny.

When she entered the house, she could hear sounds of life. Somewhere in the kitchen, a spoon scraped the side of a pot, a maid hummed as she set the table in the dining room, and hushed conversations emanated from the Servants' Hall. Melanie hastened up the stairs and went to her room.

As she sat down in front of the vanity to loosen her plait, she noticed a small twig and leaf had enmeshed itself in her hair. So she had looked as if she'd been rolling around on the ground before she went scrumping? With a sound of disgust, Melanie pulled the debris out and began to brush her hair with more vigor than was necessary.

Admittedly, she had erred by trespassing on a neighbor's property, but the man had treated her as if she were a common criminal. He was loathsomely handsome, by anyone's reckoning, and was likely used to having his way in life as a result.

"He probably uniformly forbids birds from stealing fruit and undoubtedly castigates the butterflies from deigning to alight on his branches!"

Unfortunately, Daisy stepped into the room just then. "Excuse me, miss? I didn't quite catch what you said."

"Oh, nothing." Melanie sighed. "I must drive into town this morning. Please pick out something suitable for me to wear."

"Yes, miss."

••••

Melanie gave Genevieve a pained glance over the top of her teacup. As she lowered it to its saucer, she let out the breath she'd been holding.

"I've gotten into a scrape this morning, I'm afraid."

Her aunt blinked. "I cannot imagine how."

Melanie described her adventurous morning stroll and unfortunate encounter with the gooseberry man.

"He was terribly put out even after I said I was sorry." Melanie bit the inside of her cheek. "If he should complain to you about me, I apologize in advance."

Genevieve peered at her. "He was put out over a few berries? How terribly disagreeable of him. Out here in the country, neighbors are not usually so unfriendly."

"Nevertheless, I've embarrassed myself. I just hope I haven't embarrassed you as a result."

Her aunt shook her head. "If the fellow dares say a word, I shall laugh in his face." She paused. "Did you get his name?"

"Under the circumstances, I was not inclined to observe niceties." Melanie shrugged. "It's the property on the far side of the lane, not far from your driveway."

Genevieve grimaced. "That would be the former Sebastian estate. You don't suppose you met Lord Peyton, do you?"

Melanie's mind was filled with the memory of the man's loose linen shirt. The garment had been tucked into the fellow's tight breeches in a desultory fashion, leaving his bare skin open to the morning breeze.

"He wasn't dressed like a lord. Then again, I was clad like a milk maid." Melanie sighed. "If he was indeed Lord Peyton, I hope he won't recognize me when I'm properly dressed. I shouldn't worry, I suppose. Men like him never pay attention to anyone's appearance other than their own."

"What?" Genevieve's eyes widened. "What can you mean?"

"He has the face of Narcissus." Melanie shuddered. "I imagine he spends most of his time gazing at himself in the mirror."

"Oh, dear." Genevieve stabbed a bite of ham on her fork. "My husband was much admired and admired himself tenfold in return. As a result, I've come to share your distaste for good-looking men."

"Really?" Melanie nibbled on a piece of bacon. "I thought you liked men to be *stirring*."

"I really hadn't thought about it too much but I suppose that particular quality isn't inextricably linked to a man's looks." A blush crept onto

Genevieve's cheeks. "It has more to do with how he awakes all my senses." She averted her gaze. "I'm sure I read too many novels."

"Lord Peyton, if that was indeed his name, made all my senses recoil." Melanie finally managed to laugh. "I shall leave him to Mrs. Wheeler."

Genevieve bit back a smile. "A match made in heaven."

••••

The morning was still fresh and cool when Melanie set off for Ledbury in her aunt's trap. She wore a smart black and white checked gown with tiny red embroidered roses scattered on the skirt, and her straw bonnet was lined with crimson silk as well. Her ensemble was both saucy and fetching, in her opinion, and she felt confident as she drove toward town. Now that she knew the way, the distance did not seem quite so long as it had before. Nevertheless, she had time enough to enjoy the countryside — although she kept her gaze trained on the road as she passed the former Sebastian estate.

Melanie lifted her chin. "Hmph."

She brushed all thoughts of Lord Peyton from her mind, took a deep breath, and sang something she'd recently seen in *The Mikado.*

"Three little maids from school are we..."

The song took her only a short way, at which time the image of Lord Peyton began buzzing in her brain like an annoying bee. The man had resembled a reprobate pirate that morning, so she no longer wondered why he was fond of *Pirates of Penzance.* Melanie shook her head, bemused. He had made such a good impression with the children and their matron at the orphanage and yet had been so unpleasant to *her*. Perhaps he was one of those people who presented one image to the public and an entirely different one in private. It was a great pity, but she would have to take great care to avoid him while giving her piano lessons. At least Lord Peyton would be busy with his choir practice, so the chances were good their paths would never cross.

Melanie drove to Abernathy's Fine Instruments and hitched the pony to a post set in the pavement. As she turned toward the shop, however, she noticed a familiar black horse hitched nearby. She crossed over to greet him and stroke his neck.

"Good morning, sir. I'm very sorry you have such a disagreeable owner."

"I'll thank you to step away from my horse." Lord Peyton appeared. His harsh words seemed to hang in the air as he frowned. "Matador nearly nipped me this morning."

Although Melanie was not afraid of the horse, she was obliged to step back. Lord Peyton's appearance was greatly altered from that morning, admittedly, but she did not find him much improved. His long wavy hair was tied back, his clothes were impeccably tailored, and he looked very much a gentleman.

"Is that so?" Melanie shrugged. "I imagine Matador's saddle girth is too tight."

His gaze settled on her face and his eyes narrowed. "Oh, it's *you* — Miss Scrumper."

She sketched a brief, mocking curtsy. "What a pleasure to see you again, Mr. Gooseberry."

"That's *Lord* Gooseberry to you." He stepped off the pavement and went to check his saddle's girth. "What do you know of horses anyway?"

Melanie gave him a level glance. "My skill at scrumping is only outpaced by my knowledge of horsemanship."

As Lord Peyton passed his hand underneath the strap, his expression changed. "Blazes, it *is* too tight." He loosened the girth. "You may have just saved me from getting tossed on my head or losing a finger."

"I didn't do it for *you*, I did it for the horse. I don't like to see an animal in pain."

With that, she whirled around and went into the music shop without a backward glance.

••••

The following afternoon, while Genevieve worked on a painting of the garden, Melanie tucked her new sheet music into a satchel and drove to the orphanage to give her first piano lessons. The temperature was uncomfortably warm, and she was glad she'd donned a broad-brimmed hat. When she arrived, she discovered Matador tethered under the shady tree, but a trough had been added to afford the creature a drink of water. She parked her rig close enough to allow Plaid to drink from the trough as well and was pleased to see the two horses greet one another with a nicker and a friendly snort.

As soon as she entered the main building, she could hear music from Lord Peyton's choir practice. She knocked on Mrs. Wheeler's open door, where the woman was once again bent over her desk, working sums in ledgers.

"Good afternoon, Mrs. Wheeler."

"Yes?" The woman glanced up but it was clear her mind was still engaged in her paperwork. "Oh, Miss Starhope!" The matron reached for a piece of paper filled with columns and names and gave it to her. "Here are the girls interested in lessons. As we discussed, I assigned them twenty-minutes slots over the next few days, so you can assess their needs. They are very excited to begin!"

"Excellent." Melanie peered at the names on the paper. "Well, I'd best get to the classroom, hadn't I?"

She left the office and hastened down the corridor. A large cluster of girls stood outside the dining hall again, pressing against one another for the opportunity to catch a glimpse of Lord Peyton, she presumed. Melanie murmured, "Excuse me," to get past, but she nearly trod upon several feet in the process. She shook her head in dismay as she eased her way through and continued on her way. Was she so easily swayed by handsome men when she was that age? If she had been, her mother would have made sure she didn't put on such a display. With a pang, Melanie suddenly realized these girls had no one to show them how to be ladylike.

When she arrived at the classroom, a pale young girl was waiting for her just outside the door.

"Hello. I'm Miss Starhope." Melanie consulted Mrs. Wheeler's list. "You must be Catherine Hodges?"

"Yes, miss." The child dipped into an awkward curtsy. "Mrs. Wheeler said you would teach me how to play the piano." Her eyes were too big for her face, and she shifted her weight from foot to foot.

"That's exactly why I'm here." Melanie hoped her bright smile would put Catherine at ease. "Have you ever studied the piano before?"

"No, miss. I've not been so fortunate."

"How old are you, Catherine?"

"I'm nearly thirteen."

"Wonderful." Melanie gestured toward the room. "Let's get started."

••••

Two hours later, Melanie had worked with six girls and had tasked each of them with the obligation to practice their scales before their next lesson. As the last child was leaving, she made a squeaking noise. Melanie glanced up to see what might have caused it. Lord Peyton was leaning against the doorjamb with his arms crossed.

"Good afternoon, Lord Peyton." The wide-eyed girl curtsied. "Excuse me."

"Don't forget what I said about practicing, Willa," Melanie said.

The girl paused. "I won't. Thank you."

Lord Peyton straightened so the girl could scurry past.

Melanie cocked her head, puzzled. "Can I help you, sir?"

"I must speak with you Miss Scrumper."

"Starhope."

He frowned. "What?"

"Miss Starhope." She began gathering up her sheet music. "Since we are never to be acquainted socially, I don't mind introducing myself."

"And I don't mind telling you how much your piano lessons have disrupted my choir practice. I could hear disconsonant notes all afternoon." Lord Peyton frowned. "The least you could do is shut the door."

Melanie rose. "It's too hot to work in a closed room of this size."

"There's an old saying." He pushed the door closed and crossed the room. "Something about when God closes a door..." Lord Peyton unlocked the sash and lifted the window, "...He opens a window somewhere."

She gaped. "Did you just compare yourself to God?"

"No!" He made a sound of disgust. "Why must you be so purposefully disagreeable?"

Melanie hastened over to open the door once more. "I would ask you the same thing but it's clear you've made a study of it."

His color grew pale even as pink spots appeared on his cheekbones. "Move your lessons to the morning and our problem will be solved."

"Since my aunt prefers to paint in the afternoon, I've made arrangements to be out of the house. I cannot move my lessons to the morning." Melanie crossed over to the open window and lowered the sash. "I will, however, keep the door closed from now on."

"Thank you!" He wheeled around and strode from the room, seemingly quivering with indignation.

She did not know what possessed her to stick out her tongue at his retreating back, but when he turned unexpectedly, he caught her at it.

He peered at her in shock. "How utterly childish and horribly rude!"

Although she was embarrassed, something about the infuriating man would not allow her to apologize. "It was a rude gesture for a rude man. You could think of it as an homage."

His eyebrows rose and he seemed to struggle with a response. When he burst out laughing, however, she struggled not to join in. She busied herself with her sheet music and valise until he disappeared from view.

Once Melanie was alone, she took a deep breath, let it out, and shook her head in dismay. She'd departed Bromley with the hope of beginning a new life in Ledbury, but her behavior lately had really fallen short of the mark. Lord Peyton might be pompous, arrogant, and vain, but her incivility had been unpardonable. Well, it was never too late to apologize. She pinned on her hat, tucked her valise under her arm, and strode toward the door.

Suzanne G. Rogers

Chapter Four

Lord Gooseberry

Once she reached the hallway, however, Lord Peyton was nowhere to be seen. Worse, when she emerged from the building, he had already mounted Matador and was riding off at a fast clip. She climbed into her rig and started for home. Lord Peyton was in the far distance when she reached the road and she felt more than a pang of remorse. Clearly, she could not let the situation fester any longer than it already had.

When she entered her aunt's home, she went directly into the sitting room and wrote a note of apology at the desk under the window. Afterward, she went below stairs to find someone to take it to Lord Peyton right away. Fortunately, one of the groundskeeper's assistants was at loose ends and volunteered to complete the task.

She extended the envelope to the young man. "Wait long enough to see if there is any reply, would you, Paul?"

He nodded. "Yes, miss."

Even though Melanie had done all she could do, her conscience made her restless. She went in search of her aunt, who was having a cup of tea in the conservatory.

Genevieve smiled when Melanie entered the room. "There you are! How did your lessons go?"

"They couldn't have gone better." Melanie poured herself a cup of tea from the cart and sat down. "The girls were polite, eager to learn, and I enjoyed myself thoroughly. Only..." her voice trailed off.

Genevieve gave her an expectant glance. "Only...?"

"I got into another disagreement with Lord Peyton." Melanie sighed. "I don't know why I detest him so much, but I was horribly uncivil."

Her aunt laughed. "I cannot imagine how."

Melanie had no intention of describing her bad behavior, but the memory of it brought a blush of humiliation to her countenance. "Let's just say I'm embarrassed and leave it at that. I sent over a note of apology by way of Paul just now, but Lord Peyton might send it back, ripped to pieces."

"If he does, he's no gentleman." Genevieve nudged a plate of biscuits toward Melanie. "Have something to eat and tell me more about your lessons."

As Melanie chatted with her aunt over tea and biscuits, her humiliation receded somewhat. It was far more diverting to talk about each of her new pupils and their abilities at the keyboard.

"Denise has an excellent sense of rhythm for one so young and Elizabeth concentrates beautifully." Melanie smiled. "I'm not sure I was such a good student when I was a child."

"I'm sure you were far better than I was." Genevieve rolled her eyes. "Mama insisted I take piano lessons, but I refused to practice. My tutor became so exasperated, he quit in the middle of our lesson, left the house, and never came back!"

"Blanche is much the same way but when I reminded her that she would be expected to exhibit her skills once she was out in society, she became more diligent."

Genevieve refilled her cup. "But you didn't need to be coaxed?" She dropped a teaspoon of sugar into her tea and took a sip.

"No, I love to play." Melanie paused. "I also love to read and sew. I think I'm far more singular than is good for me, but there you have it."

Unfortunately, she had also discovered her tongue was quite sharp. Perhaps she was naturally singular because she was best suited to remain a maiden.

Paul entered the conservatory a few moments later with a branch in his hands. "Excuse me, Miss Starhope. I delivered your letter to His Lordship."

Genevieve peered at the branch. "What have you there?"

The young man glanced down at the greenery. "Er...His Lordship gave it to me by way of reply." He held it up. "It's a cutting from a gooseberry shrub."

Melanie's heart sank. "Did Lord Peyton say anything else?"

"Er...only that you can use the cutting to grow another gooseberry shrub."

"That much I know." Melanie sighed. "If you would be so kind as to put it in water for me, I would appreciate it. It must grow roots before I plant it."

Paul nodded. "Yes, miss." He ambled out.

Genevieve beamed. "What a lovely gesture on Lord Peyton's part! It seems your apology has been accepted and the quarrel is behind you."

Although Melanie murmured her agreement, she was not so certain the gooseberry cutting was kindly meant.

••••

The following day, Melanie arrived at the orphanage on edge. Although the summer afternoon was exceedingly warm, she nevertheless kept the door of her music room closed and opened all the windows. As each new pupil arrived for her introductory lesson, however, Melanie concentrated on the task at hand and forgot about everything else. Just like the day before, she met with six girls — some of whom had taken piano lessons before they became orphans. Since the lessons were already short, she didn't have time to ask about how and when they had come to live at Ledbury Country Home for Children. Even so, it seemed clear to Melanie that many of the girls had a modicum of breeding and all of them were charming.

After the last girl had finished her lesson and disappeared into the hallway, Melanie wiped her perspiring brow and crossed over to wrench the door open. To her surprise, Lord Peyton stood there with a raised fist.

"Oh!" Melanie stepped back with alacrity. "How may I help you, Lord Peyton?"

The man dropped his fist to his side. "Why are you scampering away like that? I only meant to knock on the door." He strode into the room. "Merciful heavens but it's hot in here."

Determined to remain civil, she bit back a sharp retort and covered her exasperation with a smile. As she returned to the piano to pack up her sheet music, she cast about for something polite to say. "Thank you for the gooseberry cutting. It was very thoughtful."

Lord Peyton chuckled. "It wasn't meant to be thoughtful. It was meant to say you should stay off my property and pick your own gooseberries."

She gritted her teeth. "Yes, I know, but I'm determined to behave like a lady toward you from now on. Therefore, I shall mistake your ill intent for good."

"I am your humble servant." His tone was slightly mocking. "Miss Starhope, you don't like me."

Melanie's gaze flickered toward him on her way to shut the windows. "I'm sure if we were better acquainted, my opinion would improve."

"I doubt your sincerity. Let me make something perfectly clear. I treated you harshly the other day because I value my privacy."

Melanie latched the last window and turned toward him. "You need have no reason to fear I will ever set foot on your property again." She paused. "Especially now that I'm to have a gooseberry shrub of my own."

Mirth played with his lips. "Would that all such altercations be resolved so equitably. I don't like you, Miss Starhope, and you don't like me. Amid our mutual antipathy, I suggest we form an uneasy friendship of sorts."

She gave him a puzzled frown. "What an odd suggestion. I'm not sure how to respond."

"It's really rather easy. Since we've no possibility of romance with one another, we might as well be friends." He shrugged. "It's far better than an entrenched enmity and as least we can be honest with one another."

A knock came at the open door. "Hello?"

When Melanie glanced over, she saw a young tow-headed boy standing in the doorway. "Why, hello."

"Come in, Ethan." Lord Peyton beckoned.

The lad stepped forward, his gaze flickering from Lord Peyton to Melanie and back again. "Is this the piano lady?"

"Yes, this is Miss Starhope...the piano lady."

Ethan gave her a beseeching smile. "I'd like to take lessons. I've taken a few lessons before...before my parents..." his voice trailed off. "Anyway, I want to play the piano more than anything."

His poignant expression stung Melanie's eyes. "If you want to take lessons, I'm very happy to teach you, Ethan."

His expression brightened. "You are?"

"The only difficulty is my schedule. I'm here for two hours every afternoon, and every moment is spoken for."

Ethan's face fell. "I understand."

"Nevertheless, if you can come at four o'clock, I'll add one more lesson, just for you."

"You would?" He beamed. "Thank you!"

"Let's begin tomorrow, shall we?"

"I'll be here!" He did a little dance. "You were right, Lord Peyton!" Ethan ran toward the door before he stopped, turned, and gave Melanie a gentlemanly bow. "See you tomorrow." He careened from the room like an excited colt.

"That was very kind of you, Miss Starhope." Lord Peyton nodded. "Ethan is one of my best sopranos."

"You encouraged the lad to ask me for lessons." She cocked her head. "How did you know I would agree?"

He shrugged. "I suspected you must like children, otherwise you wouldn't have volunteered your time at an orphanage."

"That's true." Melanie gave him an appraising glance. "Ethan is the reason you wished to be friends, I suppose."

"Not entirely." Lord Peyton chuckled. "I find you intriguing, actually. When my brother,

Edmund, arrives, perhaps I will invite you and your aunt to dine with us."

"Ah, but you've forbidden me from stepping foot on your property."

"It's Edmund's property, to be perfectly honest and I merely manage the place. Therefore, I'm allowed to make an exception for the occasion." He bowed. "Have a good afternoon, Miss Starhope."

He sauntered from the room, leaving Melanie more puzzled than ever before. Having never met a man of such contradictions, she didn't know what to make of him. Lord Peyton had admitted to his dislike of her and yet wished to be friends. Even odder, he wished to introduce her and Aunt Ginny to his brother, the marquess. Presumably, that would include the man's wife and family as well. Considering her dreadful manners, why would he want to do that?

"As if I needed any additional reasons to remain unmarried, I cannot understand men at all."

She sighed, gathered up her things, and drove home.

••••

Over the next few days, Melanie established a routine. She spent her mornings at Asphodel, writing letters or reading, and in the afternoons, she drove the trap to the orphanage for her piano lessons. Although some of her students showed more promise than others, she enjoyed their company as well as their eagerness to learn. The children all seemed grateful for her attention and their vulnerability tugged at her heartstrings. Ethan in particular made an impression. Not only was he more musically advanced than she had imagined, but his cultivated manners and means of expressing himself set him apart.

After his lesson had concluded on Friday afternoon, Melanie knocked on Mrs. Wheeler's door. The woman was busy with ledgers, schedules, and menus, as usual, but she paused from her work long enough to give Melanie a beaming smile.

"The children are enjoying their lessons, I hear."

Were those dark shadows under the woman's eyes or was it a trick of the light?

"I've been enjoying our lessons as well." Melanie paused. "You are doing a wonderful job here, Mrs. Wheeler."

The woman sat back in her chair with a sigh. "You're very kind to say so, Miss Starhope. Few people take the time to notice what I do." She glanced at her ledgers. "Sometimes I think this is a thankless job."

"I cannot imagine the day-to-day challenges you face as matron."

"I do what I must." The woman's eyes grew misty. "How can I help you, dear?"

"What can you tell me about Ethan Dornan?"

"He's a lovely child, isn't he?" Mrs. Wheeler frowned. "Ethan's parents were taken from him last year by a brief illness. His mother was quite genteel, as I understand it, but she married a man with very little money."

"Did he not have any relatives to take him in?" Melanie peered at her. "I can scarcely believe there was no one at all."

"His mother had an aunt still living — a Mrs. Pendergast, from Worcester — but she refuses to meet the boy." Mrs. Wheeler sighed. "Mr. Dornan made his living as a musician, you see, and she disapproved."

Melanie's lips parted. "Mr. Dornan's profession is not Ethan's fault!"

"No, but some members of society simply cannot bend under any circumstances. After the Dornans passed away, Mrs. Pendergast made a sizable donation to our orphanage and instructed that her great-nephew be sent here to live."

"If she had ever met Ethan, she would not have done so." Melanie forced a smile to her lips. "Good afternoon, Mrs. Wheeler. I'll be back on Monday."

She went out to the rig, where Plaid was waiting under the shady tree. Lord Peyton and Matador had long since departed, which was no surprise. Lord Peyton uniformly arrived in the afternoons before she did and left earlier, and she hadn't seen him at all since he introduced her to Ethan.

Melanie climbed into the rig and released the brake. "Plaid, if Lord Peyton and I are friends, I'm a fairy queen."

The pony's ears swiveled toward her and he snorted — as if in laughter.

••••

When Melanie finally arrived home, it was well after teatime and she was famished. As she entered the house, however, she was greeted by a strange sight. Two maids and the cook were hovering near the drawing room, taking turns peeking through the opening between the double doors. A murmur of conversation was audible in the room beyond and Melanie realized her aunt had a guest. Although she had been meaning to beg the staff for something to eat, she realized her hunger would have to wait. Even so, what sort of visitor could have excited so much attention?

She cleared her throat. "Daisy?"

The three eavesdroppers jumped in a guilty fashion. The cook and the second maid curtsied and hastened off while Daisy stared at her wide-eyed. "M-May I take your things, miss?"

Melanie gave the maid her valise, cape, gloves, and hat. "Who has come to call?"

"Er...Lord Peyton."

Melanie no longer had to wonder why the female staff had lost their minds. "Oh." Her gaze flickered to the mirror on the wall nearby and she smoothed her hair. "That will be all."

Daisy dipped into a brief curtsy and left. Melanie took a deep breath, opened the drawing room doors, and plastered a pleasant smile onto her lips.

"Hello."

Lord Peyton broke off his conversation with Aunt Ginny and they both rose to their feet.

"You're very late, Melanie. You almost missed Lord Peyton altogether." Despite the scolding words, Genevieve didn't seem at all bothered to have been left alone with the man. Lord Peyton had the ability to charm all manner of women, evidently.

"Yes." Melanie crossed straight to the tea cart, relieved to see plenty of sandwiches left on the platter." I'm so glad I'm not too late."

Lord Peyton's smile was sardonic. "As am I."

Genevieve gestured toward her visitor. "Lord Peyton was just telling me how he plans to rename the former Sebastian estate to Prospero's Retreat."

Melanie poured herself a cup of tea. "Prospero was the sorcerer from *The Tempest*."

"You've put your finger on it, Miss Starhope."
Lord Peyton sank into his chair. "*The Tempest* was
my inspiration."

"Do you see yourself as a sorcerer, sir?"
Melanie carried her plate to the low table next to
the sofa and returned for her teacup.

He chuckled. "I think my brother is more the
sorcerer whereas I view myself as Caliban."

"You have an extraordinarily developed sense
of the absurd, I see." Genevieve laughed. "I could
never see you as Caliban."

"We all have a streak of Caliban in us, I think."
Melanie finally settled herself on the sofa. "Well,
perhaps not *you*, Aunt Ginny."

Genevieve seemed eager to change the
conversation. "Were you delayed at the orphanage
this afternoon, Melanie?"

"As a matter of fact, I stopped to speak with
Mrs. Wheeler about one of my pupils." She glanced
at Lord Peyton. "Ethan Dornan, actually."

He leaned forward. "Ethan is not unwell, is
he?"

Melanie shook her head. "The child is in
perfect health, but he doesn't belong in an
orphanage."

"I remember Ethan Dornan from last summer.
He really is a lovely boy, although a trifle small for
his age." Genevieve frowned. "Are you saying he's
not an orphan?"

"He *is* an orphan but he's not without family.
He ought to be living with his grandaunt, Mrs.
Pendergast. Unfortunately, she disapproved of his
father and now refuses to take Ethan in."

Lord Peyton recoiled. "I may have a streak of
Caliban, but Ethan's grandaunt is truly a full-

blown monster. She must truly be an unhappy woman."

"I don't know if she's monstrous or not, but I think if she had the opportunity to meet Ethan, she would change her mind." Melanie frowned. "I intend to write her a letter, offering to bring Ethan for a visit. Perhaps her curiosity will be piqued, and she will agree."

"Let me write to her."

Lord Peyton's unexpected offer nearly caused Melanie to drop her ginger biscuit into her lap. "What?"

"A letter from a Lord Cedric Peyton might carry a little more weight than one from a Miss Starhope." He paused. "I mean no offense."

"I'm not offended in the least." Melanie gave him an appraising glance. "As it so happens, I agree with you."

"Ah...a rare alignment of the stars."

When he chuckled, his straight, white teeth were revealed. Why did the perfection of his features set her nerves on edge so much?

"I commend you on your generosity, Lord Peyton." Genevieve gave Melanie a pointed glance.

Melanie took the hint. "Yes, indeed. Thank you."

A lock of Lord Peyton's dark wavy hair had come free from its binding and fell across his forehead in an insouciant manner. He looked so much the handsome devil, she wondered if he were about to sprout horns and a tail.

He brushed the lock of hair back with his fingers. "I shall ask Mrs. Wheeler for the address on Monday — or sooner if I should see her in church."

"You go to church?" Melanie blurted the question without thinking.

"Melanie!" Genevieve stared at her, wide-eyed.

"Er...I beg your pardon, Lord Peyton." She winced, inwardly. "What I meant to ask is, which church do you attend?"

"St. Michael's." Lord Peyton did not appear to be bothered by Melanie's rudeness in the least. "I hope to see you there this Sunday."

He took his leave at last, and Melanie drew a sigh of relief. As soon as the front door closed, Aunt Ginny made a sound of exasperation.

"Are you out of your senses to be baiting the man? In the space of a few minutes, you compared him to Caliban and implied he was too wicked to set foot on hallowed ground!"

Melanie sighed. "I truly don't mean to speak to him that way. It just...slips out."

"You really ought to hold your tongue." Aunt Ginny scowled. "I cannot have a young woman under my roof acting like a shrew!"

Her aunt's tone was so sharp, Melanie was cut to the quick. "I'm sorry, Aunt Ginny." She swallowed the lump in her throat. "I will redouble my efforts to be civil to Lord Peyton. I'm very glad he wishes to help Ethan Dornan reunite with his grandaunt."

Genevieve's posture relaxed. "I don't understand why you dislike the fellow so much. He seems kind and gentlemanly."

"The unfortunate manner of our first meeting has probably prejudiced me against him." Melanie bit her lip. "I doubt he took offense to anything I said. He dislikes me too much to take my remarks to heart."

"Don't be so certain, dearest." With that, Genevieve left the drawing room.

Melanie took another biscuit from the tea cart and moved over to glance out the window. Lord Peyton was striding down the driveway with his hat in his hand, swinging his arm as if he hadn't a care in the world. As if he could sense her watching him, he turned long enough to catch her eye. He laughed and continued on his way.

Melanie couldn't help but laugh, too. Yes, Lord Peyton was quite an oddity indeed.

••••

Melanie and Aunt Ginny found seats next to the aisle a short while before the service was to begin. Although she gave the congregation a cursory glance, she saw no one who resembled Lord Peyton. She did spot Mrs. Wheeler, however, seated with the staff and children from the orphanage. The group took up several rows, and Melanie gave a little wave to any of the children who happened to meet her gaze. Although the orphans wore their Sunday best, she noticed the shabbiness of their garments. She yearned to do something to help but her allowance would never stretch far enough to furnish each child with a set of new clothes.

Mrs. Wheeler was clearly doing the best she could, but because the orphanage was sustained by private donations, Melanie realized every penny that came in must be carefully spent. Hopefully, at some point in the future, Ethan would go to live with Mrs. Pendergast and Mrs. Wheeler's costs would lessen — at least until another orphan took his place.

As Melanie opened her hymnal, she heard a sort of stirring amongst the churchgoers. A moment later, Lord Peyton approached her pew. As their eyes met, he gave her a little wink and a smile before he made his way to one of the pews closer to the altar. Heads turned as he passed by and a low murmur of conversation ensued. Apparently, Lord Gooseberry caused a stir, even in the House of God.

Genevieve nudged her with an elbow. "Do you see? Lord Peyton doesn't dislike you at all."

"Hmph." Melanie tossed her head. "Think that if you wish, Aunt Ginny, but he meant to annoy me."

"Judging from the adoring expressions on the women within my view, I suspect they wish he would annoy them as well."

Melanie ignored Genevieve's whispered comment and chose to concentrate on the hymn instead. Her aunt simply did not know Lord Peyton the way she did, and could not possibly understand.

Although Melanie didn't mean to be inattentive, her mind kept wandering during the service. If Lord Peyton was successful in persuading Mrs. Pendergast to see her great-nephew, what then? Perhaps she ought to teach the talented lad something he could play for the woman, in order to charm her. Then again, maybe Ethan's musicality might remind her unpleasantly of his father. Well, if Mrs. Pendergast was that difficult, it might be better for him to remain at the orphanage.

As the vicar gave his homily, Melanie cast a quick glance back at Ethan. If — no, *when* — he met his grandaunt, his clothes would make a poor impression. Could she afford to outfit him properly? She could write her father for an advance on her allowance, but the request would undoubtedly be met with all manner of awkward questions. Lord Peyton possessed that kind of money, but she could not imagine imposing on him for the funds. Genevieve was wealthy and would probably be happy to help, yet Melanie could not ask her either. Her aunt had already spent a small fortune on Melanie's clothes when they were in London and had also spent a great deal of money redecorating Melanie's bedroom. It simply wouldn't be right to ask Aunt Ginny for more.

If she had a bolt of plain fabric, she could sew a sailor suit or a pair of short pants and a jacket. Unfortunately, fabric cost money she didn't have, especially since she was about to put some of her dwindling funds into the collection plate. She could tear out the seams of her gardening gown and make it into something for Ethan if the fabric was in better shape and a different pattern...

Genevieve rose and tapped Melanie on the shoulder. Melanie suddenly realized the postlude was playing and she belatedly stood as well.

Her aunt leaned over to whisper, "Were you daydreaming?"

Melanie smiled. "In a way."

After they emerged from the church, Aunt Ginny's friends clustered around for an introduction to her niece. Although Melanie did her best to be polite, she was watching Lord Peyton out of the corner of her eye. He'd managed to get Mrs. Wheeler off to the side, presumably to inquire about Mrs. Pendergast's address. From the envious glances cast toward the matron, evidently, many ladies would have liked to change places with her. Melanie tried her best to ignore him after that. The task became easier when she was mobbed by her pupils, who wished to reassure her how hard they had been practicing since their lesson.

Mrs. Wheeler clapped her hands. "Come along, children! The wagon is here."

A chorus of good-byes ensued and as the orphans left, Melanie found herself face to face with Lord Peyton.

She curtsied. "Good morning, sir. I hope your conversation with Mrs. Wheeler was productive?"

He winced. "Sadly, the woman refuses to tell me Mrs. Pendergast's address."

Melanie was aghast. "Why?"

"Something about confidentiality or some such claptrap." He shook his head. "I'm not without the resources to discover the address on my own, however. I will make some inquiries."

"Thank you for your persistence, Lord Peyton. I'm really exceedingly grateful."

He gave her a sidelong glance. "I didn't do it for *you*, I did it for Ethan. I don't like to see a child in need."

As she recognized her words thrown back at her, she forced a smile to her lips. "Touché, sir."

He smirked at he doffed his hat. "Good day, Miss Starhope."

Lord Peyton sauntered off toward his horse, which was tied to a hitching post within view. Why had he seen fit to meet her civility with a subtle reproach? Melanie brushed aside a wave of hurt feelings as she rejoined her aunt and her friends.

To her surprise, the ladies were staring at her in shock.

Melanie gave them a puzzled glance. "Is anything amiss?"

The women talked over one another while Aunt Ginny bit back a smile.

"You are acquainted with Lord Peyton?"

"How well do you know him?"

"I confess, he's the most handsome man I've ever seen."

As Melanie waited for the volley to subside, she wondered if she could turn their avid interest in Lord Peyton into something beneficial.

"The gentleman and I both give music lessons at Ledbury Country Home for Children. I can tell you that children are near and dear to his heart." She paused. "He's to volunteer at the orphanage over the summer, if you wish to get involved on some level."

"I gave art lessons last summer," Genevieve said. "I found the experience very rewarding."

The ladies fluttered, cooed, and began discussing their time and talents amongst themselves.

Melanie cleared her throat. "I know that the children are always in need of new uniforms. Perhaps some of you sew?"

By the time the group dissipated, Melanie had extracted promises from the ladies to call on Mrs. Wheeler. As she and Genevieve climbed into the trap for the drive home, a sense of satisfaction overcame any lingering hurt she'd felt at Lord Peyton's rebuke.

Her aunt laughed. "Well done, Melanie. I daresay you just attracted a great many new volunteers for the orphanage."

"I'm delighted...although the real draw is Lord Peyton." She shrugged. "It's like the William Cowper hymn we sung today in church, entitled

"Light Shining Out of Darkness"; 'God moves in a mysterious way.'"

Genevieve beamed. "That He does."

"Lord Peyton is still committed to contacting Mrs. Pendergast on behalf of Ethan." Melanie glanced at her aunt. "Do you think he can persuade her to see the boy?"

"If Lord Peyton visits the woman, I suspect he can." She smiled. "Most women seem to find him irresistible."

"I simply cannot understand how Mrs. Pendergast can refuse to take in her own blood." Melanie shook her head. "It's almost as if family doesn't mean anything at all to her."

Genevieve said nothing for several seconds before blurting out, "You don't blame me for breaking off contact with your father, do you?"

Melanie stared at her. "Of course not. You have every reason to be resentful."

"Mrs. Pendergast may feel the same way." The woman frowned. "I wouldn't like to feel as if I resemble her in any fashion."

"The biggest difference is that you've not taken out your grudge on me."

Genevieve's frown deepened. "Implacable resentment and permanent grudges?" She sighed. "I might as well add an invisible cloak of self-righteousness and have done with it."

Melanie reached out to touch her aunt's arm. "If I've done or said anything that implied any criticism of you, I apologize. You have nothing but my complete respect and admiration."

"Thank you." Genevieve's frown ebbed. "It's more a question of seeing myself in the bad behavior of others. I'm quite happy with my life now, so perhaps it's time to end my feud with James."

Melanie averted her gaze. "I'm not in any position to judge."

Indeed, she was not. After all, hadn't she left Bromley because of her growing resentment of Blanche? To be brutally honest, since her sister hadn't done anything other than to be in possession of extreme beauty, Melanie could be regarded as jealous and selfish.

"I believe I'll write my sister when I get home," she murmured. "It's been several days since I sent a letter, and she must be wondering if I've forgotten her."

"While you are doing that, I'll compose a letter to James." Genevieve drew a deep breath. "Sunday is an excellent day to make a fresh start."

"Yes." Melanie gave an emphatic nod. "Yes, it is."

Chapter Five
Ladies' Sewing Circle

Melanie sat back at her writing desk to read over what she had written. Her letter to Blanche was full of her news and observations, although she omitted a great deal of pertinent information about Lord Peyton. For some reason, she didn't want her sister to know about his looks or their tumultuous relationship. Although she was making an effort to rise above her petty jealousies where Blanche was concerned, she was still entitled to keep a few things to herself, wasn't she?

As Melanie was addressing the envelope, Daisy came into the room with sheets in her arms. "Oh, I beg your pardon, Miss Starhope. I'll come back later."

"No, please come in. I was just about to go downstairs."

By the time Melanie had affixed a stamp to her letter and got to her feet, the maid had stripped the bed and was making it up with fresh linens. As Melanie's gaze settled on the pretty counterpane, she had a flash of inspiration.

"Daisy, what was done with the drapes that used to hang in this room?"

The maid straightened. "Er...after they were laundered, I folded them up and stored them in the attic."

"So nobody has any plans for them?"

Daisy shook her head. "I don't believe Mrs. Hornsby cared for the color. They were dark blue and very plain."

"But the fabric was still in good shape, wasn't it? No holes or frayed edges, I mean."

"No, miss. The lining might have been a trifle lightened by the sun, I think, but the drapes themselves were sound."

"Thank you."

Melanie brought her letter downstairs, left it on the entryway table for the postman to pick up the following morning, and met her aunt in the conservatory for lunch. After a maid served them roast chicken and summer vegetables, Melanie felt a pang of longing for Penguin. If her kitty had been there, she would have fed him chicken until his little tummy was full.

"You look as if your mind is elsewhere, dearest?" Genevieve gave her a concerned glance. "Is anything amiss?"

"No, not at all. Do you suppose I could have the drapes stored in the attic? I'm referring to the ones that used to hang in my room."

Genevieve blinked in surprise. "They were Reginald's taste rather than mine and you may have them, with my blessing. Why do you want drapes?"

"I imagine there's enough fabric to make a suit for Ethan."

"Yes, there's more than enough for a child's suit of clothes."

"Well, perhaps I may sew clothes for the other children as well."

"What an excellent idea. Perhaps you can stop at the fabric shop in town tomorrow and glance through patterns." Genevieve's expression brightened. "Why don't we go up into the attic together after lunch? You may have the drapes, of course, but you might also like to sort through Reginald's clothes."

Melanie peered at her. "Are you absolutely sure?"

"I would be delighted to get rid of them, to be honest." Her aunt waved a dismissive hand. "Reginald always used the finest tailors in London and Paris, and his wardrobe isn't doing any good folded up in trunks."

"Your generosity astonishes me."

"You're the one who will be doing all the work." Genevieve smiled. "Perhaps I might be coaxed into picking up a needle to help."

••••

Melanie and her aunt spent a very pleasant Sunday afternoon browsing through the attic. The drapes had been wrapped in butcher paper and stacked on a rickety old table. Once Melanie had inspected them, she pronounced the fabric serviceable. Genevieve had to search a little harder for her former husband's trunks since they had been hidden behind spare pieces of furniture. For Melanie, Reginald Hornsby's wardrobe was a trove of wonderment. She'd never seen so many silk scarves in a myriad of patterns, suits fashioned of the finest wool, top hats made of silk and beaver, and gleaming hand-tooled shoes.

Genevieve popped open an opera hat and plopped in onto her head. "The first time I laid eyes on Reginald, his beauty made my mouth go dry." She sighed. "Of course, I was very naive and innocent back then."

"Have you any paintings of him?"

"None done by me, I'm afraid, since I burned them shortly after the wedding." She laughed. "He commissioned so many oil paintings of himself, however, they filled the drawing room walls. I took them down when he departed for Greece and stored them up here somewhere."

As Genevieve collapsed the opera hat and tossed it aside, Melanie searched the dusty attic for Reginald Hornsby's portraits. Finally, she spotted several framed paintings stacked against the wall. She picked up the smallest one and brought it over to the window. The man depicted in the portrait was as beautiful as a woman, with exceedingly fine features and curls arranged just so.

Genevieve came to peek over her shoulder. "Yes, that's a good likeness of him." She turned away with a sound of disgust. "I cannot believe I wasted so much of my life married to a man who couldn't bear my company."

"I'm sorry. I didn't mean to bring back painful memories." Melanie returned the portrait to the stack.

"Not at all. Actually, I'm feeling renewed. Not only did I unburden myself in a long letter to James, but the possibility of turning Reginald's belongings into something useful have made me exceedingly cheerful."

"I hope Papa answers your letter the way you would like."

"If not, I will have done my best." Aunt Ginny picked up an armful of clothes and tossed them back into a trunk. "I'll have the servants empty a room where you can sew. I'll also ask them to bring these trunks down so you'll have everything you need at hand."

"That will be perfect." Melanie stifled a sneeze. "Let's go downstairs, shall we? I've had enough dust for one afternoon."

She gathered up the drapes, carried them down the stairs, and put them in her bedroom until a sewing room could be arranged. All that remained was to take Ethan's measurements the following afternoon and purchase a pattern for the suit. In the next moment, her gaze fell on her handbag, and she wondered if she had enough pocket money to manage the purchase.

Melanie turned her coin purse out onto the counterpane and counted the meager sum. Her shoulders drooped as she realized her funds simply would not last until the end of the month. With few other options, she sat down at the desk to write to her father. As she composed a plea for an advance on her allowance, she told him what she intended to do with the money. Perhaps, once he realized she needed funds for a charitable purpose, he would be more inclined to agree.

••••

When Melanie arrived at the orphanage the following afternoon, she was taken aback to see a number of carriages parked in front and along the driveway. She was even more surprised to discover Lord Peyton standing next to Matador, stroking the horse's neck. There was no room for her trap, and she wondered if she ought to park somewhere down the lane. As she drew near, however, Lord Peyton beckoned her forward and pointed toward the grass on the far side of the tree.

"What on earth is happening here today, sir?" Melanie set the brake. "Nobody told me there was a special occasion."

"It's all your doing — or so I am told." As she climbed down, he took Plaid's reins and tied them onto a low-hanging branch. "The Ladies' Sewing Circle from St. Michael's descended on the orphanage this morning and took over the dining hall."

She shook her head. "Not at my direction, I can assure you."

Lord Peyton chuckled. "I believe you gave them the impression that the children needed new uniforms."

"Well, yes, they do."

"The ladies are in the midst of taking the girls' measurements for new ones."

Melanie's eyebrows rose. "I had no idea their response to my suggestion would be so prompt." Evidently, the opportunity to speak with the effortlessly perfect Lord Peyton had probably been too irresistible for the church matrons to resist. "What about your choir practice?"

"Since the ladies will be taking the boys' measurements this afternoon, the practice is cancelled."

She gasped, "I'm so sorry!"

"Compared to the need for new uniforms, the cancellation is of little consequence." He shrugged. "Besides which, I've been lending a hand."

Melanie gave him a sidelong smile. "I didn't realize you knew how to wield a needle and thread."

His glance was level. "My contribution has been more of an administrative one." He sighed. "I told the ladies I needed to tend to Matador for a few minutes, otherwise I would be in the dining hall at this very moment."

"Take all the time you need." She bit back a laugh. "If anyone should inquire, I shall pretend I didn't see you."

"How thoughtful, Miss Starhope." He paused. "By the way, I sent a letter to a solicitor of my acquaintance who lives in Worcester. If Mrs. Pendergast is a leading member of Worcester society, he'll know her address."

"That sounds promising." As Melanie gazed at Lord Peyton, she noticed a dark smudge on his chiseled features. She extracted a handkerchief from her sleeve and extended it toward him. "You've a bit of dirt," she tapped her own chin, "just there."

She walked off toward the main building, humming under her breath. As she opened the door, she glanced over her shoulder. Lord Peyton was dipping her handkerchief into the horse trough and passing the dampened cloth over his chin. It was a pity, really, since the dirt had made him a trifle more likable.

••••

Over the next few days, Melanie did not see Lord Peyton at all. Similar to the week before, he always arrived early at the orphanage for his choir practice and left before her last lesson with Ethan. Undoubtedly, he would have sought her out if he'd heard something from the Worcester solicitor, would he not? Then again, he was the sort of man to keep his own counsel. Nevertheless, she assigned Ethan to learn a simple Mozart lullaby, just in case he had the opportunity to perform for his grandaunt.

Friday morning, while Melanie and Genevieve ate breakfast in the conservatory, three letters arrived in the morning post. Genevieve sorted through them and gave two envelopes to Melanie. Her expression was oddly strained. "These are for you."

Melanie peered at her. "Is anything amiss?"

"Oh...James has answered my letter." Her voice was breathless. "I had convinced myself that I didn't care about his opinions any longer, but from the way my heart is beating, it seems I do."

"Please feel free to read your letter, Aunt Ginny. I know it's important."

"Thank you. You should do the same."

As Melanie has suspected, one of her letters was from her father and one was from Blanche. She opened the one from her father first.

Dearest Melanie,

Although I commend you for your charity work, you must learn to live within your means. I will put your allowance for July in the post a few days early, but that's all I can do.

Very Truly Yours,
Papa

Melanie could not help but be disappointed. Would it really have violated her father's strict moral code to have advanced her the relatively small sum she required? July was weeks away and—

"It's better than I had hoped. James has apologized." Genevieve laughed. "He says he had misgivings even before the wedding, but thought he was doing the right thing. He now knows he was horribly wrong and has been riddled with guilt all these years."

"I'm so glad the two of you have cleared the air."

Genevieve wriggled with excitement. "Now I can invite the rest of your family to Asphodel!"

Melanie hoped her lack of enthusiasm was not apparent. "Wouldn't that be lovely!"

"It probably wouldn't be until the end of summer." Genevieve pushed back her chair. "If you'll excuse me, I'd like to have a look at my calendar and make notes."

Her aunt hastened from the conservatory with her brother's letter in her hand. Now that Melanie was alone, she didn't bother to hide her frown. Although she was happy Aunt Ginny and Papa had made up their quarrel, a fresh wrinkle now presented itself as a result. She had come to Ledbury to establish a life of her own, but as soon as her sister arrived, Melanie would be relegated to the shadows again. Undoubtedly, Lord Peyton would be enchanted by her sister's looks and all her new friends would comment on how he and Blanche made a beautiful couple.

Melanie grabbed a hot cross bun and took a savage bite. Even though the sweet treat was fresh and perfectly prepared, she took little pleasure in the taste. She and Lord Peyton might not be the best of friends, and perhaps he was somewhat despicable, but he was the thorn in *her* side, and she wasn't ready to share him with Blanche.

After she had finished eating the bun and licked the icing from her fingers, she opened Blanche's letter and unfolded the sheet of paper inside. To her surprise, a pound note fell out and into her lap.

Dear Melly,

After Papa read your letter, he went on and on about the merits of having a budget and spending money wisely! Since you are trying to do something wonderful for that poor little orphan boy, I could not believe he refused to send you an advance on your allowance.

Therefore, I am enclosing my small contribution to the cause. It's all I can spare at the moment, since I never stay within a budget or spend money wisely. Even so, I expect it will be enough to buy your patterns.

Let me know if you are able to arrange a meeting with the boy's grandaunt. It's all very exciting and everything here in Bromley pales in comparison. I can't wait to hear what happens next!

Love and Kisses,
Blanche

P.S. Penguin has taken to sleeping at the foot of my bed. It seems we are friends at last.

Melanie hung her head in shame. Despite her lofty notions of improving herself, she'd made no progress at all. Blanche had sent her the money she needed and encouraged her with an open heart, while *she* had been stewing in old, petty resentments. Her vision blurred and a tear traced its way from the corner of her eye. *She* was the one who was conceited, not Blanche, and she deserved to feel the remorse filling her from head to toe.

She would redouble her efforts to have a cheerful and generous nature and welcome her sister to Asphodel with open arms when the time came. And if her sweet sister should happen to catch Lord Peyton's fancy, perhaps that was as it should be.

Melanie jumped to her feet and made her way to her room. She would write Blanche a glowing letter of gratitude and tonight, when she said her prayers, she would ask to be delivered from jealousy. If that didn't work, she would at least endeavor to keep her uglier feelings to herself.

••••

That afternoon, Melanie left the house a little earlier than usual so she would have enough time to visit the Ledbury fabric shop and select a pattern for Ethan's suit. As she approached the driveway of Lord Peyton's estate, the man himself appeared on Matador. He doffed his hat and fell in next to her gig.

"Hullo! Matador and I usually ride to the orphanage on our own." He grinned. "To what do we owe the pleasure of your company?"

She pretended not to hear his sarcasm. "I have an errand to run in town, if you must know. I'm sewing a suit for Ethan, so he'll have something to wear when he visits his grandaunt."

Lord Peyton gave her a piercing glance. "You've placed a great deal of faith in my ability to convince Mrs. Pendergast to see him."

"I have." Melanie saw no reason to say otherwise. "Your talent with fascinating women is akin to a snake charmer."

He chuckled. "I have failed to fascinate you, it seems. Why is that?"

Melanie smiled. "Evidently, I am not a snake."

Lord Peyton's hearty laugh gave Matador a start. Clearly, the horse was not used to hearing good humor from his rider.

She nodded at the creature. "I hope you've had a word with your stable hand about the tightness of his girth."

"Actually, the fault that day was mine. The wife of the fellow who tends my horses was lying-in, so I gave him a few days off. As a result, I saddled Matador myself — badly, as it happened."

Melanie's gaze flickered toward Lord Peyton. "You allowed a servant a holiday due to a baby?"

Their eyes met." Shouldn't I have done?"

She glanced away. "It's just unusual, that's all."

Only the sound of horses' hooves and the squeak of her carriage wheels broke the silence that ensued. As she was casting about for some innocuous topic of conversation, Lord Peyton spoke first. "I have Mrs. Pendergast's address. I intend to call on her tomorrow."

Her eyebrows rose. "In that case, I shall have to get Ethan's clothes ready more quickly than I had anticipated."

"I cannot promise to persuade her, but I shall do my best."

"I have faith in you...that is, y-your ability to induce Mrs. Pendergast to see reason."

Although she seemed to have stammered, she preferred embarrassing herself in front of Lord Peyton rather than risk giving the impression she admired him in any significant way.

"Er...my aunt wishes to invite the rest of my family to Asphodel before too long." She paused. "That would be my parents and my younger sister, Blanche. They live in Bromley."

Lord Peyton nodded. "My brother and his children have been touring Europe for the last year. They will likely be joining me in a fortnight."

"Your brother and his children?" Melanie cocked her head. "What about the marchioness?"

His voice took on a strange hoarseness. "Audrey is dead."

"Oh, dear. I didn't realize your brother was a widower."

Lord Peyton's grip on Matador's reins tightened. "Forgive me, but I really should ride on. I'm usually at the orphanage by now."

Without waiting for an answer, he urged his mount into a trot. Bewildered, Melanie stared at Lord Peyton's back as he increased the distance between them. What had she said to anger the man so thoroughly? She certainly would have liked to hear more about his brother's children and the circumstances of their mother's death, but he apparently couldn't bear her company a moment longer. For some inexplicable reason, the slight stung. Then again, he had insulted her so frequently since they met, she ought to be used to it by now.

•••

Melanie sat next to Ethan on the piano bench and gave him a beaming smile. "I can tell you've been practicing but your fingering is a trifle awkward just here..." She placed her hands on the keyboard to play the passage in question. "If you'll just work on that part, it will sound lovely."

"Thank you, Miss Starhope." He averted his eyes. "Sometimes the other boys make fun of the way I'm always practicing."

"Never you mind. I imagine if they were as talented as you are, they would practice too."

He lowered his voice, as if he were imparting a secret. "I like playing the piano more than anything."

"I understand your Papa was a musician."

"Yes." Ethan's face fell. "I miss my parents."

"I don't blame you one bit." Melanie took a deep breath and let it out. "It's very sad when life takes such a dark turn, especially for children."

Ethan's thin shoulders moved up and down in a shrug. "Lord Peyton says that, too."

"Does he? Well, if he says it, it must be true." Melanie stood up to retrieve the carryall she'd set on top of the piano. "Before you leave, I'd like to take your measurements."

"The church ladies already did that."

Melanie produced a tape measure and a notepad. "Yes, but that was for a new uniform. I like to sew and I'm going to make you a suit."

Ethan's eyes widened. "For me?" Without warning, he flung his arms around her waist and gave her a big hug. When he didn't let go right away, she returned the hug with one of her own. The child's artless display of affection brought tears to her eyes, but she covered her emotions with a bright smile.

"Now, hold still while I record what I need."

He stood ramrod straight. "Yes, Miss Starhope."

After Melanie was finished, Ethan ran off with a smile on his lips. As she gathered up her things and tidied the room, her spirits were buoyed. If a set of new clothes would make the child happy, she couldn't wait to get started. Earlier that afternoon, she'd purchased the pattern, thread, pins, scissors, and a tape measure. Just as she'd started to select buttons, however, she remembered the extraordinary ones she'd seen on one of Reginald Hornsby's jackets. Once she sewed them onto Ethan's suit, he would look perfectly splendid.

Melanie made her way from the orphanage, listening to the sounds of children playing on the grounds outside. When she emerged and crossed toward her rig, she was surprised to discover Lord Peyton lounging against the shady tree. He straightened as she approached and swept the hat from his head.

She gave him a puzzled glance. "Were you waiting for me, sir?"

"Actually, I was somewhat brusque with you earlier and I wished to apologize." He averted his eyes. "The subject of my sister-in-law's untimely death is still painful."

"Forgive me, Lord Peyton. I shan't mention it again."

"You've done nothing wrong, I assure you. I just wanted you to know."

With that, he returned the hat to his head, seated himself on Matador, and rode off. As Melanie climbed up into her gig, she wondered why he had bothered to apologize for his behavior that afternoon, but not for any of the other previous slights she had suffered at his hand. She would likely never know why, but at least she had discovered he cared about something other than himself. Admittedly, that wasn't an entirely fair assertion. Not only had he been considerate toward a servant, but he'd also demonstrated concern for Ethan Dornan. In fact, the man was going to considerable effort to establish the lad's relationship with his grandaunt and so couldn't be all bad. Of course, a slightly worm-eaten apple wasn't all bad, either.

As she drove away from the orphanage, she tried to sweep all thoughts of Lord Peyton from her mind. She couldn't afford to let down her guard with a man who'd repeatedly proven himself to be rude and arrogant. Let all the other ladies in the county fawn and simper over His Lordship, while *she* attended to more important matters.

Like afternoon tea.

••••

An ostentatious carriage was parked in the courtyard when Melanie arrived home. When she entered the house a few minutes later, she heard the murmur of conversation in the drawing room. As Daisy came to meet her, Melanie whispered, "Who has come to call?"

"Mrs. Steed."

Melanie recognized the name right away as the leader of the Ladies' Sewing Circle.

"I see." She gave the maid her things. "Kindly put my carryall in the sewing room, Daisy."

"Yes, miss."

Melanie entered the drawing room. "Good afternoon."

Genevieve glanced up from her conversation with Mrs. Steed. "Good afternoon, Melanie. We have a visitor."

The two women rose.

"How lovely to see you again so soon, Mrs. Steed." Melanie curtsied before lowering herself into the nearest chair. "I must say, the generous response by the Ladies' Sewing Circle has exceeded my expectations."

"I'm glad you think so, Miss Starhope." Mrs. Steed settled herself onto the sofa once more. "I thought you might wish to see what the new uniforms will look like." She gestured toward the tea-table nearby, which held several fabric samples and drawings.

Melanie smiled. "I would indeed."

As Melanie examined the sketches and fabric, Mrs. Steed resumed her conversation with Genevieve.

"As I was saying, my friend in London wrote to say she is well acquainted with Edmund Peyton, the Marquess of Warwick, and his brother, Lord Peyton."

Although Melanie feigned interest in the uniforms, she listened, nonetheless.

"And has your friend anything notable to report?" Genevieve asked.

"Well, they are both eligible, for one thing. Lord Peyton is a bachelor, and his brother is a widower. The Marchioness of Warwick passed away last year and sadly left two small children behind."

"Oh, how dreadful." Genevieve shook her head. "Had the woman fallen ill?"

"Lady Warwick never fully recovered from delivering her second child, apparently." Mrs. Steed sighed. "After her death, the two brothers withdrew from society."

Genevieve frowned. "I can very well imagine."

"There's something else." Mrs. Steed lowered her voice. "Lord Warwick and Lord Peyton are not at all close. Rumor has it that they quarreled years ago and never fully reconciled."

"What a pity!" Genevieve shook her head. "Unresolved resentments can weigh upon one's heart rather dreadfully."

Melanie finally spoke up. "Lord Peyton and his brother may have put their difficulties behind them. I was informed that Lord Warwick and his children will be joining him at Prospero's Retreat in the near future."

Mrs. Steed peered at her. "I'm so glad you told me! I was going to ask Mr. Steed to call on Lord Peyton but I'll wait until Lord Warwick arrives instead."

Melanie raised her eyebrows. "Poor Lord Peyton."

She was perfectly serious, but Mrs. Steed laughed. "Yes, it's terrible for the man, always being overshadowed by his brother." She shrugged. "Alas, life is not always fair."

"No, it is not." Melanie gave the woman a bright smile. "Thank you for showing me your plans for the uniforms. The children will be delighted with their new clothes."

Mrs. Steed beamed as she gathered up her materials. "I'm so glad you think so. The sewing circle is hard at work, even as we speak. Uniforms for the girls should be completed within a fortnight and then we'll get to work on the boys." She stood. "Well, I must be off. I certainly hope Lord Warwick arrives soon because I would love to invite him to dine!"

After the woman left, Genevieve gave Melanie an amused glance. "You and Lord Peyton have something in common, it seems."

"If you are referring to him standing in his brother's shadow, I refuse to feel sorry for him. With his looks and talent, he need never feel inferior."

"You have come a long way if you can acknowledge the man's virtues so freely. It sounds very much as if you are defending him."

"Not at all." Melanie waved a dismissive hand through the air, as if brushing aside an annoying fly. "Has tea been set out in the conservatory? I'm famished."

Chapter Six
Sunday Picnic

Melanie and her aunt filed into St. Michael's on Sunday morning. As Melanie moved down the aisle, she smiled and nodded at orphans and sewing circle ladies alike. It was easy to pick out Frederick Ingram because of his cowlick and Anne Leighton because of her curly red hair. After she settled into a pew next to Genevieve, she flexed her hands several times.

"It's a good thing I'm wearing gloves, otherwise everyone would see my reddened fingertips."

"You needn't sew from sunup to sundown, dearest," her aunt murmured. "For all you know, Lord Peyton will be unsuccessful."

Melanie shook her head. "He won't, and the suit must be ready beforehand."

Genevieve peered at her. "You have a great deal of faith in him."

"I wouldn't call it faith in *him*, exactly." She paused. "I think I have faith that Mrs. Pendergast will be persuaded."

Genevieve gave an unladylike snort. "You may twist things as you wish, but it amounts to the same thing. You just don't want to admit it."

Melanie made a noncommittal sound. Why was Aunt Ginny being so purposefully obtuse? With a frown, she reached for the hymnal and turned to the opening hymn. Just as she was humming the first few bars to herself, she noticed movement out of the corner of her eye.

"May I sit with you?"

To her shock, Lord Peyton stood in the aisle, fixing her with his usual sardonic smile.

She gulped. "Oh...certainly."

Melanie nudged Genevieve and they both scooted over in order to make room for the gentleman.

He sank down into the pew. "I have news."

She stared at him, expectantly. "Yes?"

He frowned and shook his head. "We'll discuss it after church." His gaze flickered to the hymnal in her hands. "Shall we share?"

Melanie thrust the hymnal toward him. "W-Would you prefer to hold it?"

Lord Peyton chuckled. "I wouldn't dream of taking the hymnal away from you, Miss Starhope."

For the entirety of the service, Melanie could not concentrate on what was said. She tried to tell herself it was entirely due to Lord Peyton's unspoken news. That was partly true, of course, but... what if people noticed the two of them sitting together and decided to make something innocent into the subject of gossip? Furthermore, she could not escape his scent, or the occasional physical contact when his arm happened to brush against hers. Why hadn't he chosen to sit elsewhere, for mercy's sake?

His close proximity had other, more physical effects as well, and she became increasingly cross with herself as a result. In Bromley, Mr. Jones had raised a blush with his boyish looks, but Lord Peyton radiated a *manliness* that could not be ignored. Melanie did not understand the peculiar sensations rocketing throughout her body, but she'd never felt them before. Evidently, despite her best intentions, she was not as immune to Lord Peyton's charms as she might have imagined.

She straightened her spine and redoubled her resolve to control her emotions. Although she might enjoy the taste of onions, she had discovered they disagreed with her. Similarly, she might relish the delicious sensations that Lord Peyton had awakened within her but admittedly, she knew they would lead her astray. More importantly, if Lord Peyton truly understood she had a weakness, his triumph would be complete.

The notion was anathema.

Melanie made an effort to recall how nasty Lord Peyton been to her at their first meeting, so she could hold onto her feelings of revulsion...but as she formed a mental picture of the way he had looked, all she could think about was his unbuttoned shirt and the smoothness of his skin. Blast the man for torturing her in this fashion! He was all things despicable, unworthy, and beneath her notice.

And yet...

Did it bother him to be outranked by his brother in much the same way Blanche outshone her? If so, Lord Peyton had a weakness as well. In his case, unfortunately, she found the vulnerability appealing. Gah! Unless she could steel her resolve, her existence in Ledbury would become unbearable. She must not lower her guard under any circumstances from now on or she might as well throw herself into the nearest bramble bush and have done with it.

After the service had concluded, Melanie's pew was obliged to wait for the pews in front to empty before the occupants could file out with everyone else. As the pew in front began to empty, Lord Peyton glanced down at her.

"Have you planted my gooseberry cutting yet?"

The question caught her unprepared. "What?"

"The gooseberry branch I sent over with your manservant. Have you planted it?"

"Er...no. It's still in a vase of water, growing roots."

"I'll be over this afternoon with a spade — and a picnic lunch for two." Lord Peyton stepped out into the aisle and left before she could protest.

Genevieve blinked. "What was that all about?"

"It seems that Lord Peyton is intent on planting a gooseberry shrub on your property this afternoon."

Her aunt peered at her. "Why?"

"I imagine he wishes to discourage me from scrumping."

"You're joking."

"Not entirely." Melanie sighed. "Lord Peyton has something to report regarding his conversation with Mrs. Pendergast. He says he's bringing over a picnic for two."

"That sounds delightful." Aunt Ginny peered at her. "Why do you look so vexed?"

Melanie would have rather eaten a raw onion and suffered the effects than confess the true nature of her disgruntlement to anyone. "I didn't care for his high-handed manner."

"There must be more to it than that. You're exceedingly flushed."

"Am I?" She cast about for another plausible explanation. "Er...I'm put out because I shall have to set aside the time I need for sewing."

"Nonsense! Sunday is a day of rest, dearest. Besides which, you need to give your fingers time to heal."

Her pupils rushed over to greet Melanie just then and she was spared the necessity of a reply. On the drive home, however, she began to fret about Lord Peyton's impending visit. If she were forced to spend any length of time alone with the man, her guard might slip. The risk of revealing herself was too great. Should her words, deeds, or expressions suggest she found Lord Peyton attractive, he would take every opportunity to mock her.

"Aunt Ginny, you must come with Lord Peyton and me on our picnic. I need to know where you would like the gooseberry shrub planted."

The woman laughed. "I wouldn't dream of intruding. And as for the gooseberry cutting, place it wherever you wish. The property is so extensive, you have many spots from which to choose."

"No, but...i-it's not proper for us to picnic alone without a chaperone."

"Considering the antipathy you have for one another, I don't think anything untoward could possibly occur." Aunt Ginny gave her a sharp glance. "He's not tried to take liberties, has he?"

"Heavens, no!" Melanie recoiled. "I assure you, such things have probably never entered his mind where I am concerned. It's just that people gossip, and I don't wish to be the unfortunate target of unkind rumors."

"How will anyone know? Besides which, I intend to skip lunch and paint on the patio all afternoon. The clouds in the sky are unusually beautiful today and I hope to capture them in watercolors."

Tension began to build in Melanie's neck. "But Papa and Mama would not approve!"

"In that case, take Daisy along. She can help serve you and Lord Peyton and I'm sure she knows better than to repeat anything she overhears."

"Yes, all right." The compromise allowed Melanie to lower her shoulders somewhat. "That is an excellent idea."

When Melanie returned home, however, she discovered that the housekeeper had given Daisy the afternoon off and no one else could be spared from their duties. She returned to her room, removed her Sunday gown, and paced. What should she wear to picnic with a fatally attractive man she despised? Her gown could not be pretty, lest he imagine her to be flirting with him. Perhaps she ought to wear something ugly, in order to repulse him even more by her than he was already.

She gasped as an idea came into her head. "I know the exact thing!"

Melanie hastened into her closet and sorted through her clothes until she found her gardening gown. Not only was the pinafore ill-fitting and old, but she'd been wearing the garment when she and Lord Peyton first met. He would be instantly reminded of why they disliked each other and probably treat her with his usual arrogant disdain. His rudeness would entitle her to retaliate and then he would storm off in disgust.

It was perfect.

••••

Melanie was in her sewing room when the housekeeper tapped on the open door. "Lord Peyton has arrived, Miss Starhope."

"Thank you."

Melanie put down her basting, checked her hair in the mirror, and chuckled. She'd taken her hair down from its pins, twisted it into a plain black braid, and tied the end with a ribbon. Although it was difficult for her to judge, she suspected Lord Peyton would deem her indifferently dressed and as attractive as a croquet mallet. She retrieved a broad-brimmed hat from her room and made her way downstairs.

When she entered the drawing room, however, Lord Peyton was not there and he wasn't in the library across the hall, either. Baffled, she glanced out the window and discovered him lounging outside, next to gig.

"How very ill-bred!" She stormed outside and confronted him directly. "Lord Peyton, don't you know a gentleman is supposed to wait for a lady inside her house?"

When he turned, she discovered he was an indifferently clad as she was. In fact, unless she missed her guess, he'd donned the same clothes he'd worn on the morning he'd caught her picking gooseberries. This time, however, his shirt was properly buttoned, and he held a hat in his hand.

He grinned at her. "The house belongs to your aunt, not you. Besides which, I'm no gentleman and you're no lady."

Melanie's eyes narrowed but before she could take him to task, he threw his head back and laughed.

"Can't you tell when you hear a joke? I waited outside because my boots are dirty, and I didn't want to track mud into the drawing room."

"Oh." She wished she had not overreacted since the man evidently enjoyed making her angry. "Where are we going for our picnic?"

"You tell me." He stuck his thumb toward the open, two-wheeled carriage parked in the courtyard. "I have the hamper and spade in back.

Your housekeeper also brought out the gooseberry cutting, wrapped in a wet towel."

"Gooseberry shrubs like a great deal of sun so..." she pointed, "let's go to the top of that knoll."

"Done."

After he helped her climb up into the gig, he began to drive across the lawn.

Melanie nodded toward the dapple-gray mare in the harness. "You didn't sell Matador, I trust?"

"Oh, no, but the proud creature is not interested wearing a harness." He gestured with his left hand. "This is Phoebe. Although she's far more even-tempered, she has her moments."

"I hope she gets along well with Matador."

"They...tolerate one another."

Melanie laughed. "I suppose an uneasy truce is better than nothing."

"Exactly." He gave her a sidelong glance. "I underestimated you, Miss Starhope."

The brim of her hat was so broad, she had to tilt her head back to meet his gaze. "In what way, sir?"

"I approve of your attire." He shrugged. "Most women would have worn something fussy and feminine to a picnic, but you look as if you are ready for a planting."

Melanie glanced down at her pinafore gown. "I wear this when I'm gardening."

"And scrumping."

Despite herself, she smiled. "That, too." Melanie's curiosity finally overwhelmed her. "What news have you to impart regarding Mrs. Pendergast?"

A wince crossed his handsome face. "When she discovered why I had come to call, she nearly had me tossed out on my head."

Melanie's jaw dropped along with her heart. "What a horrible woman!"

"I tried my best to tell her about Ethan's disposition, manners, and talent, but she didn't want to listen." His expression softened. "I hope you don't blame me for failing to convince her."

"No. I'm quite certain nobody could have done more." She groaned. "What are we going to do now?"

"I...well, I have some ideas, actually, but let us talk more about that later. Where do you wish to plant the cutting?"

She pointed to a spot. "Just there, I think."

Lord Peyton reined Phoebe in and set the brake. "If you will carry over the branch, I will dig a hole."

He helped Melanie down from the gig, draped the damp towel and cutting across her arms, and retrieved a spade from the back of the carriage. After he stuck the spade into the ground, he slid out of his jacket, hung it on a cleat attached to the back of the gig, and began to unfasten the buttons on his shirt.

Melanie's eyes widened. "What are you doing?"

He didn't bother to spare her a glance. "Taking off my shirt so it doesn't get dirty."

With a rising sense of panic, she took a half-step back. "Stop that this instant!"

Lord Peyton paused his disrobing long enough to look at her askance. "Are you repulsed by the human form?"

Melanie glared. "Not at all, but it simply isn't proper for you to remove your clothes."

He fixed her with an appraising glance. "You're not afraid of me, are you?"

Her spine straightened. "Don't flatter yourself. I'm just shocked at your lack of propriety."

Lord Peyton chuckled as he unfastened his buttons on his cuffs. "Turn your back then, if you are so squeamish. My shirt is made out of fine linen, and I refuse to go the rest of the afternoon wearing dirt."

She made a sound of disgust." You're an animal."

He laughed louder. "You wound me."

Lord Peyton hung his snowy white shirt on a second cleat and crossed over to the spade. Melanie averted her eyes for a short while — until she realized he was paying her no attention at all. Then, and only then, did she allow her gaze to linger on his bare torso. Lord Peyton's male beauty nearly took her breath away. His sleek, hard muscles rippled as he worked, and his smooth skin seemed to glow in the sunlight. Melanie felt her toes curl inside her sturdy boots, and she leaned against the gig to steady her weak knees — just like Aunt Ginny had described. *When God made this creature, he must have made him in the image of a heavenly angel.*

Lord Peyton finally tossed the spade to one side and beckoned to Melanie. "It's your turn."

"All right."

She averted her gaze as she moved toward him. Fortunately, by the time she positioned the cutting properly and covered its newly formed roots with dirt, Lord Peyton had donned his clothes.

She gave him a puzzled glance. "How did you clean your hands?"

"I brought several jugs of water for the task. If you bring that towel over here, I'll help you wash yours."

After he poured water over her hands, he wiped them clean with the towel. Unfortunately, his gaze missed nothing.

"What happened to your fingertips?"

"Oh." She put her hands behind her back. "I've been working on Ethan's suit, trying to complete it as quickly as possible."

"I don't mean to make you self-conscious. In my opinion, there's absolutely nothing wrong with hard work." His smile was uncharacteristically kind. "I'm only sorry Ethan won't be wearing the suit to meet his grandaunt."

"I'm eager to hear your ideas about how to move forward."

"In due time." He brought the jug over to the gooseberry cutting and emptied it of water. "Well, we've done our best. Let us hope what we planted takes root and flourishes."

"The cutting has as good a chance as any."

"Yes, and perhaps more than most." He retrieved the spade and returned it and the jug to the gig. "Do you know of a shady spot for our picnic?"

"We passed a lovely weeping willow on the way here."

"That should do nicely." Lord Peyton took hold of Phoebe's bridle. "It's not far. Shall we walk?"

A short while later, Melanie and Lord Peyton had settled themselves on a large blanket underneath the graceful willow, which had a view of Prospero's Retreat. Although she tried to help as he unpacked the large hamper, he waved her off with a smile and a shake of his head. "I invited *you* today and so you must allow me to manage things."

Since he would not permit her to even unfold a napkin, she reclined on the blanket, closed her eyes, and listened to him work. The warm breeze moved the branches overhead just enough to let patches of light through and she found the temperature exceedingly pleasant.

Minutes went by and Melanie suddenly realized Lord Peyton's movements had ceased. She opened her eyes and caught him staring at her.

"What is it?" Melanie sat up. "Have I done something wrong?"

He frowned. "You're really quite pretty when you're not acting like a shrew."

"That sounded partly like a compliment. Since it was coming from *you*, however, I shall take it with a pinch of salt."

"It was a compliment." As Lord Peyton passed her a plate filled with small sandwiches, his gaze flickered toward her skirt. "How did you get those holes in the fabric? It almost looks as if a cat mistook you for a tree."

"That's just what happened." She laughed. "I was out walking one day when I came across a black and white stray kitten. I petted the little creature for a little while but when I tried to leave, he jumped on my skirt and wouldn't let go."

"What did you do?"

"What else could I do? I brought him home, named him Penguin, and he's been excellent company ever since." She averted her gaze. "I had to leave the sweet boy in Bromley."

"I expect you miss him." Lord Peyton picked up an empty glass. "Would you prefer tea or water?"

"Tea, please."

They nibbled on sandwiches, fruit, cheese, and slices of cake. After a short while, Melanie was too full to eat anything else and simply watched Lord Peyton polish off a second helping of everything.

She shook her head. "How do you stay so trim while eating so much?"

He chuckled. "So you *were* watching when I had my shirt off."

Melanie made a sound of disgust. "If you've nothing more civilized to contribute to the conversation, I shall bid you good afternoon."

Before she could move, he reached across to encircle her arm. "Please don't. I have a proposal."

His touch sent her heart racing, but fortunately he released her instantly.

"I was thinking about Ethan's situation," he continued. "I believe he has made an indelible impression on both of us."

She gave him a puzzled glance. "Yes."

Lord Peyton's color was high. "The lad needs a stable home, with a married couple as guardian."

"That would be the best possible situation for Ethan." She cleared her throat. "Yes."

The blood began rushing in her ears. After all the acrimony that had taken place between them, could Lord Peyton really mean to propose?

He swallowed. "Would you ever consider entering into such a marriage — for Ethan's sake, that is?"

"I-I hadn't planned on marriage at all..." The next words tumbled from her lips before she could think too much., "...but I suppose if the proper person came along, I might change my mind."

Lord Peyton heaved a sigh of relief. "I was hoping you would say that." He grinned. "You've got pluck. I believe you and my brother, Edmund, will get along famously. You'll adore his children, I think. We'll say nothing to him about Ethan until he forms an attachment to you. After that, I believe things will fall into place. What do you think?"

For several long moments, Melanie was too shocked to make a reply.

He peered at her. "Well?"

"I'm...flattered you think me worthy of your brother, sir, but I rather wonder why you think he and I might suit one another."

"I know his taste in women. The only real challenge is to overcome Edmund's reserve. Since his wife passed away, he's been withdrawn and difficult to reach."

"No doubt he's still in mourning." Melanie focused on Lord Peyton. "Why don't you consider matrimony yourself? After all, you've grown fond of Ethan and would likely make an excellent guardian."

"I've little desire to marry, I'm afraid. My heart will always belong to another."

Melanie's spirits were already as low as possible, so why did it feel as if someone had reached down her throat and was squeezing her heart?

"I don't understand." She was unable to draw a deep breath. "If you are in love with a lady, why not make her your bride?"

"The lady *was* my fiancée years ago, but decided to marry a man with a title instead." He frowned. "Sadly, I love her still."

"I'm truly sorry for you." Melanie reached for her hat. "Forgive me, but I've developed a headache. I'll go in now but thank you for the picnic."

He jumped to his feet and helped her to rise. "You'll like Edmund. He's always been a favorite among women."

Melanie forced herself to smile. "It remains to be seen if he will like me."

"He will. It's almost a certainty."

She hastened off across the lawn in a sort of stunned haze. How could she have hoped for even a moment that Lord Peyton was proposing to her? She was an utter and complete fool, profoundly stupid, and extraordinarily naïve. Evidently, she'd gone against all her principals and had allowed herself to care for him. As soon as she was certain he could no longer see or hear her, she sank down into the grass and laughed until mirthless tears were streaming from her eyes.

She despised Lord Peyton — but she despised her own weakness even more.

••••

Melanie curled up on her bed, sobbing, while Genevieve sat in a chair nearby. Her aunt said little while Melanie had told her what had happened in a choked voice, but her countenance was etched with sympathy. Finally, when Melanie grew calmer, the older woman spoke.

"I *had* wondered if your antipathy toward Lord Peyton didn't mask some deeper regard."

"That's not helpful, Aunt Ginny."

Genevieve sighed. "I wonder why Lord Peyton is so convinced that you and his brother will suit one another."

Melanie mopped her face with a handkerchief. "Probably because he dislikes his brother and wishes to see him unhappily wed."

"Come now." Genevieve gave her a reproachful glance. "Cynicism will get you nowhere."

"Perhaps not." Melanie sat up and rested her back against the headboard. "I'm not feeling optimistic, nevertheless."

"I know you don't want to hear this, but why don't you wait to form an opinion until you've met Lord Warwick? Lord Peyton knows his brother better than you do, after all, and the man might be delightful. Besides which, there are worse things than becoming a marchioness."

Melanie scowled. "I cannot believe you said that."

Her aunt shrugged. "Why not? No one will force you to marry Lord Warwick if you don't like him, but consider that he has two young children who need a mother. In addition, you can provide a home for Ethan Dornan. Furthermore, you can have children of your own, if God sees fit to bless you in that way."

Melanie was in no mood to be fair or reasonable, but she knew her aunt was just trying to look on the bright side. "I suppose." She took a deep, cleansing breath. "Truth be told, I'm disappointed in myself. I wanted to be like you — a strong, independent woman who is happy to remain unmarried. Instead, I discovered I'm just as vulnerable as any other girl to a ridiculously handsome man like Lord Peyton."

Genevieve averted her gaze. "The things we tell ourselves are often merely to console us for the things we cannot have." She swallowed hard.

"If I've made you believe I wouldn't trade my independence for the chance to have a child, I was less than honest." She got to her feet. "Give Lord Warwick an opportunity to win your affections, Melanie. I do not think you will regret it."

As her aunt left the room, Melanie stared after her in disbelief.

Suzanne G. Rogers

Chapter Seven

A Musical Soiree

Aunt Ginny waved a card in the air. "You and I have been invited to a soiree."

Melanie glanced up from her breakfast. "Oh?"

Genevieve focused on the invitation. "Lord and Lady Dellingpole request the pleasure of your company at a soiree this Saturday evening. Please be prepared to contribute to the entertainment in some way." She beamed. "It seems you will have the opportunity to play the piano for Ledbury society."

"I look forward to the evening." Melanie gave her aunt a sidelong glance. "What about you, Aunt Ginny? Have you some musical talent of which I am unaware?"

The woman snorted. "Alas, no. but I'm always included in our local soirees because I draw amusing caricatures. No one likes to be poked fun at more than people with money. It flatters their sense of self-importance."

Melanie laughed. "I expect you're right."

"What will you play?"

"Er...I don't know." She frowned. "It's been a long time since I performed for anyone."

"Don't take too long to select music, if you need to practice. I don't have a piano, so you'll have to use the one at the orphanage."

"All right."

Melanie spent the rest of the morning working on Ethan's suit, although not at such a frantic pace as before. While she sewed, she fretted about the soiree. Should she play Mozart's

"Rondo alla Turca" to demonstrate her finesse or something romantic, like Beethoven's "Moonlight Sonata?" Perhaps she ought to select a piece less commonly performed, lest she be compared to ladies who had played it for local society before. Although she realized she needn't worry overmuch, she preferred to focus on music rather than her disastrous picnic with Lord Peyton. At least playing the piano was within her control.

As Melanie drove to the orphanage that afternoon, she was relieved not to see Lord Peyton on the road. If she could avoid the man altogether, her heart might have time to heal. She decided to ask Mrs. Wheeler to shift her lessons to the morning. Now Genevieve had grown used to Melanie, surely her presence in the house would not be so very bothersome, especially if she kept to her sewing room. Perhaps she could also visit some of the ladies she'd met from church.

When she proposed the change to Mrs. Wheeler, however, the matron shook her head. "That won't do at all, I'm afraid. I need our girls to work in the garden in the mornings, and the lads help the groundskeeper with chores."

Melanie covered her frustration with a smile. "Never mind, then. It was just a thought." She paused. "I hope you don't mind if I stay after my lessons this week and practice on the piano? I'm to attend a musical soiree and I have to prepare."

Mrs. Wheeler brightened. "I'm glad I can help *you* for a change, Miss Starhope. Feel free to use the piano as long as you wish."

"Thank you."

As Melanie made her way to the music room, she greeted the young ladies clustered around the dining hall doorway. Although the door was ordinarily closed, at the moment it was wide open — likely because of the unusually warm temperature that afternoon. When she heard a clear, high soprano singing a phrase from the Lacrimosa movement from Mozart's "Requiem," she paused to listen. The voice belonged to Ethan, not surprisingly, as Lord Peyton directed him. Melanie was touched when the expression on the young boy's face reflected his emotional involvement in the music. She stepped back, unseen by anyone in the dining hall, and moved down the corridor. Once she entered the oppressively hot music room, she threw open all the windows and hoped the space would cool down a little before her pupils began to arrive.

She sat down on the piano bench and began to fan herself with a stack of sheet music. Ethan Dornan really was the most talented child she'd ever met, and she yearned to help him develop his abilities. Would she really consider marrying Lord Warwick in order to take Ethan as a ward? Melanie shook her head and frowned. Even if the marquess turned out to be attractive and affable and his children managed to capture her heart, the prospect of living in the same house as Lord Peyton was unappealing. Indeed, she would have to fall madly in love with the man's brother to feel Lord Peyton's grip loosen.

Her first pupil arrived just then and for the remainder of the afternoon, Melanie lost herself in tutoring. When Ethan walked into the room at four o'clock with his sheet music in hand, she gave him a smile.

"Hello! I heard you singing earlier. I thought you were brilliant."

The skin across his cheekbones glowed pink. "It's Lord Peyton's direction that makes it seem that way."

"I'm sure his direction helps." She patted the piano bench next to her. "Shall we begin?"

Ethan set his sheet music on the rack and focused all his attention on the lesson. Melanie glanced at the boy from time to time as if he were a precious jewel. Mrs. Pendergast would never know what she had missed, but she had very little sympathy for the woman's loss. As incredible as it seemed, she felt as if she'd opened her mind to a different future than the one she'd planned. Perhaps, as each day went by, the possibility of becoming Lady Warwick would seem increasingly palatable.

"Very nice," she murmured, once Ethan's twenty minutes had passed. "Next time, I'd like to see you concentrate on your phrasing."

"Yes, Miss Starhope." He gathered up his music and bowed. "Thank you!"

The door opened and Lord Peyton appeared. "Merciful heavens but it's hot in here." He winced and opened the door completely. "On a day like today, I should be horsewhipped for asking you to keep it closed."

"It's not that bad." Melanie blotted her upper lip with a handkerchief as surreptitiously as possible.

"Will you be able to stay for a few minutes, Ethan?" Lord Peyton held up some sheet music. "We need your help turning pages."

The boy smiled. "Oh, yes!"

"Excellent." Lord Peyton crossed over toward the piano and arranged the music on the rack. "Miss Starhope and I are going to play a duet."

She peered at him, puzzled. "To what purpose, sir?"

"You and Mrs. Hornsby have been invited to Lord and Lady Dellingpole's upcoming soiree, have you not?"

"Y-yes."

He shrugged. "Since you and I are newcomers, I thought we should play something seldom heard in these sorts of gatherings."

Melanie glanced at the music. "Shubert's *Fantasia in F Minor*, Opus 103.'" She shook her head. "I've never played piano four hands before."

"You play Primo while I'll take Secondo." He gestured for her to slide over. "You'll enjoy it, I think."

"I shall try my best."

Lord Peyton crooked a finger at Ethan. "Stand at the ready."

The lad hastened toward the piano.

Melanie peered at the notes on the composition, determined to prove she was up to the task of the duet. At the same time, however, Lord Peyton's proximity was taking its toll on her poise.

"Your hands are trembling, Miss Starhope." He frowned. "Are you all right?"

"Er...too much sewing, I imagine." Melanie gave her hands a shake and lowered her fingertips to the keys. "I'm ready to begin."

Although her playing was tentative at first, Lord Peyton's murmured encouragement gave her confidence. The duet wasn't perfect, of course, but about halfway through, she was so swept up in the music that she forgot about the partner by her side and just allowed herself to feel the emotions in the piece. When the ending notes came at last, she felt almost as if something beautiful — like an exquisite, snowy dove — had come to life and flown away.

Moments later, applause erupted. She glanced over to discover the residents and staff of the orphanage had come to listen to the music. Lord Peyton stood up and took a comedic bow. Although he gestured toward her afterward, as if to give her credit, she knew full well he deserved the lion's share of the praise.

After the impromptu audience dispersed, Lord Peyton rested one hand on Ethan's shoulder. "Thank you for your help, lad."

Melanie nodded. "Yes. indeed. Very well done. What did you think of the music?"

"I've never heard anything so wonderful." His face radiated joy. "Someday, I want to play that, too."

Lord Peyton chuckled. "You will, Ethan. Of that, I have no doubt."

"And you'll play it far better than I just did," Melanie added. "Run along now."

Ethan scampered from the room while Lord Peyton was gathering up the sheet music.

"Despite what you just said, you played the piece very well for your first time." He gave her an expectant glance. "Do you think you'd like to play the duet at the soiree?"

"I'd like nothing better." She smiled. "You must let me practice it, however, so I can perform to standard."

Lord Peyton presented her with the pages. "These are for you, then." He paused. "I'll be here tomorrow at half past four o'clock, so we can work on it together." He turned and sauntered from the room in the carefree fashion she found so characteristic of him.

Melanie packed away her things and closed up the room as she did every afternoon. Although her spirits were high, she couldn't help but be a trifle bemused at this unexpected development. She'd vowed to avoid Lord Peyton, but fate had decided otherwise. How was she to expunge her inconvenient feelings for the man when she was thwarted at every turn?

••••

Saturday Evening

Melanie tugged on her kidskin gloves and flexed her fingers. Seated in the landau next to her, Genevieve gave her a sidelong glance.

"You must stop fidgeting, dearest."

Melanie sighed and tried to relax her neck. "I can't help it. I don't want to make a fool of myself performing at the soiree — and most especially not in front of Lord Peyton!"

"You told me yourself that your practices went well." Genevieve's smile was placid. "Think about something other than yourself."

"Yes, you are quite right." Melanie nodded. "I shall concentrate on enjoying the other performances and take my own in stride." She took a deep breath and let it out. "There...I'm fine."

Genevieve chuckled. "Few ladies will be wearing Montagna originals tonight. We must take a little pleasure in that."

"We must, indeed."

Although Melanie's remark was in jest, she was genuinely happy with her ensemble. Madame Montagna had designed a cunning costume with a gray silk menswear-influenced double-breasted jacket and a graceful, full skirt with a bustle. Her white handkerchief linen blouse had a high collar with a cherry red silk tie, and the underskirt of her gown was flocked in a dainty floral pattern.

By contrast, her aunt had chosen to wear a more traditional polonaise dinner gown of violet blue floral pattern silk, with a standing collar, long, narrow sleeves, and plain underskirt of matching fabric. The darts in the bodice and the simplicity of the front lent Genevieve a very elegant air and her glossy sable mane was arranged in a flattering style.

"We make a handsome pair, in my opinion," Melanie said.

"None handsomer."

For the remainder of the drive, Melanie closed her eyes and visualized the notes she and Lord Peyton were to play that evening. After a few moments, however, she opened her eyes with a start.

"I *did* give you the sheet music, didn't I?"

"Yes." Her aunt patted the portfolio that held her sketchbook and pencils. "I checked twice before we left, just to make sure."

Melanie forced her shoulders to relax. "I confess, I'll be glad when my performance is over. I hope Lord Peyton and I will go first."

"I imagine that will be up to the hostess."

●●●●

When they entered Lord and Lady Dellingpole's stately residence a short while later, their host and hostess gave them a gracious welcome.

"Miss Starhope, Lord Peyton informed me that the two of you will be playing a duet this evening." Lady Dellingpole beamed. "What a treat!"

"We shall do our best." Melanie's gaze flickered around the entrance hall, where guests were chatting in small groups. "Has Lord Peyton arrived?"

"He sent word of a slight delay. Even if he's late, however, it's of little consequence. Your duet is our final performance."

"Ah." Melanie's smile became frozen. "That sets my mind at ease, thank you."

Lord Dellingpole gestured toward a set of double doors. "We're having the soiree in the drawing room. If you brought any sheet music, feel free to leave it with my cousin, Mr. Anton Chastain. He has graciously volunteered to be our musical director this evening."

Melanie curtsied. "Thank you."

After Genevieve exchanged a few pleasantries with the couple, she and Melanie moved toward the drawing room together.

"Aunt Ginny, I need to find Mr. Chastain. Are you acquainted with him?"

"Er...I met the young man at a Christmas ball three or perhaps four years ago. I don't remember him terribly well, but I suspect I'll recognize the fellow when I see him."

In the drawing room, sofas and chairs had been arranged to face the far end, where an ebony grand piano sat next to a graceful harp. Several early arrivals had already claimed their seats near the back, and their was an air of excited anticipation. Melanie raised her hand to wave at the few people she knew from church.

Genevieve murmured, "Oh, my. Mr. Chastain is standing next to the piano.

Melanie followed her glance. Mr. Chastain was tall, slender, and possessed straight, fair hair slicked back from his face with pomade. As an older matron spoke to him, he jotted something down on a piece of paper and gave her a sunny smile.

Melanie whispered, "He seems affable."

"Yes, the fellow was always pleasant but he used to be a trifle round in the tummy and came up to my chin. Clearly, he's grown up since the last time we met." Genevieve chuckled. "Come along and I'll introduce you."

As they approached, the matron moved toward a group of guests in the back, leaving Mr. Chastain free.

Genevieve curtsied. "Good evening, sir. You probably don't remember me but I'm Mrs. Hornsby."

The young man's expression radiated good humor. "Of course I remember you, Mrs. Hornsby. You drew a wickedly accurate caricature of me that I had to have framed. I keep it to remind myself of how far I've come."

Melanie found Mr. Chastain's ability to laugh at himself quite refreshing.

"You've changed a great deal, so I shall have to draw a more accurate one tonight." She gestured toward Melanie. "This is my niece, Miss Melanie Starhope. She's to play piano." She set down her portfolio so she could retrieve the sheet music from within.

"Mr. Chastain, I was informed you're to be musical director this evening." Melanie's smile sprang to her lips without effort. "I hope that doesn't mean you won't be performing."

His green eyes danced. "On the contrary, I'm to perform "Generoso chi sol brama," from the Handel opera, *Scipione.*"

Her respect for the gentleman rose. "I'm impressed."

Mr. Chastain feigned relief. "I'm so glad to hear it." He leaned closer to whisper, "I struggled for days trying to come up with something to impress Ledbury society."

She laughed. "I have no doubt everyone here was trying to do the exact same thing."

Genevieve slid sheet music into her hands. "Here you are, Melanie. Now if you'll excuse me, I must find a suitable spot to begin my caricatures."

She hastened off, leaving Melanie and Mr. Chastain alone.

"What have you there?" Recognition lit his eyes as he took the sheet music from her. "*Fantasia in F Minor*, Opus 103?" He made a sound of disbelief. "I'm completely stunned and delighted. With whom do you intend to play this duet?"

"Er..." Melanie glanced over her shoulder, but her partner had not yet appeared. "Lord Peyton and I are supposed to perform together, but it seems he's been detained."

"Hmm." Mr. Chastain stroked his chin. "If he does not show up, I would be honored to play this with you."

"I may be obliged to accept your offer, sir, however Lady Dellingpole has said we are to perform last. Lord Peyton may yet arrive."

"Aunt Lila said we were to end the soiree with a duet, but I thought she must be referring to someone's ghastly rendition of "The Celebrated Chop Waltz." I'm glad to be wrong." He used a pencil to scribble notes on what appeared to be the evening's schedule.

She stepped back. "Well, I mustn't monopolize your time any further."

Mr. Chastain grinned. "We're to have refreshments after the music. May I escort you into the dining room?"

Melanie inclined her head in a nod. "I would be honored, sir." She went on to circulate among the other guests with a warm feeling inside.

When Lady Dellingpole rang a little bell to announce the musical portion of the soiree, Lord Peyton had still not arrived. She would have been concerned about his welfare, had he not already sent word of his delay. Whatever his other faults, he had always been punctual. What could possibly have occurred to make him late?

Melanie and her aunt found chairs near the front of the room. Since the soiree was well attended, almost every seat was taken.

Genevieve whispered, "Lord Peyton is exceedingly late."

"I cannot imagine why, but I'm sure we'll find out in due course."

Mr. Chastain stood up next to the piano and urged everyone to be seated. When it seemed as if everyone was settled, he grinned. "Welcome to our soiree! My name is Mr. Chastain and as I watch everyone find a chair that suits their taste, I am reminded of a quote from *All's Well That Ends Well*." He cleared his throat. "'It is like a barber's chair that fits all buttocks, the pin-buttock, the quatch-buttock, the brawn-buttock, or any buttock.'"

Lady Dellingpole gasped. "Really, Anton!"

Despite her admonition, the guests erupted in uproarious laughter. Lady Dellingpole finally relented and dissolved into giggles. Melanie laughed so hard that her stomach hurt.

Mr. Chastain held up his hands for quiet. "There is nothing like the mention of buttocks to break the ice. It is like beginning something with the end."

Another round of laughter ensued.

"And so, without further ado, I shall start off the evening with an aria about unrequited love, from Handel's *Scipione*." He glanced at Melanie and gave her a saucy wink before crossing to the piano.

She bit back a smile, secretly pleased by the attention. The gentleman might not be as dashing as Lord Peyton, perhaps, but he was very likable and boyishly attractive. More importantly, he treated her as if she were worthy of his respect and admiration.

Mr. Chastain began to play the opening notes of his aria. Although the music itself was understated, once he sang, his clear tenor filled the room. Melanie spoke not a word of Italian, but she was enraptured by the emotion conveyed in Mr. Chastain's lyrical voice. The aria was perhaps four minutes long, but she felt as if she were holding her breath the entire time. As his performance came to an end, Melanie led the applause. Mr. Chastain bowed, no longer the clown in *All's Well That Ends Well*, but a respected musical talent.

Melanie continued to clap as she glanced around to soak in the enthusiasm. Out of the corner of her eye, she noticed a familiar figure standing on the far side of the room. Lord Peyton had arrived at last and was glowering at her. She gave him a tentative smile and a nod of welcome, but he merely glanced away. A servant carried a chair over for him just then, and several guests had to shift around to make room.

Melanie whispered to her aunt, "Lord Peyton has arrived and he's in none too good a humor."

Genevieve made no reply, evidently distracted by something in the back of the room. She wore an odd expression — almost as if she'd been stunned.

Melanie nudged her. "What is amiss?"

Genevieve faced forward. "There is a gentleman here who looks very much like Lord Peyton. I believe he must be Lord Warwick."

Melanie longed to catch a glimpse of the man but Mr. Chastain was announcing the next performance — Mrs. Steed in her rendition of "Slumber, Dear Maid," on the harp. As the plump, older woman sat down to pluck out the familiar tune, Melanie was only half-listening. So, Lord Warwick must have arrived at Prospero's Retreat early and that was the reason for Lord Peyton's tardiness. Considering the strained relationship between the two brothers, she no longer wondered why Lord Peyton had been scowling.

For the next hour, guests sang ballads or played piano music from Bach, Beethoven, or Mozart. To be different, one elderly baron acted out the lyrics of "God Save the Queen" in a humorous game of Charades. Another lady played the harp and recited a poem at the same time. Butterflies began to stir in Melanie's stomach as she realized the time of her performance must be drawing close. Then, Lady Dellingpole hastened to the front of the room, to whisper something in Mr. Chastain's ear.

He nodded before addressing the gathering. "We are nearly to the end of the entertainment, but we have something special to add from an honored guest. Lord Warwick will recite one of King Richard's speeches from *Richard II.*"

Melanie exchanged a meaningful glance with Genevieve before turning to watch the marquess stride to the performance area. Her aunt had been correct when she said Lord Warwick strongly resembled his brother. The man's features were more roughly hewn than Lord Peyton's, to be sure, and his demeanor reflected an aristocratic reserve. His closely cropped hair was also a shade lighter and of a finer, straight texture. Whereas Lord Peyton reminded Melanie of an untamed pirate, his elder brother reminded her of a prince. She was glad the man was to perform so she would have the opportunity to take his measure.

When the marquess began his recitation, the deep timbre of his speaking voice sent a ripple down Melanie's spine. She was not especially fond of Shakespeare's historical plays, but the role of Richard II suited him. Lord Warwick delivered the speech with suitable pathos, speaking each phrase as if for the first time.

Genevieve's pencil flew over her pad as she sketched his likeness. When Melanie glanced at the drawing, she noticed her aunt was not drawing a humorous caricature as much as a portrait. Admittedly, it would have been challenging to poke fun at such a handsome man. Then again, if Melanie were to depict Lord Peyton, she would draw him with horns, a tail, and a pitchfork.

As Lord Warwick delivered the last few lines, a tear traced its way down the man's cheek. After a long moment of silence, an overwhelming number of guests — Melanie and Genevieve included — gave the performance the standing ovation it deserved.

Despite the fact Melanie admired the man's looks and commanding presence, she was not drawn to him in the way she might have hoped. Furthermore, as Lord Warwick took a bow and glanced around at the guests, his gaze did not linger on her in any significant way. Still, the man was clearly reserved, and she suspected it would take a great deal of effort to know him well. For now, she would make no decision about him, one way or another.

Mr. Chastain beamed as he took the floor. "What a truly memorable evening it has been so far! But to borrow a phrase from Lucentio in *The Taming of the Shrew*, 'I burn, I pine, I perish'...for just one more performance! We will end with a piano duet from none other than Miss Starhope and Lord Peyton."

Melanie tugged off her gloves, left them on her seat, and took her place at the piano. Lord Peyton came to join her, very much more subdued than usual.

"You look stunning this evening," he murmured.

Had she heard him correctly? She stammered, "Th-Thank you."

Mr. Chastain came to stand next to the piano. "May I turn the pages for you?"

Lord Peyton's response was a curt nod, but Melanie returned the man's smile with one of her own. "That would be very helpful, sir."

She and Lord Peyton had practiced the duet enough to play it with confidence and Mr. Chastain's skill in turning the pages assisted their efforts. As the minutes passed, Melanie found she was enjoying the performance more than she had imagined. When it was over, she was pleased to discover their duet warranted another standing ovation. The response was so enthusiastic, Lord Peyton actually smiled.

"It's good to see you happy," she whispered.

Before they could step away from the piano, Lady Dellingpole rang her little bell.

"This concludes our little entertainment for the evening, but if you will all move into the dining room, we have refreshments!"

Genevieve stood up and raised her voice to be heard over the hubbub. "Don't forget to pick up your caricatures before you leave tonight! I think I managed to get everyone."

Several guests crossed over to her and she began to hand out the drawings. Without exception, expressions of delight ensued.

Lord Peyton's voice drew Melanie's focus. "You played well." His warm fingertips touched Melanie's wrist, sending delicious shivers throughout her body. "I would be honored to escort you into the dining room."

Mr. Chastain leaned in. "I got there before you, sir. Hard luck."

"Did you, indeed?" Lord Peyton gave Melanie a sardonic smirk. "That's a pity."

For a moment, his expression and the touch of his hand had sent her into a maelstrom of confusion. Therefore, she was almost relieved to see Lord Peyton's nastier side emerge.

She tossed her head. "I'm sure you can bear the disappointment quite well."

"I can but try."

As Melanie accompanied Mr. Chastain from the drawing room, she noticed Lady Dellingpole on Lord Warwick's arm. That was as it should be, of course, since the marquess was the highest-ranking gentleman at the gathering. A great many unmarried ladies focused on Lord Warwick with a gleam in their eyes, but he seemed oblivious.

Melanie gave her escort a smile. "You were a wonderful musical director, Mr. Chastain. Not only that, but your performance tonight was one of the most memorable. Where did you learn to sing opera?"

"Naples, Italy. I studied music at the Conservatorio di Musica San Pietro a Majella."

"I'm impressed."

"Really?" He danced a little jig. "If so, my efforts to impress the ladies have borne fruit."

As they sat down to a light supper of shrimp, salad, cold roast beef, and summer vegetables, they talked about composers and musical theory. Even though she was enjoying herself, her gaze flickered toward Lord Peyton. He was dining with Aunt Ginny, and they were engrossed in conversation.

As she recalled the sensation of Lord Peyton's warm fingers touching her bare skin, a slight shiver shook her body. Any other girl might have mistaken the gesture for some sort of romantic overture, so it was a good thing she knew better.

Mr. Chastain's voice interrupted her reverie. "Your mind seems elsewhere, Miss Starhope."

"I beg your pardon, sir." She cast about for a plausible excuse. "I believe I was thinking of dessert. Would you mind fixing me a plate of something sweet?"

"Aha! I can see we have many things in common...such as the love of dessert." He jumped to his feet. "I'll be back momentarily."

As she watched Mr. Chastain hasten off, she felt a surge of warmth. He possessed talent, good humor and charm, as well as a knowledge of music. Perhaps he didn't quicken her pulse as much as she might like, but what could she expect from a man she had just met? Her mind's eye was suddenly filled with the image of a certain wicked, bare-chested pirate, with unbound wild hair and a powerful masculine presence. Melanie bit her lip and sighed. No, it would be best to keep her mind on cake rather than torture herself with ridiculous fantasies.

Suzanne G. Rogers

Chapter Eight
Gentlemen Callers

As Melanie was waiting for Mr. Chastain to return with dessert, she noticed Lord Warwick cross over to his brother and ask to be introduced to Genevieve. Her aunt rose for the introduction, only to dip into the deepest, most graceful curtsy Melanie had ever seen. The woman's cheeks seemed brushed with crimson, her inky black eyelashes fluttered, and the smile on her full lips was at once welcoming and warm. Melanie fought to keep her countenance. Genevieve presented the marquess with his sketch, which he received with unvarnished pleasure. Was Aunt Ginny merely being polite to an aristocrat or had she finally met a gentleman worthy of her esteem?

She turned to Mrs. Steed, who was making short work of an eclair. "I enjoyed your performance of "Greensleeves." I've never studied the harp. Is it difficult to learn?"

Mrs. Steed licked icing from her fingers before she answered. "Mama made me study the harp when I was a child. I resented her soundly at the time, but I would thank her today, if she were still living." The woman nodded toward Lord Warwick. "The brothers are at it again, it seems."

Melanie shook her head. "I don't understand."

Mrs. Steed smiled. "One must outdo the other, whenever possible. I saw it all the time with my own two sons when they were boys. It's usually the younger sibling who feels the need to compete, but in this case, I think we must lay the blame at Lord Warwick's door."

Melanie stole another glance at Lord Warwick. The marquess was still chatting with Aunt Ginny, while Lord Peyton stood nearby with a stony expression.

"I'm sure if there is even a modicum of truth in what you say, Mrs. Steed, the behavior is inadvertent."

"Perhaps." The woman shrugged. "Even so, I cannot help but feel a trifle amused."

Melanie bit her lip. Mrs. Steed might be amused, but obviously Lord Peyton was not. She was reminded of how Blanche was always flirting with whichever young man happened to glance in Melanie's direction. Melanie had adjusted her life accordingly, but she could never fully trust her sister again. If Lord Peyton mistrusted his brother in the same fashion, she no longer had to wonder why he was so dour. She was a spinster, he was a pirate, and each of them were destined to go through life alone.

At evening's end, while Melanie was retrieving her cloak for the drive home, she noticed Lord Warwick made a point of saying good night to Genevieve. By contrast, Lord Peyton did not even spare Melanie a glance. She did not know what to make of his coldness and could not decide whether she was relieved or disappointed. Fortunately, she was distracted by Mr. Chastain who bowed and said, "Parting is such sweet sorry that I shall say goodnight till it be morrow."

Lord Dellingpole overheard and burst into laughter. "I should hope not, lad, since we are all longing for bed!"

"In that case, I shall just bid you farewell." Mr. Chastain's eyes lit with merriment, even as he lifted Melanie's hand to his lips for a kiss.

Lord Peyton appeared not to have noticed the exchange, but she could not be sure either way. He and Lord Warwick left a very short while thereafter, without a backward glance.

••••

Melanie was somewhat dispirited as she and Genevieve climbed into their carriage for the ride home. Moments after the coachman drove away from the resident, her aunt gave her a significant glance. "You may have made a conquest tonight."

"Mr. Chastain?" She shook her head. "He seems to be a great favorite among the ladies."

"I believe he made his preferences clear."

Melanie smiled. "Lord Warwick made his preferences clear as well. I don't believe he asked for an introduction to any other lady in the room."

Genevieve was almost giddy as she murmured, "I-I don't flatter myself it was anything more than politeness."

"I do not know, but Mrs. Steed made an interesting observation to me in private."

She related what the older woman had said about Lord Warwick's relationship to his brother. Her aunt's demeanor, which had been ebullient, turned pensive. In fact, all her responses to Melanie's comments became monosyllabic responses.

Finally, Melanie gave the woman a concerned glance. "I'm sorry if I've said anything wrong."

"You did not." Genevieve shrugged. "I'm merely overtired."

Melanie cast about for some levity. "I expect a great many ladies were vexed when Lord Peyton escorted you into the dining room."

"He was very attentive to me." Genevieve's answer was soft. "Looking back, I wish he had not been."

Melanie was perplexed. "Did you find his company to be tiresome?"

"Not at all. From what Mrs. Steed told you, however, Lord Warwick apparently wishes to put Lord Peyton in his place whenever possible."

"I still don't understand."

Genevieve sighed. "Do you remember when I told you about my exceedingly stringent requirements for any future husband? As soon as I laid eyes on Lord Warwick, I knew he exceeded them."

"But that's wonderful, isn't it? The gentleman apparently returns your regard."

The sheen of emotion in Genevieve's eyes was visible even in the dim lighting of the carriage. "How can I be sure Lord Warwick wasn't merely trying to twit his brother?"

Melanie was taken aback. "Oh."

Her aunt's logic was impeccable and applied to her as well. Lord Peyton had planned to escort her into the dining room because he must have known his brother would take it as a challenge. Obviously, he had been attempting to lure Lord Warwick into asking for an introduction, but Mr. Chastain had unwittingly interfered. Did that mean Lord Peyton's caress after their duet had been sincere? As she remembered the cold manner of their parting, the truth was difficult to fathom. "Surely he would not toy with your affections in such a scandalous fashion."

She did not realize she'd spoken aloud until her aunt responded.

"I would hope not, but I've never felt this way about a man before." Genevieve leaned forward, her face etched with concern. "Forgive me for seeming to be insensitive. I *did* tell you to consider the marquess, so I hope I've not injured you."

"Don't worry about that, Aunt Ginny. You asked me only to give Lord Warwick the opportunity to win my affections. Clearly, he prefers your company to mine." Melanie's laugh was mirthless. "Even if that wasn't so, I'm afraid my affections have long been engaged elsewhere."

"Lord Peyton, I presume." Genevieve pause. "What about Mr. Chastain?"

"He and I got along famously tonight. Nevertheless, if he should press his suit, I could not promise him anything more than friendship."

"This is a pretty pickle." Genevieve closed her eyes and shook her head. "We've both met the men of our dreams, but we cannot be certain of them."

"Whether Lord Warwick is truly taken with you remains to be seen." Melanie fixed her gaze out the window. "As for me, I'm quite certain of Lord Peyton. There can be no room in his heart for anyone else but himself."

••••

When Melanie and Genevieve arrived at church the following morning, Mrs. Wheeler and the orphans were just pulling up to the curb in their wagon. As Melanie stepped down from the gig, children jumped out and rushed over to give her a hug. Ethan's embrace was so tight, Melanie let out a squeak. Frederick turned a cartwheel for her amusement, nearly stepping on elderly Mrs. Teeter in the process. Mrs. Wheeler and a few members of her staff corralled their wayward charges moments later, but the episode put a smile on Melanie's face.

Mrs. Steed, who'd been chatting with friends nearby, crossed over. "Good morning!" She nodded toward the orphans, who were now queuing into two columns and marching into church. "Those children really are the sweetest little dears."

Genevieve smiled. "I quite agree."

"I cannot tell you how glad I am to be volunteering at the orphanage." Melanie gestured toward her aunt. "It was Aunt Ginny's suggestion and I'm very grateful for it."

"As I must thank you for yours." Mrs. Steed beamed. "The Ladies' Sewing Circle is thrilled to be sewing new uniforms for the children. Our activities had grown somewhat stagnant lately, so it's lovely to be doing something meaningful. I've just been told that the first batch should be ready later this week."

Melanie exchanged a delighted glance with Genevieve. "I can't wait to see them."

As she filtered into church alongside her aunt, she couldn't help but glance around for Lord Peyton. Before she settled into a pew, she finally spotted him up front, sitting alongside his brother. Lord and Lady Dellingpole sat next to them and Mr. Chastain was on the aisle.

She whispered, "Lord Warwick is here already."

Genevieve's expression became wistful. "I noticed. We shall see if he makes a point to greet me after church."

Melanie frowned. "I had no right to repeat gossip, Aunt Ginny. I wish I hadn't said it."

"Nonsense." Genevieve shook her head. "I've learned that gossip can be quite useful. Besides which, I would rather be put on my guard than to hope for something impossible." She patted Melanie's hand. "You did the right thing."

Melanie smiled but she was filled with genuine regret. She vowed to mind her own business from now on — which evidently did not include Lord Peyton. Was he annoyed at her failure to attract Lord Warwick's notice? What did it matter if his brother chose Aunt Ginny instead? Lord Peyton's irritation reflected an unflattering tendency toward officiousness, but she could say nothing under the circumstances. Should the marquess intend to court Genevieve, Melanie could not afford to treat Lord Peyton publicly with the disdain he deserved.

After the service was over, the pews up front began to empty as usual. As Melanie and Genevieve waited their turn to step into the aisle, Lord Warwick and Lord Peyton approached. The younger brother kept his focus elsewhere, but Lord Warwick nodded at Genevieve and touched the brim of his hat as he passed. Pleased beyond measure, Melanie slid her aunt a knowing glance afterward.

Genevieve whispered, "That means nothing, dearest."

Melanie tried not to smile. "Whatever you say, Aunt Ginny."

As they emerged from the church several minutes later, however, Melanie caught a glimpse of Lord Peyton and his brother riding off down the street in a sporty gig. Her view was suddenly blocked by Mr. Chastain, whose cheerful countenance never failed to lift her mood.

"Good morrow, sir." Melanie winked.

He gasped, as if with delight. "She is pretty, and honest, and gentle; and one that is your friend." He sketched a graceful bow. "I praise heaven for it."

She tapped her chin and furrowed her brow. "The words sound familiar, but I cannot place it."

He chuckled. "*The Merry Wives of Windsor.*"

"Yes, that's it. You're really very clever, Mr. Chastain."

"High praise from a fair lady."

Lady Dellingpole called out from inside a nearby carriage. "Make haste, Anton!"

He rolled his eyes and sighed. "Forgive me, Miss Starhope, but my chariot awaits."

Mr. Chastain bounded off as Melanie laughed. The fellow was all lightness where Lord Peyton was dark — so why couldn't she fall in love with him?

She spoke under her breath. "Because that would be too easy."

••••

"Lunch was delicious, but I cannot eat another bite." Melanie tucked her napkin by her plate and sat back in her chair. "I'll going to spend the afternoon working on Ethan's jacket — unless you have other plans."

"No, nothing special." Her aunt shrugged. "I was going to start the vampire novel I just purchased."

"You haven't read it yet?" Melanie groaned. "I suppose I must wait a little longer, then, to read it myself."

"I tell you what; why don't you fetch your sewing to the drawing room and I'll read the novel aloud." Genevieve waggled her eyebrows. "We'll kill two birds with one stone that way."

"Ooh, what a marvelous idea." Melanie stood. "I'll meet you in ten minutes."

She rushed upstairs to gather her materials and made her way to the drawing room with eager anticipation. Not only did Genevieve have a lovely speaking voice, but the gothic novel was bound to be exciting.

As Melanie picked up Ethan's jacket, she was pleased to see the progress she'd made. Since it only lacked buttons, she would be able to finish the garment in an hour and make a start on the trousers tomorrow. Should she wait until the suit was completely finished before taking it to the orphanage or would the lad enjoy having the jacket once it was ready? Undoubtedly, he would be thrilled to receive anything new, so she decided to give it to him after his piano lesson the following afternoon. Since she had time, she would also embroider the lad's initials on the inside lining of the lapel, in gold thread. What a thrill he would get when he saw his very own monogram!

A short while later, she was settled on the sofa with the jacket and a handful of buttons she'd cut from one of Reginald Hornsby's garments. The polished gold buttons sported a fleur-de-lis and gave the jacket an unusual cachet. Ethan would look the proper little gentleman, which was how it should be.

Genevieve opened her novel and began to read. "The old house on the hill had been unoccupied for as long as anyone could remember..."

Melanie continued to sew as she listened, although she glanced at her aunt from time to time with widened eyes. By the end of the first chapter, she'd sewn on all the buttons, and it was time to begin the monogram.

Genevieve paused. "Do you want me to continue with the next chapter?"

Melanie's nod was emphatic. "That is, if you feel up to it. Once I'm finished embroidering these initials, I can take over reading."

"What a good idea. Since I didn't draw your caricature at the soiree, I would love to sketch you as you read."

Melanie wrinkled her nose. "Ordinarily, I would be far too self-conscious to let you take my likeness, but if I'm reading *Blodwen and the Bloodless*, I'll be far too engrossed to mind."

As Genevieve continued on with chapter two, Melanie prepared her embroidery needle and thread. As she turned the jacket inside out, however, she suddenly remembered an overlooked detail. "Bother!"

Her aunt paused. "What's wrong?"

"I need Ethan's middle initial for his monogram." Melanie frowned. "I could do the monogram with his first and last initials only, of course, but I always think a three-initial monogram looks more impressive."

"I agree." Genevieve shrugged. "Perhaps you could embroider the letters you know and then ask Mrs. Wheeler for Ethan's middle name when you go to the orphanage tomorrow?"

"That's exactly what I must do." Melanie made a sound of exasperation. "I wanted to give Ethan the jacket tomorrow, but I shall just have to wait one more day."

She finished embroidering the two initials, annoyed with herself for having neglected to ask

Mrs. Wheeler for the middle name beforehand. Then again, it's not as if she didn't have a great deal on her mind.

"All right." Melanie stuck the embroidery needle into a pincushion and laid the jacket to one side. "It's my turn to read."

"I'll fetch my sketchbook from the conservatory." Genevieve rose. "I won't be but a moment."

Melanie stood up to stretch and then retrieved *Blodwen and the Bloodless* from where her aunt had left it in her wing chair. She marked the place they had left off with a length of ribbon from her sewing basket and strolled over to the window to gaze out at the courtyard. To her utter shock, two well-dressed gentlemen were strolling up the driveway, side by side. She leaped back out of view, turned, and began to pace. Should she go upstairs to avoid receiving the visitors or would it be better to stay where she was?

In a panic, she rushed from the room, nearly knocking headlong into Genevieve. "Oh, I'm sorry!"

"What on earth is the matter?"

"I-I'm not at home," Melanie stammered. "Lord Peyton and Lord Warwick are coming to call."

The heavy door knocker sounded just then and she made a squeaking noise.

"I cannot receive both gentlemen by myself." Genevieve gave Melanie's sleeve a tug. "Calm yourself and sit down. Most assuredly, they won't be here for more than a few minutes."

Although Melanie felt foolish for her panic, she returned to the drawing room with her aunt most reluctantly. Very shortly thereafter, the butler announced Lord Warwick and Lord Peyton and showed the men inside.

Melanie rose. Try as she might to feign indifference, the moment she saw Lord Peyton, she felt the same familiar tug from deep within. His gaze met hers only briefly before he glanced away.

"Lord Warwick, you remember my niece, Miss Starhope, from the soiree?" Genevieve gestured toward her. "She and your brother brought the entertainment to a close."

Indeed, I do." The marquess gave Melanie a polite bow. "Your piano duet was quite the triumph."

"Thank you, sir...but I believe the credit should go almost entirely to your brother."

Lord Warwick chuckled. "You'll forgive me if I beg to differ." He shrugged. "Truth be told, I'm not an aficionado."

She cast about for a diplomatic response. "One cannot possess expertise in everything." Why wouldn't Lord Peyton look at her? "Erm, Lord Peyton, I'm embroidering Ethan Dornan's jacket with a monogram. Do you happen to know the lad's middle name?"

He gave her a mocking smile. "A monogram for a boy of twelve? I might have reserved that for a member of the royal family, not an orphan."

Melanie's blood ran cold.

Genevieve peered at him. "I think that is the point, sir. The boy has had such few privileges in his young life, Melanie is trying to make him feel special."

A muscle worked in Lord Peyton's jaw. "Fitzhugh." He strode over to the window and sat down in a chair out of Melanie's direct viewpoint.

Lord Warwick made himself comfortable in the wing chair Genevieve had recently vacated. "Mrs. Hornsby, I came to ask you for some assistance. I intend to give a ball, but I'm wholly unfamiliar with the neighborhood. Could I lean on you for advice?"

As the marquess and Genevieve began to discuss the prospective ball, Melanie sat down in a rather ungainly manner. She reached for her embroidery, but the shaking of her hands prohibited her from making any progress. Lord Peyton had made his displeasure with her known last night, but his antipathy had seemingly deepened overnight. Her throat began to swell with emotion, and she began to fear she would embarrass herself.

The conversation between Genevieve and Lord Warwick broke off when Melanie stood.

"I have a headache, I'm afraid. Please excuse me while I go upstairs to rest."

Her aunt and Lord Warwick murmured something polite, but Lord Peyton said nothing as she left the room. The moment she set foot on the stairs, tears came rolling down her face. She did not know what she had done to offend Lord Peyton, but it seemed clear they were no longer friends — uneasy or otherwise.

He could go to Hades for all she cared.

••••

Monday

Melanie joined her aunt for breakfast, despite the fact she had no appetite. Instead of helping herself to the food laid out on the sideboard, she poured herself a cup of tea.

Genevieve gave her a worried glance. "You didn't eat anything at dinner last night, Melanie. Why don't you have some eggs and ham?"

"I'm not hungry."

Her aunt frowned. "Lord Peyton's behavior toward you was inexplicable and ungentlemanly but you mustn't let it linger in your mind a moment longer."

"It doesn't matter." Melanie stared into the amber liquid in her teacup. "All that's important is you and Lord Warwick. The fact that he sought your advice is significant."

A smile sprang to Genevieve's lips. "It is, isn't it? He wishes to have the ball the first week in August."

"I'm sure the news will gladden many hearts." Melanie could not interject much enthusiasm into her voice. "The Season will have come to a close by then and I...I will be going back to Bromley."

Genevieve's merriment disappeared and several long moments of shocked silence ensued.

"I can't believe it," she said finally. "You're running away again."

"Again?" Melanie stared at her, stung. "What does that mean?"

The furrow between her aunt's eyebrows deepened. "You ran away from your problems in Bromley and now you're running away from Lord Peyton!"

"That's unfair! I came here to find a new life apart from being Blanche's sister. Now that I have proven myself, it's time to go home again. By August, I will have trespassed far too long on your kindness."

"Nonsense. I don't know what's wrong with Lord Peyton, but you've made many other friends here in Ledbury. Furthermore, you've rendered an invaluable service to the orphanage. Don't throw it all away because you let a gentleman hurt your feelings."

Melanie scowled. "I didn't *let* him. He was deliberately rude."

"Admittedly, he was. That being said, you can choose how to feel about it." Genevieve tossed her head. "If it were me, I wouldn't care a jot."

"You're not in love with him!"

Melanie hadn't meant to blurt it out, but from the expression on Genevieve's face, the confession was not a surprise.

"Many young women bestow their affections on gentlemen who are unworthy, Melanie. If you allow this to be your downfall, I will be very disappointed. You're made of sterner stuff."

"I thought I was, too."

"All right, then." Her aunt pushed a rack of toast toward Melanie. "Eat breakfast, put on a pretty frock, arrange your hair in a new fashion, and move forward. You've done something quite lovely for Ethan Dornan. Take pleasure in his happiness and cast about for other meaningful activities to fill your time."

"Trousers."

Genevieve peered at her. "What?"

"My next meaningful activity." Melanie bit back a tiny smile. "Ethan's trousers."

Her aunt laughed. "A very meaningful activity, indeed."

••••

Before Melanie left for the orphanage that afternoon, she donned a fetching summer gown made of fine cotton lawn. The fabric was white, with a delicate red toile pattern that gave the overall impression of pink. Although the neckline was square-cut and low, her décolletage was covered with illusion all the way up to the high collar. The ensemble was one she'd purchased from Madame Montagna in London, and it was at once demure and flirtatious. She planned to avoid Lord Peyton completely, of course, but it did no harm to wear something beautiful. Furthermore, the pretty gown lifted her spirits and gave her confidence.

She hung Ethan's finished jacket on a wooden hanger and covered it with a hastily stitched muslin bag. The bag would keep the dust of the road off the fabric and ensure its pristine arrival. Once she was ready, she stopped into the conservatory to tell her aunt good-bye.

Genevieve's eyes lit up with pleasure when Melanie appeared. "What a lovely dress!"

Melanie turned a pirouette. "I took your advice and wore something to make me feel cheerful."

"I feel cheerful just looking at you." Her aunt beamed. "You must let me sketch you in that gown when you have a moment. I didn't get the opportunity to take your likeness at the soiree, as I'd planned."

"No, you were more agreeably occupied." Melanie smiled. "Do you suppose Lord Warwick will call on you this afternoon?"

"I doubt it. I think he's far too reserved to rush into anything so forward."

"We'll see." She paused. "If things work out well for you and the marquess, however, would you consider taking Ethan in as your ward?"

"You don't even have to ask. In fact, even if Lord Warwick has no interest in me at all, I might consider taking Ethan in anyway." She wrinkled her nose. "The only drawback is that I would have to acquire a piano."

"You are a sweetheart." Melanie deposited a kiss on her aunt's cheek. "I'm off to give lessons."

"I hope Ethan likes his jacket. He can have no earthly idea how much work and effort it cost you."

"Sewing the jacket afforded me more pleasure than I would have thought possible. Perhaps I should thank *him*." She smiled. "I hope to be back before teatime."

During Melanie's drive to the orphanage, she felt light-hearted and full of purpose. She discovered she could keep her mind agreeably occupied by planning what sort of children's clothes she could create with the resources she had at hand. Not only did she have fabric left over from the drapes, but she also had Reginald Hornsby's wardrobe at her disposal. In addition, her allowance would be arriving soon, so perhaps she could afford different patterns, thread, and a bolt of fabric or two. The creative mind was a happy mind, she decided. That might explain why her aunt was generally contented.

When Melanie arrived at the orphanage, Matador was tethered to his usual post under the tree. She took a moment before going in to stroke his neck. "Lord Peyton might be a devil, but I hope that won't affect our friendship," she murmured. "You're really a splendid animal."

The horse's ears swiveled back as she spoke, but he said nothing in response.

Melanie chuckled. "Your loyalty to your master is commendable. I wouldn't have expected anything less."

She retrieved the garment bag from the gig and made her way inside the building. The distant strains of "It Is Well with My Soul," by Horatio Spafford filled the corridor. Since the hymn was one of her favorites, she began humming along with the tune. Whatever grudges she might bear against Lord Peyton, she admitted his style of teaching was insightful. He had started an unmanageable group of boys learning fun, engaging operettas. Now that they were used to singing in a choir, he was now transitioning them to more classical compositions. It was a pity he couldn't speak to women with such clarity of thought.

As she passed Mrs. Wheeler's office, she noticed the woman was listening to the music with her eyes closed and mouthing the lyrics along with the choir. Melanie bit back a smile and tiptoed past to allow the matron to enjoy the uplifting hymn. When she approached the dining hall, the girls watching from the hallway outside clustered around her and gave her hugs in what had become a ritual. Melanie was obliged to hold her finger over her lips to keep them from speaking aloud. The last thing she needed was for Lord Peyton to burst into view, reproaching her for disturbing his work. Then again, she could respond with a kick to his shins — a punishment he so richly deserved.

Once she entered her music room, she shut the door, hung Ethan's jacket on a coat hook, and opened all the windows. She had refused to glance into the dining hall as she passed by and took pride in overcoming the temptation. Lord Peyton's disapproval meant nothing to her from now on. Furthermore, whatever troubles came her way, she would find the means to defeat them.

Melanie crossed over to the piano to play, "It Is Well with My Soul." Since she did not have the sheet music, she realized her rendition was likely not faithful to the original Nevertheless, she took comfort in the knowledge that it was, at least, faithful in spirit.

"When peace like a river, attenders my way,
When sorrows like sea billows roll;
Whatever my lot, Thou hast taught me to know
It is well, it is well with my soul…"

Her first pupil arrived just then and so Melanie broke off to spend a very pleasant two hours tending to her duties. Quite a few of the girls mentioned how much they were looking forward to their new uniforms and how nice the ladies from the Sewing Circle had been. When Ethan arrived at four o'clock, she decided to give him his new jacket at lesson's end. Before he could play a note, however, Mrs. Wheeler burst into the room in a dither.

"Forgive me, Miss Starhope, but Ethan is wanted in my office. His grand-aunt is here to see him."

Melanie rose from the piano bench. "Mrs. Pendergast?"

Ethan stared at Mrs. Wheeler, seemingly frozen. "Aunt Ruby is here?"

"She is, lad." The woman beckoned. "Come along. We mustn't dawdle."

"Wait a moment." Melanie rushed to unwrap Ethan's jacket. "Put this on."

He donned the garment, still too shocked to say anything. Even when Melanie made an effort to comb his hair with her fingers and straighten the shirt collar under his jacket, he meekly submitted without so much as a squeak. By contrast, Mrs. Wheeler stood by the door practically vibrating with nerves.

Melanie stepped back and gave the boy a smile of encouragement. "You look very handsome."

"I'm scared," he whispered.

She knelt. "She's your grand-aunt, not a stranger."

He gulped. "Will you go with me?"

"Absolutely." Melanie stood and took him by the hand. "Let's go meet your Aunt Ruby."

Chapter Nine

Headwinds

Melanie did not understand how word spread around the orphanage so quickly, but children lined the corridor as she, Ethan, and Mrs. Wheeler made their way to the front of the building. Girls and boys whispered so many words of encouragement to Ethan, Melanie was nearly brought to tears. When they stepped into Mrs. Wheeler's office, Lord Peyton was there, standing with his arms crossed. An older woman, dressed in an exquisitely tailored travel suit made of lightweight wool, was seated in a corner chair. She stood when Melanie led Ethan into the room.

"Merciful heavens." The woman peered at the boy. "You look like your dear mother."

Mrs. Wheeler squeezed past. "Mrs. Pendergast, this is your great-nephew, Ethan Dornan."

Melanie loosened her grip on the child's hand and gave him a little nudge.

He bowed. "Er...it's a pleasure to meet you, Aunt Ruby."

Mrs. Pendergast said nothing, but she fumbled for a handkerchief. The silence was deafening, so Melanie blurted out, "I've been giving Ethan piano lessons. H-He's the most talented pupil I've ever had and...and he has the most beautiful manners." She swallowed the lump in her throat. "As you can see for yourself, he is a little gentleman."

"Yes." Mrs. Pendergast wiped her eyes and took a deep breath. "Would you like to come live with me, little gentleman?"

"I..." Ethan glanced at Lord Peyton, who gave him a curt nod. "Aunt Ruby, could I have piano lessons? I like music."

Mrs. Pendergast laughed through her tears. "You may have all the lessons you wish, lad."

Ethan fixed her with a solemn smile. "In that case, I'll go."

"I was hoping you would agree." Mrs. Pendergast turned to Lord Peyton and extended her hand. "Thank you for coming to visit me, sir. I've regretted being inhospitable that day, but you gave me a great deal to think about."

"I'm glad." He took her hand and bowed.

To Melanie, the next few minutes were a blur as Ethan made his good-byes to his friends. Everyone went outside, where Mrs. Pendergast's cab was waiting. He waved before climbing into the carriage with his aunt and they drove off. Melanie glanced neither right nor left as she returned to the building, went into her music room, and closed the door. Then she collapsed onto the piano bench and sobbed her heart out. She hadn't realized before now how much she had counted on having Ethan as part of her family. He was better off with a blood relative, of course, but somehow, she felt bereft.

Melanie was crying so hard, she didn't hear the door open. When Lord Peyton sat down beside her, however, she nearly jumped out of her skin.

"Forgive me for startling you." He gave her an appraising glance. "Those don't look like happy tears."

As he pressed a handkerchief into her hand, she stole a glance at his countenance. His expression was sober to the point of being morose.

"You don't look happy, either."

"I'm happy...for Ethan." He shook his head. "I'm only sorry for myself. I had grown used to the idea of having the boy as a ward."

"I understand your feelings completely and share them." In the next moment, she tossed his handkerchief in his lap and scrambled to her feet. "Nevertheless, I shall not commiserate with a man I despise."

He grabbed her wrist before she could walk away. "You don't despise me, and I don't despise you."

"Unhand me, you...you..." she struggled to think of a bad enough word, "...*pirate.*"

Lord Peyton laughed as he released her. "I'm a pirate, am I? I rather like that." He stood and walked toward her with a gleam in his eye.

"Stop it!" She scampered back as he closed the distance between them. "Stay away from me."

"No." He pulled her close. "Pirates take what they want, don't they?"

Melanie glared at him, even as her heart hammered against her chest. "You forget yourself, sir. We are enemies."

"*I* am my own worst enemy, not you."

She held his gaze. "Stop teasing me, Lord Peyton. It's unbecoming."

"Ah, but I'm a pirate, according to you."

"Even a pirate is not entitled to take liberties with a lady."

"I suppose not." He loosened his embrace so she could escape.

Melanie straightened her clothes. "I shouldn't have to say this, but you really ought not tease women that way. Although *I* understand you have no romantic interest in me, a less sophisticated girl might misunderstand."

"I didn't realize you were so jaded."

She scowled. "And I didn't realize you were so daft."

"No?" The man shrugged. "I'm also known as Cedric the Daft."

"I can believe it." Melanie began to close and lock the windows. "Why did you follow me in here, other than to torment me."

"I came to apologize for my cold behavior toward you Sunday afternoon."

She paused long enough to peer at him. "Cold behavior? I would have called it rudeness of the highest order."

"Yes, and I owe you an explanation." A muscle worked in his jaw. "My brother has a history of inserting himself between me and any lady who catches my fancy. I had hoped he had grown bored of the game by now, but I discovered at the soiree he had not."

"You think that is the reason Lord Warwick asked to be introduced to Aunt Genevieve?"

"He may have mistakenly assumed I wished to court your aunt." Lord Peyton shrugged. "She may be a few years older than I am, but she's a very fine-looking woman all the same."

"My aunt is indeed a true beauty in every sense of the word." Melanie frowned. "How many times has this happened between you and your brother?"

"Many, many occasions but..." His color grew pale, but his cheekbones had red spots on them, "...only one time that truly mattered."

Something in the hoarseness of Lord Peyton's voice triggered a memory. She had heard him speak that way once before in their acquaintance...when he'd mentioned the death of his brother's wife. Certain pieces of the puzzle began to fall into place.

"Oh." Melanie's exclamation was soft. "The late marchioness was your fiancée before she became your brother's wife."

Lord Peyton's hands became fists clenched at his side. "Yes."

"And you believe she married Lord Warwick only because of his wealth and title?" Melanie shook her head. "Forgive me for saying so, but you don't know much about women." She began to gather up her things.

"What exactly don't I know?"

"You really are your own worst enemy." Melanie frowned. "Any woman truly in love with you would never be tempted by anything your brother has to offer. If the objects of your affection strayed from your side, it meant they were not worthy of your admiration."

As she spoke, she suddenly realized the same principle applied to her and any beaux she had lost to her sister. What a fool she had been, to resent Blanche for their perfidy! She would never, ever have been happy with such shallow gentlemen and her sister had performed an unwitting service on Melanie's behalf.

She shook her head. "Admittedly, I've no right to judge since I've been guilty of the same mistakes but leave your brother and my aunt to sort things out for themselves." Melanie pinned her hat onto her head.

"You seem quite sure of your conclusions." His eyes narrowed. "If I make my admiration for another lady known and Edmund abandons your aunt for her, what would you say then?"

Melanie grabbed the hanger and empty muslin bag from the hook on the wall. "I would say Aunt Genevieve made a narrow escape and your brother is an ass." As she strode from the room, Lord Peyton's laughter spilled out into the corridor.

••••

Melanie sailed into the conservatory, where her aunt was lingering over tea.

"Good afternoon, Aunt Ginny I'm sorry to be late." She poured herself a cup of tea from the cart next to the table, took a biscuit from a platter, and sat down. "I have news."

"Oh?" Genevieve glanced up from a pad of paper which contained notes and lists. "What's wrong? You look as if you've been crying."

"I had been, earlier." Melanie sighed. "Mrs. Pendergast came to the orphanage this afternoon and took Ethan away."

Her aunt gasped. "The woman gave no notice of her intentions?"

"None of which I am aware." Melanie related what happened, from the moment Mrs. Wheeler had summoned Ethan, to his departure with his grandaunt. "After he left, I came undone."

"I don't blame you, dearest." Her aunt's eyes shone with emotion. "He was a sweet boy and we'll miss him."

Melanie managed a weak smile. "It seems Lord Peyton managed to persuade Mrs. Pendergast after all."

"Did you speak with Lord Peyton?"

"For a short while." Melanie had no intention of confessing *that* particular conversation. "He made an apology of sorts for his rudeness yesterday."

"I'm glad to hear it." Genevieve cocked her head. "Did he give you any explanation?"

"Erm...no, but I accepted his apology anyway. If you and Lord Warwick are to be friends, it wouldn't do for Lord Peyton and I to be at odds."

"That's very mature, Melanie, and I'm quite glad to hear it. I've been thinking about having an intimate dinner party and I would like to invite Lord Warwick and his brother as guests."

The notion of dining with Lord Peyton gave Melanie pause. "Who else will you invite to round out the party?"

Genevieve plucked a tea pot from the cart. "It would just be the four of us." She refilled her cup.

Melanie's eyes widened. "I'm not sure that's proper!"

"I don't see how having the neighbors over to dine will be so very scandalous." Despite Genevieve's assertion, a flicker of doubt crossed her features. "Besides which, I cannot make the numbers work out any other way. I could invite Lord and Lady Dellingpole but I would have to ask Mr. Chastain as well. Then, we would be short one lady."

"I see your point." Melanie nibbled her biscuit. "What about inviting the vicar and his wife instead?"

"Since they have a daughter of marriageable age, it would be unpardonable not to include her. Unfortunately, we would then be short one gentleman."

"That's true, but what if you invited Lord and Lady Dellingpole, Mr. Chastain, the vicar and his wife, and their daughter? That balances perfectly."

"Yes, but then it's no longer an intimate dinner party."

Melanie popped the rest of her biscuit into her mouth and wiped the crumbs away with a linen napkin. "All right, then. What if you were to invite the gentlemen to tea or luncheon here in your conservatory? A daytime event is more than acceptable and not leave us vulnerable to gossip."

"You are right." Genevieve nodded. "I've lived so long by myself that I've forgotten how meddlesome people can be." She took a deep breath and let it out. "I'll send over an invitation for Saturday afternoon tea at four o'clock."

Melanie giggled. "If Lord Warwick comes alone, I shall just have to develop another headache and go to my room."

"You'll do no such thing. Lord Warwick will get the impression you are sickly."

"I can always be called away on an errand that cannot wait."

"Stop teasing me!"

The phrase reminded Melanie of Lord Peyton and she was instantly contrite. "I'm sorry, Aunt Ginny. I don't mean to make you uncomfortable."

"I know. Forgive me if I snapped at you just now." Genevieve sighed. "As silly as it may seem, I'm nervous as a cat where Lord Warwick is concerned."

"I understand."

Indeed, truer words were never spoken. Melanie had grown exceedingly flustered whenever a certain rapscallion was nearby. Although Cedric the Daft had embraced her in jest earlier that day, the warmth of his body made her senses tingle even now. She ought to have slapped him for his temerity, but her heart wouldn't have been in it. Well, since she had the misfortune to fall in love with a pirate, there could be only one cure. Blanche would be coming to visit at the end of the summer, Lord Peyton would be instantly smitten, and Melanie would be free. It would be akin to a wolf chewing off his own foot to escape from a trap, but at least she could lick her wounds in private.

She reached for another biscuit, but the image of Lord Peyton gazing passionately at Blanche made her gorge rise.

"I think I'll go upstairs to rest for a little while." Melanie stood. "It's been a long day."

••••

When Melanie entered the orphanage Friday afternoon, a group of girls were waiting for her. They wore dresses styled in a sailor suit fashion, with square white collars, blue neckerchiefs, and blue pleated skirts that brushed the tops of their boots.

Elizabeth beamed. "The Ladies' Sewing Circle brought our uniforms this morning."

Willa turned a pirouette. "Do you like them, Miss Starhope?"

"Oh, yes." Melanie sighed with pleasure. "You look like young ladies."

Denise hid a giggle behind her hands. "The boys are so envious! They have to wait for their new uniforms until next week."

"I'm sure the Ladies' Sewing Circle is working as fast as they can." Melanie glanced at Catherine. "I hope you've been practicing?"

"Yes, Miss Starhope." The girl bobbed up and down in a curtsy. "Now that Ethan isn't here, I can practice all I want."

The mention of Ethan sent a poignant wave of sadness through Melanie, but she forced herself to smile. "I expect to be impressed, then. I'll see you later."

When she passed by the dining hall, the boys' choir was singing the hymn, "Holy, Holy, Holy! Lord God Almighty." The girls lingering in the hallway broke off from peering through the glass in the doorway long enough to give Melanie a hug. They were all clad in their new uniforms and she whispered, "You look beautiful!" It tugged on her heartstrings to see the pleasure her praise gave them. She continued on to the music room, opened up the windows to let in some fresh air, and prepared for her first lesson.

Over the next two hours, Melanie noticed a marked lack of concentration in her pupils, but she let it pass. No doubt, the new uniforms had sent their spirits soaring and so she was loathe to criticize. At the end of each lesson, however, she urged the girls to continue to practice.

"Imagine that you have a recital for Her Majesty coming up at the end of the summer," she said. "Think about how proud you would be to show her all you've accomplished!"

After her last pupil left, Melanie began closing windows and tidying the room. As she worked, she decided to speak with Miss Wheeler about actually having a recital in August. Even her beginning students could play something simple, and it would give the girls a goal.

Just as she reached for her hat, Lord Peyton appeared. "There's a staff meeting in the dining hall and Mrs. Wheeler thought we ought to attend."

"I can't imagine why." Melanie shook her head. "Do you have any idea what the meeting is about?"

He shrugged. "I don't know, but the staff has already assembled."

"Hmm." Melanie picked up her carryall. "All right."

As they walked down the hallway together, she mentioned her idea about a recital at the orphanage. "Do you think your choir would like to participate?"

Lord Peyton's eyebrows rose. "The lads would enjoy performing. It's a very good idea, Miss Starhope."

"I'm glad you think so." The rare moment of cooperation made Melanie smile. "I'll discuss the recital with Mrs. Wheeler as soon as may be."

He gestured toward the open doorway of the dining hall. "After you."

The men and women employed by the orphanage had assembled inside and were seated at the long tables ordinarily occupied by children. Amid a hubbub of conversation, Melanie and Lord Peyton took seats in the back and waited for the meeting to commence. A tall, thin gentleman was chatting with Mrs. Wheeler at the podium in front, and Melanie caught Lord Peyton's eye.

"Do you know that chap?" She nodded toward the podium.

Lord Peyton shook his head. "No, but he looks like an undertaker."

Melanie stifled a laugh. Shortly thereafter, Mrs. Wheeler rang a little bell and the room fell quiet.

"Thank you all for coming." She glanced at the fellow standing at the podium. "This is Mr. Fletcher, who is Trustee for the Ledbury Country Home for Children. He has come to make an announcement."

The man surveyed the room with pursed lips before gesturing toward Mrs. Wheeler.

"Mrs. Wheeler, the Board of Governors has asked me to say you've done an outstanding job over the years, managing this facility with the resources at hand."

The matron beamed.

He continued, "The task has been challenging, but you've performed your duties in a sterling fashion. The Board wishes to thank you for your efforts."

Applause ensued, and the groundskeeper even stood up to whistle between his teeth. Mrs. Wheeler blushed and waved off the praise in her usual modest fashion. The Trustee waited to speak until the staff had settled down once more.

"Unfortunately, the orphanage has very recently lost its largest donor. Given the strong headwinds going forward, the Board has voted to sell the property and close the orphanage before the end of the year."

The staff erupted in protest, Mrs. Wheeler's face lost all color, and she collapsed into the nearest chair. Melanie felt her own blood run cold as she realized the entirety of the blame was hers. Obviously, Mrs. Pendergast had withdrawn her financial support along with her great-nephew, leaving the orphanage underfunded. Melanie had been the one to suggest Ethan be reunited with his aunt, with no thought of any other ramifications. How could she have been so thoughtless?

She shot to her feet, shouting to be heard over the cacophony. "What if we could raise money from other donors?"

The noise died down as all eyes focused on Mr. Fletcher's response.

He shook his head. "It would do no good, I'm afraid."

Lord Peyton stood. "I'm sure we could replace what was lost, sir."

Melanie gave Mr. Fletcher a level glance. "I agree with Lord Peyton. The orphanage has many friends who—"

"*No.*" The Trustee's voice held a note of finality. "The Board of Governors has long wished to close the facility and it has already been sold. Losing the donor merely made the vote easier."

Her head swam. "What about the children? Where are they to go?"

"Our young residents will be sent to various public institutions in England, wherever space can be made." Mr. Fletcher's expression was sanguine. "The children will be well looked after, I assure you."

The staff began shouting questions of their own regarding their employment and Melanie sank into her seat. She had volunteered her time to help the children, but she'd been the unwitting instrument of the orphanage's demise. How could she live with herself? As she remembered how the orphans had lined the halls to lend Ethan support not so long ago, her heart broke. A recital was pointless since it could never lift their spirits now.

Melanie barely listened as Mr. Fletcher answered questions about letters of reference, pensions, dates of separation, and when the children would be transferred. Mr. Fletcher ended the meeting with a curt, "I will be in touch soon," before striding off. Lord Peyton bolted off in pursuit, but Melanie held out little hope he could make a difference this time.

Mrs. Wheeler and the staff filtered out of the dining hall with stunned expressions and slumped shoulders. Once the room was empty, Melanie rose from her seat and walked over to gaze out the window. The dining hall had a view of the grounds, where the children were playing games of tag or chatting in groups. The idyllic scene was at once uplifting and yet devastating, since she knew it must come to an end. The ties of friendship the children had forged with one another would be severed when they were scattered to the winds. They had already suffered enough with the loss of their parents and now they would lose each other.

She felt someone rest a comforting hand on her shoulder. "Are you all right, Miss Starhope?" For once, Lord Peyton's countenance was free of his customary smirk.

Melanie sighed. "No, I am not all right. The closing of the orphanage is my fault."

He dropped his hand to his side. "In point of fact, *I* am to blame far more than you. If I hadn't convinced Mrs. Pendergast to take Ethan, she would have continued her financial support."

"You wouldn't have visited the woman if I hadn't insisted on it. I knew if she met you, she would be persuaded." Melanie gave Lord Peyton a sharp glance. "What if you were to visit the Board of Governors? Perhaps you could convince them to reverse their decision."

He grimaced. "I took Mr. Fletcher aside just now to beg for just such an audience but it was no use."

Melanie frowned. "I hope the new owners realize their acquisition comes at the expense of defenseless children." She swallowed the lump in her throat. "I feel so horribly guilty and...helpless."

"You're the least helpless woman I know." He paused. "Perhaps there *is* something we can do. We found Ethan a home, after all. What if we were to find homes for the other children?"

She peered at him. "Are you mad? There are nearly two dozen children at the orphanage, Lord Peyton."

"Ten lads and eight young ladies."

Melanie made a sound of dismay. "Even so, we could never find homes for them all."

"I admit, the prospect is daunting. Nevertheless, we might be able to find homes for some. We won't know unless we try."

"I'm willing to do anything to make up for what I've done." She studied him. "Do you have a plan?"

"Well..." he scratched his head, "...I'll write an editorial about the orphanage for the local newspaper and end with a plea for help. Perhaps some families will be moved to take in a child or two."

"That might work." Melanie warmed to the task. "We could also write profiles about each boy and girl, mentioning the activities they enjoy and things like that."

Lord Peyton cocked his head. "Perhaps your aunt could sketch the children and the newspaper could run the portraits along with the profiles."

"Aunt Ginny would love to help, I think." As a modicum of hope was born, a glimmer of a smile curved Melanie's lips. "I'll approach the sewing circle to beg the ladies to consider taking a child. They became acquainted with the children when they took their measurements, after all, and several mentioned how winsome they were."

"Hmm..." His eyebrows drew together as he stared off in the distance. "I'll call on the vicar and his wife next week. My boys' choir know a few hymns now and if the lads sang during a service, members of the congregation might be moved enough to take a ward."

Melanie grabbed his arm. "Lord Peyton, you're brilliant!" When he met her gaze, she realized what she'd done and released him. "I beg your pardon." She stepped back.

"It's perfectly all right."

"I should be going. Aunt Ginny will wonder where I am."

She strode off, hoping he hadn't noticed the painful blush creeping across her face.

The man's voice echoed through the dining hall. "You're afraid of me, Miss Starhope."

Melanie turned long enough to give him a scathing glare. "You wish that were so!" She tossed her head and disappeared into the corridor.

She intended to get to her gig and drive off before Lord Peyton had emerged from the building but when she glanced through Mrs. Wheeler's open door, however, her plans changed. The matron was sitting behind her desk with tears running down her face. On the bottle in front of her sat an uncapped bottle of amber liquid and a glass.

"Oh, dear." Melanie stepped into the room to comfort the woman. "I'm so awfully sorry, Mrs. Wheeler."

The matron brought her glass to her mouth, took a long swallow, and shuddered. "I'm to be pensioned off and shunted aside." She took another drink. "I have nowhere to go."

Melanie sighed. "You've had a bad shock and this is no time to be making decisions about your future. Once you've gotten used to the idea that your life will change, however, perhaps you'll be able to see the possibilities."

Mrs. Wheeler refilled her glass. "I'm sure you are right but it's the children who worry me most."

Melanie glanced at the doorway to make sure a certain annoying gentleman wasn't listening. "Lord Peyton is worried about them, too, and he has a brilliant plan to find them homes in Ledbury. If anyone can succeed, he can."

The woman met her gaze. "You believe in him that much?"

"Indeed, I do." Melanie gave her a sympathetic smile. "He's the most persuasive, magnetic man I've ever met."

"In that case, my optimism is rekindled." Mrs. Wheeler capped the bottle on her desk and lowered it into the drawer. "I keep that whiskey only for medicinal purposes, Miss Starhope. I would appreciate it if you don't mention it to anyone."

Melanie nodded. "Your secret is safe with me."

She left the office and turned down the corridor, only to see Lord Peyton leaning up against the wall not five paces away with a grin on his face. Obviously, he had overheard the entire conversation — including her generous praise of him.

Melanie's eyes narrowed and she strode past without a word.

Chapter Ten
Tea Party

Melanie gritted her teeth as she left the building and made her way to her gig. No sooner had she untethered Paint, however, when Lord Peyton arrived.

"You find me persuasive and magnetic, do you?"

She gave him a scathing glance. "Gloating is unbecoming, sir."

The man shrugged. "I'm just glad to discover you don't detest me as much as you pretend."

Melanie lifted her chin. "I was merely trying to comfort Mrs. Wheeler as best I could. If I were you, I would endeavor to prove me right."

"And so I shall." He moved closer. "I believe I also heard the word, 'brilliant.'"

She stepped back. "I know what I said, so you may stop toying with me. For now, I am determined to put aside our differences for the good of the children." Melanie climbed into her gig without waiting for Lord Peyton's assistance. "Good afternoon."

Melanie turned into the road and began the drive home, congratulating herself on handling a difficult situation with aplomb. Admittedly, however, her reprieve was only temporary. She should have realized Lord Peyton would be lurking outside the door and tailored her words accordingly. Now, he would suspect she admired him and tease her as a result.

"Fair moon, to thee I sing..."

She glanced back, only to discover Lord Peyton was riding directly behind her, singing a song from *H.M.S. Pinafore*. His baritone rang out in a lusty manner for everyone to hear but she knew it was directed at her. Melanie urged her horse to move a trifle faster, but to little avail. When Lord Peyton had finished singing, "Fair Moon, To Thee I Sing," he launched into, "Time Was When Love and I Were Well Acquainted," from *The Sorcerer*. She let him go on for several minutes before reining in her horse.

Lord Peyton rode up beside her. "Have you any requests?"

"Yes. I respectfully request you leave off your serenade as we pass through town. We don't want to cause a stir, and I doubt if you wish to appear addled."

"I will leave off, on one condition." He gave her a sidelong glance. "Once we've left town, you must sing a duet with me."

She groaned. "You really are mad. I don't sing nearly as well as you do, Lord Peyton. Do you mean to make a fool of me?"

"No, I only mean to sing a duet." He paused. "Are you familiar with *Iolanthe*?"

"Yes, but—"

"Splendid! We shall sing, "If We're Weak Enough to Tarry," from the second act."

"Lord Peyton, it's out of the question. I—"

He cut her off with a reprise of, "Time Was When Love and I Were Well Acquainted." Although she did not know what may have possessed him, she suspected he meant to sing it all the way through town.

"Stop!"

He broke off. "Do you agree to my terms?"

She made a sound of frustration. "I've little choice, it seems, but you must promise not to laugh at me."

"I'd sooner throw myself into a bramble bush, naked as a robin."

Melanie recoiled in horror. "You cannot speak to a lady in that manner!"

Lord Peyton wore an expression of innocence. "I meant only that the bramble bush would be unadorned, not I. What did you think I meant?"

She picked up her reins and continued on her way without venturing any remark at all. What on earth could be wrong with the fellow today? One would think after receiving bad news about the orphanage, he would be sober and reflective. Instead, he seemed determined to misbehave at every turn.

Once they had reached Ledbury, she gestured toward him. "Ride on, sir. I don't want anyone to imagine we are together."

He chuckled. "That's not part of the bargain, Miss Starhope. You must suffer my company awhile longer."

Melanie glared. "Hmph!"

After that, she did her best to ignore him. She smiled and nodded at any acquaintances she happened to drive past, but she dared not glance at or speak to the gentleman riding abreast of her. Surely anyone watching them would see Lord Peyton's company was uninvited and unwelcome, wouldn't they?

As soon as they had left the town behind, Melanie scowled at him. "How could you subject me to gossip in such a cavalier fashion? You should have ridden ahead, as I asked."

He took a deep breath and sang, "If we're weak enough to tarry..."

Melanie rolled her eyes and sighed, but she could not go back on her word. When it came time for her part, she sang the lyrics as best she could. By the time she and Lord Peyton were singing together, she was surprised to discover she was enjoying herself. Furthermore, when Prospero's Retreat and Asphodel drew near, Melanie's spirits were greatly improved.

She gave Lord Peyton a grudging smile. "I hate to admit it, but you've cheered me."

"Why do you hate to admit it?"

"Because you're always so difficult." When she glanced over, the usual shadows on Lord Peyton's countenance had lifted and he was almost ebullient. "What has come over you, sir? You were quite dour after the staff meeting and now you seem almost intoxicated."

Lord Peyton chortled with laughter. "Perhaps I keep a flask of whiskey in my pocket — for *medicinal* purposes." He winked.

"You overheard that, too?" Melanie shook her head. "Please keep Mrs. Wheeler's secret to yourself, I beg you. If anything should get out about her drinking, she'll think I'm responsible."

"I don't know a thing, I assure you." Lord Peyton doffed his hat. "I shall see you tomorrow afternoon, Miss Starhope."

"You will?" Melanie suddenly remembered Aunt Ginny's invitation to tea. "Oh, yes. You will. Good afternoon."

They parted ways and Melanie drove on. Just before she turned into her own drive, she glanced back. Lord Peyton waved farewell and, to her amusement, began to sing, "If we're weak enough to tarry..." His voice followed her as she continued toward her aunt's home. Perhaps he hadn't been joking about the flask after all.

••••

When Genevieve fussed over the floral arrangement on the table for the third time, Melanie gave her a sidelong glance. "Are you nervous, Aunt Ginny?"

"Most decidedly not." The woman hastened toward a window, to check her reflection once more. "How do I look?"

"Like a painting by Renoir."

Melanie's praise was not exaggerated. Genevieve wore a lovely blue-and-white striped gown with a lace collar and cuffs, and her sable hair was arranged in a flattering and elegant fashion. She was the embodiment of femininity, sophistication, and beauty.

Her aunt paced. "How can you remain so calm?"

"I don't know, really. Perhaps it's because I'm not seeking Lord Warwick's approval and Lord Peyton has lost his mind."

"What do you mean?"

"Yesterday afternoon, on the way home from the orphanage, he would not stop singing." Melanie shrugged. "I cannot account for it."

"He must have had his reasons."

"Considering the serious situation in which we find ourselves, his jocularity was inexplicable. Still, I suppose it's better than sobbing into one's tea." Melanie rose from the table and turned a pirouette. "Do I pass muster?"

Her gown was also extremely feminine, with its lilac pattern, lightweight fabric, and dainty darts. Melanie had chosen the garment for its bodice, which accentuated her tiny waistline and feminine curves.

"You look lovely, as you very well know...although your neckline makes me think I should have worn something lower." Genevieve glanced down at herself. "Do I have time to change?"

The butler appeared. "Lord Warwick and Lord Peyton have arrived."

Genevieve's took a deep breath and let it out. "Show them in, Newman."

The butler frowned. "Mr. Chastain has come to call as well. All three gentlemen arrived at the same time."

Genevieve and Melanie exchanged a glance of consternation.

"We can't turn Mr. Chastain away," Melanie whispered. "Not if he's waiting in the drawing room with the other two!"

"Heavens, no." Her aunt sighed. "Quickly, Newman, bring another place setting while my niece and I greet the gentlemen in the drawing room. Tell Cook we'll be five for tea."

The man wore a pained expression. "Mr. Oglethorpe, Mrs. Oglethorpe, and Miss Priscilla Oglethorpe have also come to call."

Melanie gasped, "The vicar and his family? Merciful heavens!"

Genevieve stared at the butler for several long moments. "Tell Cook we'll be eight for tea, Newman. We'll need four more place settings and a second table. Use the one on the patio."

"Right away, Mrs. Hornsby."

As Melanie accompanied her aunt from the conservatory, she slid the woman an apologetic glance. "I suppose, upon reflection, teatime wasn't a good time for an intimate gathering."

"Apparently not." Genevieve spread her arms wide in a shrug. "Nevertheless, we shall make the best of it."

She accompanied Melanie to the drawing room with a broad smile of welcome. "I'm so delighted to see all of you! Please say you'll stay for tea."

Melanie's gaze flickered toward Lord Peyton, who was biting back a smile.

The vicar's wife shook her head in a sheepish manner. "I wouldn't dream of imposing, Mrs. Hornsby." She gestured around the room. "Unfortunately, we all arrived here at the same time and—"

Mr. Oglethorpe finished her sentence. "—and as a result, we decided to stop in for only a few minutes and be on our way."

Genevieve handled the situation with aplomb. "Nonsense! Melanie and I would be delighted to have you to tea, wouldn't we, Melly?"

"Indeed, tea is being laid out in the conservatory as we speak." Melanie nodded. "The conservatory is not to be missed."

Mrs. Oglethorpe exchanged glances with her husband and daughter. "In that case, we would be delighted to stay."

Mr. Chastain beamed. "I'm always delighted to stay wherever I'm wanted!"

"Mrs. Hornsby, I'm afraid I will take my leave." Lord Warwick's expression was tight. "Perhaps we shall take tea together some other time."

Genevieve's smile slipped. "Oh...I..."

Melanie stepped forward. "Forgive me, Lord Warwick, but I would be so grateful if you would tarry awhile. A dire situation has developed about which I could use your advice. In fact, each individual here will have an opinion I will find useful."

Lord Peyton stirred. "I echo Miss Starhope's sentiments. Our gathering is rather fortuitous, actually. Now that you're all here, I'm spared from having to visit you about this matter individually."

Mr. Chastain's eyes widened in a comical fashion. "I confess, the mystery is killing me."

At that, Miss Oglethorpe smothered a giggle with her hand.

Lord Warwick seemed disgruntled, but he nodded his head in acquiescence. As for Melanie, she was not impressed with the marquess's generosity of spirit. Their plans for an intimate tea had indeed been thwarted, but he could have been more gracious about it. By contrast, Lord Peyton showed no signs of huffing off in a pique.

Genevieve gestured toward the doorway. "Shall we go through?"

Lord Peyton extended his arm to the vicar's daughter. "Miss Oglethorpe, may I escort you to tea?"

Melanie's momentary surge of good will toward Lord Peyton ebbed. Lord Warwick took a step toward Genevieve, but she ignored him in favor of the vicar.

"Mr. Oglethorpe, I would be honored if you would lend me your company."

The snub was one which Melanie approved of, whole-heartedly. If the marquess intended to court her aunt, he must make more of an effort to be sociable. Lord Warwick may have impressed Genevieve with his looks, but it would be a pity if he fell short of the mark in all other ways.

In the end, Lord Warwick deigned to escort Mrs. Oglethorpe to tea and Mr. Chastain bounded over to Melanie.

"The fates have smiled upon me today, Miss Starhope. Not only do I have the pleasure of your company, but we are also to have sweets."

Mr. Chastain could always make Melanie laugh.

••••

Over tea, Melanie held the floor long enough to announce the orphanage's impending closure. "The children are almost like siblings, and it would be a shame to see them scattered all over England," she said finally. "I was hoping to solicit your advice, Lord Warwick."

He shrugged. "If you are suggesting someone ought to buy the place and keep the orphanage open, I would say there are few people willing to invest in an establishment that loses money."

"Yes, you are right, but there is another possibility." Melanie's glance flickered toward Lord Peyton. "Your brother and I are hoping the children could be placed locally with Ledbury families."

Lord Warwick's face was a mask. "I think your expectations are too high. The odd farmer might like to have an extra hand or two but I cannot imagine anyone genteel would take on an orphaned child out of the goodness of their heart."

"Can you not?" Genevieve's tone was slightly brittle. "I certainly hope our community would evince more interest than that. These are children, after all, deserving of protection."

"One must be realistic, Mrs. Hornsby. Orphans are created every day and their lives will never be made completely whole — not by you or anyone else."

She lifted her chin. "That doesn't mean their lives can't be improved, sir."

"Not every injury can be fixed with sugarplums and kisses." The marquess cocked his head. "Besides which, would you be happy, raising another woman's child?"

"Why, yes. I *had* been willing to take Ethan Dornan as a ward, but his grandaunt came for him instead." Genevieve's color was pale. "I shall definitely consider taking another child."

The atmosphere was so thick, Melanie cast about for something to break the tension. Fortunately, Lord Peyton came to the rescue.

"I admire and respect your generosity, Mrs. Hornsby." He smiled. "I'm sure there is another worthy orphan who will interest you as much as Ethan did."

Miss Oglethorpe glanced at her father. "Papa, in Matthew 25:40 it is written, 'Inasmuch as ye have done it unto one of the least of these my brethren, ye have done it unto me.'" Therefore, shouldn't the vicar lead by example?"

Her mother's eyes shone. "Oh, I agree. Quincy, dearest, would you be willing to take in a ward? As a member of the Ladies' Sewing Circle, I've met the children firsthand. Willa Bains is an adorable little girl."

Melanie seized the opportunity to encourage the vicar's wife. "I've been teaching Willa how to play the piano. She's been very diligent with her practicing, I must say. She also likes to draw and sing."

"It breaks my heart to think Willa shall be sent off to an institution where she doesn't know a soul." Mrs. Oglethorpe retrieved a handkerchief from her handbag and dabbed at her eyes.

Mr. Oglethorpe frowned. "I don't know, Harriet. This is not a decision to be taken lightly."

"Papa, you're always talking about Christian charity," his daughter said. "Is this not an opportunity to demonstrate exactly that?"

The conversation became lively at that point, with people talking over one another, almost to the point of acrimony.

Melanie jumped to her feet. "I'm sorry. I didn't mean to start a row."

Mr. Chastain rose. "You didn't start a row, Miss Starhope. I just think the topic is one that stirs deep emotions." He gestured toward the garden. "I would love to see your rose bushes if you would care to give me a tour."

The vicar stood as well. "I'm afraid we must be going, Mrs. Hornsby, but I thank you for your hospitality."

"You are always welcome, any time." Genevieve crossed over to Mrs. Oglethorpe and Miss Oglethorpe, to give them both a warm embrace.

Lord Peyton cleared his throat. "I'll walk out with you, Mr. Oglethorpe."

"Forgive me, but I must take my leave as well." Lord Warwick stood. "Thank you for having me to tea, Mrs. Hornsby."

Genevieve's lips tightened. "I'm so glad you could come, sir. The conversation was most illuminating."

Melanie's heart sank. Not only had she started an argument between friends, but she had also driven a wedge between Lord Warwick and her aunt. Once Genevieve accompanied her guests from the conservatory, Melanie and Mr. Chastain were left alone.

She sighed. "Shall we walk outside, sir? I would love some fresh air."

The gentleman sketched a flowery bow. "I am your humble servant."

••••

Mr. Chastain escorted Melanie along the white gravel pathways crisscrossing the flower garden.

She frowned. "I didn't expect that tumultuous reaction, to be honest. I confess, I'm a trifle discouraged."

His expression was sober. "As a bachelor, I'm not sure how I could be helpful to you. I'll definitely talk to my cousins about the orphanage, but I doubt they would be interested in taking in a ward. They mentioned just the other day how they wish to begin traveling extensively."

Melanie squeezed his arm. "Thank you, Mr. Chastain. Perhaps they might know someone who would like to take in a child."

"Perhaps." He gave her a dimpled smile. "I like children, you know. I've often been accused of remaining one myself."

Once again, Mr. Chastain's good nature managed to cheer her. "Perhaps that is because you have managed to retain the fresh innocence of youth. It's far more appealing than cynicism, I must say."

He pretended to ponder her words. "I accept your compliment, Miss Starhope, but you must allow me to repay it in kind. It's wonderful of you to help those orphans. Your efforts are exceedingly noble."

"I don't know about that but you're kind to say so."

Mr. Chastain bent to draw in the fragrance of a lovely red rose. When he straightened, he gasped. "I've just had a splendid idea!"

She blinked. "About the children?"

"In a very real way." He regarded her with delight. "If you and I were to marry, we could take in five wards — one for each spare bedroom in my cousins' residence. What do you say?"

Melanie's first instinct was to take the proposal as a jest, but his earnest expression said otherwise.

"Mr. Chastain, I could never consider marriage just to take in a ward." Of course, she had felt differently when she thought Lord Peyton was proposing, hadn't she? "Besides which, we are barely acquainted with one another. I would need to feel a deep and abiding affection to even consider matrimony."

The man pouted only for the briefest of moments. "So, you're not ruling me out, I take it?" He stroked his chin. "I cannot sweep you off your feet but then I'm not a broom. If I play my cards just right, I might yet be a groom. I must find a way to make you want to swoon. Perhaps if I play exactly the right tune?"

She laughed. "You are full of wit, Mr. Chastain, and your words are like perfume. To your charms the right lady will never be immune."

"Ooh, good one." He brought her hand to his lips. "Don't dismiss my proposal completely, Miss Starhope. We could have so much fun together."

The crunch of footsteps on gravel grew louder as someone approached. "Miss Starhope, might I have a word?" Lord Peyton's manner was curt.

"Forgive me, sir." Melanie extricated herself from Mr. Chastain's grasp. "Thank you for being so supportive."

"Anytime, Miss Starhope. Anytime at all." He bowed. "I bid you a fond adieu." The gentleman danced a jig before striding toward the house.

Lord Peyton nodded toward the gazebo. "We can talk over there."

As they made their way down the path, she gave him puzzled glance. "I thought you had gone with your brother."

"I merely accompanied Mr. Oglethorpe to his carriage in order to speak with him. I asked him to say nothing about the orphanage during the service tomorrow since the children have not yet been told." His words were terse. "The vicar agreed to allow the boys' choir to sing at the Sunday service next week."

"Oh, I'm glad you managed to persuade him." Melanie proceeded him into the gazebo. "Nevertheless, I sense you are angry with me." She turned to face him.

"Am I?"

"I'm afraid so. I know the tea didn't go especially well, but I was trying my best to solicit help."

A muscle worked in his jaw as he scowled at her. "Are you enjoying yourself, leading that lad around by the nose?"

"What?" She peered at him in alarm. "You cannot be referring to Mr. Chastain."

"He's barely one and twenty, Miss Starhope and has not a serious bone in his body. You are wasting your time."

Melanie couldn't believe her ears. "You're not my father, Lord Peyton, nor my guardian. What business is it of yours?"

He crossed his arms over his chest. "We have work to do, Miss Starhope. I had imagined you were focused on the orphanage, but it seems you are easily distracted by a flirtation."

"I am focused on the orphanage completely, sir. Since I need your help with the children, I'm going to pretend you're not the most officious, arrogant gooseberry of my acquaintance." She turned on her heel and began to walk back to the house.

His voice followed her. "That's *Lord* Gooseberry to you."

••••

Over dinner that night, Melanie and her aunt engaged in little conversation. Finally, Melanie put down her fork and pushed her plate away. "Forgive me, but I seem to have no appetite this evening."

Genevieve put her fork down as well. "Neither do I." She rose. "Would you like go to the drawing room for a brandy?"

"Oh, yes." Melanie dropped her napkin by her plate and stood. "I think we've earned it."

A short while later, she had removed her shoes and was sitting on the sofa with her legs tucked up next to her. Genevieve brought over two snifters of amber fluid, gave her one, and then sank down into a wing chair.

"The beauty of living alone is that nobody criticizes you for having a drink." She took a sip. "As you said, however, we've earned it."

Melanie drank a mouthful of brandy and grimaced. "It burns, but it's a good sort of burn."

"Yes."

"Aunt Ginny, I'm terribly sorry for what happened today." Melanie frowned. "I seem to spoil everything I touch."

"That's not true, dear." Genevieve frowned. "If you are referring to Lord Warwick's boorishness, I'm glad his cold-hearted nature was revealed sooner rather than later. I now need only feel sorry for his late wife and children."

"You say that quite bravely, but I know you are disappointed."

"I confess, I am."

Truth be told, Melanie was exceedingly disappointed in Lord Peyton as well.

Genevieve emptied her snifter. "Why did Lord Peyton come back to speak with you this afternoon? He seemed to be in a towering temper when he left."

Melanie swallowed a mouthful of brandy before responding. "Ostensibly, he wished to say that the vicar will permit his choir to sing in church. Thereafter, however, Lord Peyton scolded me for my friendship with Mr. Chastain and accused me of flirting with the gentleman."

Genevieve gaped. "What must have possessed him to do such a thing?"

"I don't know, but he said some insulting, unwarranted, and dismissive things about Mr. Chastain."

"What a ghastly way to behave! It's almost as if Lord Peyton was jealous."

Melanie's laugh was mirthless. "I know that's not true. He was probably vexed with me for the way I discussed the orphanage at tea."

"If that's the case, I'm as deeply disappointed in Lord Peyton as I am in his brother."

Melanie drained her glass and stood. "Would you care for another brandy?"

Her aunt held out her glass. "Yes, please. Perhaps it will burn the memory of Lord Warwick out of my mind."

Melanie splashed more brandy into both their snifters, adding a little more to hers than was good for her. The entire bottle would not burn away her thoughts of Lord Peyton — but it might singe them a trifle.

Suzanne G. Rogers

Chapter Eleven
Intentions

Melanie was muzzy-headed the next morning, but a headache remedy set her right again. When she went down to breakfast, her aunt seemed to be moving in a gingerly fashion as well.

"A full glass of water and headache powder," Melanie murmured. "I recommend taking it before we leave for church."

Genevieve groaned. "Why didn't I think of that?"

As they drove past Prospero's Retreat on their way to Sunday service, Melanie scowled. "This is really a dreadful state of affairs, being at odds with our neighbors. I cannot avoid Lord Peyton because of the orphanage, and you will likely cross paths with his brother more often than you would wish."

"Once the summer is over, perhaps we should cancel all our invitations and go to London. Or maybe we should go abroad and winter in Madeira."

Melanie winced. "I don't speak a word of Portuguese."

Genevieve shrugged. "I don't think it matters, but we could always learn a few phrases before we leave."

Melanie gave her a sidelong glance. "Didn't you criticize me once for planning to run away from my troubles?"

"This is different." Her aunt shrugged. "We will be going on holiday."

"What if we have a ward?"

"We'll bring the child along, of course. It will be a wonderful opportunity for all of us to become better acquainted."

On her way down the aisle, Melanie waved at the group of orphans sitting in the back. The girls looked pristine in their new sailor suits, but the boys were scruffy. It was of little consequence, however, because the Ladies' Sewing Circle would be finished with the uniforms by the coming week.

After she and Genevieve were seated, Melanie spotted Lord Peyton and the marquess seated in the front pew again. She was willing to wager that neither gentleman had lost any sleep over her or her aunt. Well, Melanie intended to ignore them both. She would interact with Lord Peyton as necessary, of course, but her care and attention would be reserved for the children.

Once the service had concluded, she pretended to be absorbed in her Bible as the congregants in the forward pews left during the postlude. A wrapped bonbon dropped onto the open pages, and she glanced up to see Mr. Chastain file past, chuckling to himself. Melanie couldn't help but smile. He really was a lovely soul and they got along very well...but she had to admit Lord Peyton had made a good point. Mr. Chastain didn't seem capable of sober discourse for any length of time. The more intimate aspects of a marital union required passion, did they not? If the gentleman felt a deep passion for her, he had failed to show it thus far.

"Move along, dear," Genevieve whispered. "You're holding up our pew."

"Oh, sorry."

As Melanie left the church, she was mobbed by children. She was so busy hugging each and every orphan, she almost didn't care when Lord Warwick and Lord Peyton mounted their horses and rode down the street. Of course, as she accompanied her aunt to their gig a few minutes later, the snub sank in.

"Mrs. Wheeler hasn't told the children anything yet, apparently," Melanie murmured. "Otherwise, they would have mentioned it to me just now."

"Perhaps she'll make an announcement later today." Genevieve frowned. "Did you notice Lord Warwick and Lord Peyton ride off without a word?"

"I confess, I did." Melanie's shoulders drooped. "I cannot decide if it's worse to be angry with someone or for them to be angry with you."

"Both situations are equally unpleasant, I think."

As they drove home, Melanie failed to shake off a feeling of melancholy. "I must write Blanche a letter when I get home." She sighed. "Would you like to continue reading *Blodwen and the Bloodless* this afternoon? I need something to cheer me up."

"So do I." Genevieve smiled. "I'll sketch while you read if that's all right with you."

"Oh, yes. That sounds lovely."

••••

Melanie carried the novel into the drawing room. "Where would you like me to sit?"

Genevieve gestured toward the window. "Just there would be perfect. Start reading whenever you like."

Melanie turned to the bookmark where they had left off last time and cleared her throat. "Twilight was gathering when Blodwen finally spied Newt. When the pup noticed her draw near, he stood up and began to wag his tail in welcome. She could see right away the reason he had not come home; his fur been entangled in a bramble bush and the creature could not get free..."

As she read, she could hear a faint scratching as Genevieve sketched her likeness from a few feet away. Melanie was so worried about Blodwen getting home before nightfall, her own problems seemed to ebb. Page after page went by before another sound reached her ears. She glanced through the window to discover a carriage rolling up the drive.

"Oh, bother! We have a visitor."

Genevieve made a sound of frustration. "After yesterday's tea party, I would have dearly loved to have an afternoon to ourselves." She set her sketchpad aside. "Excuse me while I wash my hands. My fingers always get black from the charcoal pencil."

Melanie returned the bookmark to her novel, set it aside with a frown, and crossed over to peruse the sketches Genevieve had torn from her pad and stacked on the table. Her aunt had captured her well, in Melanie's opinion, although she judged the portraits to be a trifle too flattering.

Genevieve returned to the drawing room, examining her manicure. "It's a shame I can't wear gloves when I'm sketching. I can never be entirely certain my fingernails are clean."

From outside in the courtyard, Melanie heard a child say, "What a big house!"

She gave her aunt a startled glance before creeping back toward the window. What she saw emerging from the carriage made her gasp.

"It's Lord Warwick and he's brought his children!"

Genevieve's lips parted. "Why?"

Melanie shrugged. "You said yesterday you wouldn't mind raising another woman's child. Perhaps he wishes to see if you truly meant it."

"But I've grown to loathe the man!" Genevieve tossed her head. "His children would have to be the most adorable angels ever born to overcome my antipathy toward their father."

"Lord Peyton did say his brother had become withdrawn and difficult to reach. Perhaps this is Lord Warwick's attempt to..." Melanie cast about for the proper phrase, "...to soften his hard edges."

Genevieve peered at her. "Whose side are you on?"

Melanie crossed over to squeeze her aunt's hands. "Yours, utterly and completely."

The butler appeared. "Lord Warwick, Lord Peyton, Miss Josephine Peyton, and Master Sterling Peyton."

Genevieve cleared her throat. "Show them in, Newman, and bring a plate of biscuits."

"Right away, Mrs. Hornsby."

Lord Warwick appeared first, carrying a toddler in his arms and holding a young girl by the hand.

"Good afternoon, Mrs. Hornsby. Miss Starhope. I brought the rest of my family to meet you."

Both of his children had wavy dark hair, pink rosebud mouths, and green eyes. The little boy caught sight of Melanie and Genevieve and giggled, revealing two front teeth. By contrast, the girl wore a serious expression and surveyed the room with an appraising glance. When her eyes rested on the two ladies, she dropped her father's hand and dipped into a curtsy.

"I'm Josie."

Genevieve and Melanie answered her curtsy with one of their own.

"I'm Mrs. Hornsby and this," Genevieve gestured toward Melanie, "is my niece, Miss Starhope."

Josie nodded. "We are neighbors, did you know?" She pointed at her brother. "This is Sterling. He blows bubbles with his mouth."

As if on cue, Sterling blew a raspberry.

Genevieve laughed. "Lord Warwick, your children are delightful."

"Thank you, Mrs. Hornsby." His smile was almost self-effacing. "Your praise is worth the earning."

Melanie was shocked to discover the man's lips were cracked and somewhat puffy on one side. Furthermore, his cheekbone was sporting a faint purplish smudge. Her gaze flew to Lord Peyton, who also appeared worse for wear. He had a black eye and a slightly swollen nose to boot.

Josie tugged on Genevieve's skirt. "May we see the glass room?"

Her eyebrows rose. "Oh...yes, of course you may." Genevieve glanced at Melanie. "We'll return momentarily."

Josie took Genevieve's hand. "Papa thinks you're pretty."

Lord Warwick's color rose. "Shh, dearest. That's a secret."

Aunt Ginny accompanied Lord Warwick and his children into the entrance hall, leaving Melanie and Lord Peyton alone. Considering the acrimonious way they had parted the day before, her manner was cool.

"I wrote something for the newspaper." He retrieved a folded piece of paper from the inside pocket of his jacket and extended it toward her. "I thought you might like to read it."

As she took the paper, she noticed his knuckles were bruised. "What happened to you?"

"I took a tumble from my horse."

"Is that so?" Melanie looked at him askance. "Did Matador kick your brother afterward?"

"There is nothing wrong with your powers of observation, it seems." Lord Peyton glanced toward the doorway as if to make sure no one was standing within earshot. "As it so happens, Edmund and I had a bit too much to drink last night and settled our differences."

"I see."

Had Lord Peyton beaten some sense into his brother or was it the other way around? Evidently, since he had not apologized for his remarks about Mr. Chastain, the beating had had no effect. Then again, perhaps his head was too thick for any remorse to get through.

Melanie turned toward the window to read what Lord Peyton had written. The article detailed the closing of the orphanage and appealed to the populace to consider making room for a child in their homes. She was impressed when he concluded with the Bible verse Miss Oglethorpe had quoted to her father at the ill-fated tea.

"This is very good." She glanced over. To her dismay, he was studying the sketches Aunt Ginny had drawn of her. "Er...never mind those. My aunt was merely passing the time."

"Her drawings have real flare." His eyes met hers. "You've never looked lovelier."

Why did his glance have the power to make her heart beat faster?

"Thank you." Melanie folded the paper with trembling hands. "As I said, I like what you wrote. You made the case well."

She dropped the article on the table, turned, and fled toward a chair. A few moments later, Lord Peyton came to sit nearby.

"I meant what I said about Mr. Chastain, I'm afraid, but I'm sorry if I upset you."

"Perhaps if you knew him better, you would appreciate his better qualities."

"It's possible, I suppose."

Was Lord Peyton's response meant to be conciliatory or was it, in fact, evasive? She gave him an appraising glance. "You have a great deal in common — such as an interest in music."

"You could be right."

So, he was being evasive and conciliatory at the same time. Before she could say anything else, a footman appeared with a tray.

"Where would you like the biscuits, Miss Starhope?"

"Oh...the children are with my aunt and Lord Warwick in the conservatory. You should take the biscuits there."

"Very good, miss."

When the servant left, an awkward silence ensued. Lord Peyton's presence made it difficult for Melanie to think straight. Despite his somewhat battered features, he was the most handsome man she'd ever seen. *How would it feel to sit in his lap?* She frowned and shook her head. How could she be thinking such thoughts — and on Sunday, too?

Lord Peyton frowned. "What's wrong? You look as if you are conflicted about something."

"Um..." Melanie fumbled to produce a plausible reason for her expression. "I-I'm worried." She gulped. "The same arguments at tea yesterday might be repeated all over Ledbury in the coming days and weeks. Husbands and wives may argue between themselves about whether or not to take in a child and those people who choose to do so might squabble with one another over particular children. I'm trying to help the orphans, but I don't mean to tear the very fabric of society to shreds."

He leaned forward. "Perhaps people ought to argue, to get disagreements out in the open."

"I hadn't considered things that way." Melanie studied him. "Then again, sometimes people argue too much. Acrimony can get in the way of harmony."

"True." Lord Peyton sat back. "Consider, however, that too much harmony can get in the way of romantic passion. For a woman like you, that would be a great pity."

Melanie gaped at him. Was the man a mystic, capable of reading her mind? "You take pleasure in provoking me, sir."

She left her chair and crossed over to the window so he wouldn't notice the blush creeping across her countenance. Unfortunately, he followed, standing so near she could feel his breath stirring the delicate hair on the nape of her neck.

"At least I provoke you, Miss Starhope. Anton could never say as much."

She felt the husky whisper resonate throughout her body. "You think far too well of yourself, Lord Peyton, and far too little of me."

When Melanie turned to face him, she realized she'd made a tactical mistake. Her back was against the window, he stood inches away, and she had nowhere to retreat. Worse, she would not have retreated, even if it had been possible.

He smiled. "I wouldn't say that."

Her eyes suddenly narrowed as she realized he was making a fool of her. He knew full well the physical sensations he provoked in women and likely enjoying watching them squirm.

"You are a vampire, Lord Peyton."

His expression grew puzzled. "I don't understand."

She gestured toward the novel she'd set aside on the table. "Vampires are preternaturally attractive men who lure naive young girls close, just before they bite. You may not be an actual creature of the night, but your tricks won't work on me."

"First, I'm a pirate and now a vampire? You're quite wrong on both accounts." Lord Peyton leaned in until his lips hovered near her ear, "I don't bite, I assure you."

Before she could respond, footsteps just outside the drawing room made him step back. Moments later, young Josephine appeared with a biscuit held high.

"Uncle Ceddy, this is for you!" She crossed over to give him the treat with crumbs on her face.

"I'm not in the mood for a biscuit right now." Lord Peyton knelt, retrieved a familiar-looking handkerchief from his pocket, and wiped her chin. "You take it."

Josie frowned. "What about the pretty lady behind you?" She extended the grubby biscuit toward Melanie.

She shook her head. "Thank you, but you may have it all to yourself."

The girl giggled as she darted from the room. By the time Lord Peyton had risen to his feet, Melanie had maneuvered to put a sofa between the two of them.

She glanced at the linen square in his hand. "That's my handkerchief."

He peered at the handkerchief. "Surely not."

"It has my monogram, embroidered in red."

"Hmm." Lord Peyton frowned at the letters. "So it does."

"I gave it to you that day at the orphanage and you never returned it to me."

"As it so happens, I have no wish to return it." He tucked the handkerchief into the inside pocket of his jacket and held his arms out wide. "Although you may come and get it, if you dare."

"You cannot trifle with my affections, sir." Why was she so breathless? "It isn't proper."

His gaze was smoky. "I have no intention of trifling with your affections."

"I'm glad we understand one another." Melanie sank down into a chair. "Keep the handkerchief if you like. It means nothing to me."

"Ha!" Lord Peyton dropped his arms to his side. "Where is your sense of adventure, Miss Starhope? I had imagined you possessed more backbone that that."

She glared. "And I had imagined you possessed better manners."

Conversation in the entrance hall presaged the inopportune return of Genevieve and his brother. Moments later, Lord Warwick appeared with his daughter in tow while Genevieve carried Sterling. The four of them seemed very happy.

Lord Warwick gave his brother a beaming smile. "We've stayed too long."

"Oh, dear." Genevieve deposited a kiss on Sterling's chubby cheek and transferred him to his father's arms. "It was lovely meeting you, Sterling and Miss Josephine. I shall enjoy having you as neighbors."

Josie's mouth and chin were covered with crumbs again. "Thank you for the biscuits!"

Melanie lifted her hand in farewell as the Peyton family took their leave. As she stood at the window, watching them climb into the carriage, Lord Peyton glanced over. A slow smile curved his lips as he patted the part of his jacket where he'd tucked her handkerchief. In the next moment, he disappeared into the carriage, and it began to roll down the driveway.

Genevieve came to stand beside her. "That was a lovely visit."

"So Lord Warwick has redeemed himself?"

Her aunt gave her a sidelong glance. "Perhaps a little. Did Lord Peyton tell you about the accident he and his brother had?"

"Why, no—"

"An axel broke on their gig, and they were thrown to the ground." Genevieve shuddered. "It's a wonder they weren't more seriously hurt."

As Melanie remembered Lord Peyton's bruised knuckles, she bit back a smile. "Yes."

Genevieve crossed over to the table and began to stack her sketches into a pile. "Wait a moment..." She peered at the floor and underneath the tablecloth.

"What's wrong?"

"I finished seven sketches before, but now there are only six." She straightened. "Do you know what happened to the missing one?"

"I believe Lord Peyton may have taken it. Apparently, he fancies himself a collector of sorts."

"Oh, that's all right, then." Genevieve breathed a happy sigh. "Do you know, I think I'll get a piano as soon as may be."

Melanie blinked. "Do you wish to learn how to play?"

"No, but you would enjoy it, wouldn't you? Besides which, we've had so many musically talented guests come to visit lately, a piano will be useful." She smiled. "Shall we continue with *Blodwen and the Bloodless?*"

"Why not?"

Indeed, the afternoon was filled with vampires, it seemed. Lord Peyton had said he wasn't toying with her but what exactly *was* he doing? He might not be a vampire, but he was definitely mesmerizing her — wittingly or not. Evidently, she would need a chaperone whenever he was around.

••••

At breakfast the following morning, Melanie wondered how she could convince her aunt to give up her afternoons at home in order to chaperone her at the orphanage. As it turned out, however, she needn't have worried.

"I'm going to go with you to your piano lessons." Genevieve refilled her cup with fresh tea. "I would like to sketch the children."

"That's good."

"Edmund is going to the orphanage this afternoon as well. He suggested we read the children's histories to discover if they have extended family. If so, perhaps some of the families might be persuaded to take their blood relatives in." Her aunt gave a happy sigh. "I'm glad Edmund wishes to help after all."

Melanie peered at her. "*Edmund?*"

"Mmm hmm." Genevieve brought her cup to her lips.

"You've known the marquess for such a short time, I cannot believe you are already on intimate terms." She paused. "Perhaps you need a chaperone."

Her aunt snorted into her tea. "I'm a mature widow, Melly, not a blushing debutante. You needn't worry about my reputation."

"It's not your reputation that concerns me as much as your heart." Melanie frowned. "Has Lord Warwick given you any idea about his intentions?"

Genevieve averted her gaze. "No, but he *did* introduce me to his children. I don't think he would have done so if he didn't wish to court me."

"He merely introduced his children to his neighbors, Aunt Ginny." Melanie scowled at the sausages on her plate. "Without other assurances, I wouldn't count on anything."

Her aunt's smile slipped. "I suppose you are right." She lowered her gaze to her plate. "I will endeavor to be more circumspect from now on."

Melanie cut her sausage into bits. "I don't mean to discourage you, but I suspect the Peyton brothers have broken many hearts over the years. They don't need to add two more."

Genevieve gaze her a sharp glance. "Two? You don't mean to say Lord Peyton has been flirting with you?"

"I-I think it's in his nature to flirt with every girl he meets."

"I've not observed any such thing, dearest. He possesses the appearance of a rake, to be sure, but he comports himself like a gentleman."

"Not always," Melanie muttered.

"Oh, dear." Her aunt grimaced. "In that case, it is not *I* who need a chaperone as much as you."

"Nothing untoward has happened, I assure you. Nevertheless, he teases me dreadfully whenever we're alone." Melanie stabbed a bite of sausage with her fork.

"Why does he tease you, dearest?" Genevieve peered at her. "Do you suppose it's his manner of courtship?"

"Aunt Ginny, Lord Peyton has expressly told me he is not interested in matrimony. Therefore, I can only conclude he is trying to revenge himself for my impertinence."

"I cannot believe that." Genevieve nibbled on a piece of bacon. "Even so, I'm glad you have reminded me to be cautious. Edmund — Lord Warwick, that is — must prove himself worthy before I relax my guard."

"Even if he does prove himself, there is one way to be absolutely certain of his devotion." Melanie studied her plate. "I will be able to free myself from any attraction I harbor for his brother at the same time."

"What did you have in mind?"

"Blanche."

Her aunt's sigh was long and low. "That's simply dreadful."

Melanie peered at her. "You disagree?"

"No, it's a brilliant idea." An expression of distaste crossed Genevieve's countenance.

"Nevertheless, using Blanche in that fashion is despicable. How did you ever think of it?"

Melanie shrugged. "No gentleman has ever looked twice at me after they have seen my sister. I'm used to it in a way, but I made myself a promise never to settle in romance. I love my sister, but if Lord Peyton is captivated by her looks, my passion for the man will shrivel up and disappear entirely."

"Yes. The same logic should apply to Lord Warwick, I'm afraid." Genevieve made a sound of disgust. "I shall invite our family to visit on the third of August."

"Why then?"

"Lord Warwick's ball, of course. It's to be held on Wednesday, August fourth."

"We are agreed, then."

"Agreed." Genevieve frowned. "And I hope we will both be proved wrong."

••••

When Melanie and her aunt arrived at the orphanage that afternoon, Matador was nowhere in sight. Instead, a gig was parked in the spot where Lord Peyton's horse usually stood.

"I see Lord Warwick managed to get his axel fixed in a very short period of time." Melanie's tone was light. "It's really quite remarkable."

"Yes. Wait..." Genevieve's eyes widened, "do you doubt his story?"

"Not only do I doubt it, but I know it to be untrue." Melanie gave her an apologetic glance. "Lord Peyton told me that he and his brother settled some issues between them in a drunken brawl."

"Not really!" Her aunt's spine straightened. "Why would Lord Warwick resort to such a fabrication?"

"Don't be too hard on the fellow. He probably thought you would find a fistfight between two grown men unflattering."

"I do — especially as between brothers." Genevieve crossed her arms in a fit of obvious pique. "Why did Lord Peyton confess to you, then?"

Melanie laughed. "Lord Peyton already knows I think the worst of him."

They entered the main building, where the faint, angelic sound of the boys' choir filled the hallways.

Genevieve gasped, "That sounds heavenly, doesn't it?"

"The choir is practicing for next Sunday's service, I expect." Melanie gestured toward open office nearby. "We should let Mrs. Wheeler know you are here."

When they walked inside, the matron was huddled with Lord Warwick as they poured over files spread out on the woman's desk.

Melanie exchanged a glance with her aunt before clearing her throat. "Good afternoon."

The two broke off their conversation and got to their feet.

Lord Warwick smiled at Melanie but in the next moment his gaze slid to Genevieve. "Good afternoon." He gestured toward the files. "We are hunting for relatives."

"That's wonderful." Melanie glanced at her aunt once more, but the woman was focused on Lord Warwick. "Erm...Mrs. Wheeler, have you told the children about the closure?"

"I made the announcement last night at dinner." The matron's expression became sober.

"There were quite a few tears, I'm afraid, and the children are frightened."

Melanie frowned. "That's understandable. Did you say we are trying to help them?"

Mrs. Wheeler nodded. "Yes, but the little dears are upset all the same."

"I shall try to reassure them as best I can." Melanie gestured toward Genevieve. "My aunt has come to sketch the children for the newspaper."

Lord Warwick shook his head. "There's been a change in that regard. Cedric went to the newspaper with his story this morning. The editor agreed to publish his article and upcoming profiles of orphaned children, but he won't publish the sketches. He said there is simply no room."

"Bother!" Melanie bit her lip. "If people could see the children's faces, it would become more personal. Without appealing to people's emotions, it is altogether too easy to dismiss orphans as someone else's problem."

"I can attest to that, I'm afraid." Lord Warwick's expression was sheepish. "Can we not post the sketches elsewhere? Perhaps some local proprietors would be willing to put them in their shop windows."

Mrs. Wheeler brightened. "The postmistress is a friend of mine. I believe I can persuade Francine to post several sketches inside the post office."

Genevieve stirred. "I'll ask Mr. Abernathy if he would be willing to help. Since I intend to purchase a piano from his shop, I'll make their cooperation a requirement of the sale."

Lord Warwick chuckled. "Remind me never to bargain with you, Mrs. Hornsby."

She lifted her chin. "There is nothing wrong with a lady asserting herself, sir. Gentlemen are not the only creatures allowed to make demands."

The marquess gave her a puzzled glance. "I agree. Please forgive me if you thought I suggested otherwise."

Melanie edged toward the door. "If you'll excuse me, I must set up for my piano lessons."

Genevieve held up her sketchpad. "If you don't mind, Mrs. Wheeler, I would like to wander around the facility, drawing portraits."

The matron beamed. "The children will enjoy that very much, I think."

Lord Warwick's eyebrows drew together. "Is there anything I can do to help you, Mrs. Hornsby?"

To her credit, Genevieve barely hesitated. "The greatest help you could give me at the moment is to locate relatives for these orphans."

Melanie and her aunt left the office and headed down the corridor.

"I must give credit where credit is due," Melanie murmured. "Lord Warwick's attitude has undergone a transformation. Few aristocrats would bother to visit an orphanage, much less lend a hand personally." She glanced at her aunt. "I think the transformation must be due to you."

"I hope so." The woman let out her breath in a gust. "I had vowed to demonstrate my independence just now, but my knees were shaking so hard, I worried the noise was audible."

Melanie laughed. "If your knees made any noise at all, it was drowned out by Lord Peyton's choir."

Suzanne G. Rogers

Chapter Twelve

Dispirited No Longer

Once Melanie and Genevieve reached the dining hall, girls were pressed against the door, watching Lord Peyton through the glass insert as usual. Their ordinarily ebullient demeanor was muted, however, even when they clustered around Melanie for hugs. She held up a finger to her lips when they began to ask questions, and she beckoned them to follow her and Genevieve down the hall.

"We cannot talk here, or Lord Peyton will scowl at us," she whispered.

In the music room, Melanie shushed the girls while she opened the windows and closed the door. Then, the children let loose with an emotional outpouring until she held up her hands for quiet.

"I'm sorry this has happened to you but there are a great many people who are trying to help find you permanent homes. Please try to remain as cheerful as possible and carry on as you might ordinarily do. We may have visitors to the orphanage who might like to invite you into their families. It wouldn't do for them to see long faces, would it?"

The girls shook their heads and Denise wrapped her arms around Melanie's waist. "Could we come to live with you?"

A chorus of supplication ensued, and Melanie's heart swelled with emotion. "Please understand that I'm exceedingly fond of you all, but young, unmarried ladies don't take in wards. I have no money or home of my own, so it simply isn't possible."

"Marry Lord Peyton," Willa said. "He likes you."

The girls jumped up and down in excitement, shouting, "Marry Lord Peyton! Marry Lord Peyton!" and Melanie felt her face burn with embarrassment. "The gentleman has not asked me to marry him and there are no indications he has any such intentions. I beg you not to suggest anything of the kind to him or I will be humiliated."

The girls turned toward Genevieve. "Can we live with you, Mrs. Hornsby?"

She gave them a kind smile. "Wouldn't you prefer a family with a mama and a papa and possibly brothers and sisters?"

The children exchanged glances with one another, but nobody contradicted the assertion.

"To that end, Mrs. Hornsby has come to draw your portraits," Melanie said. "We will post them around town, so potential families will get to know you better."

That news was greeted with excitement, she was pleased to see.

She cleared her throat. "I would like for you to be on your best behavior as my aunt takes your likenesses...but don't be late for your piano lessons!"

Genevieve smiled. "Come along, girls, and let's find some quiet place to work."

They filed out of the room, leaving Melanie alone. The fear and anxiety amongst the young children brought tears to her eyes and she sank down onto the piano bench in despair. If she accepted Mr. Chastain's offer to marry her, she could take in five girls — but how could she choose among them? The ones left out would be crushed and possibly scarred forever by a rejection that had nothing to do with them personally. Even if they drew straws, it would still seem unfair and cruel. Furthermore, it did nothing to help the boys.

Melanie forced herself to take deep breaths until she grew calm again. She had encouraged the girls to remain cheerful, after all, so she must set a good example. Fortunately, when her first pupil arrived, she managed to greet her with a smile. Surely, with God's grace and the help of so many caring people, these orphaned children would find homes of their own.

After her last pupil had finished her lesson and skipped outside to play, Melanie went about closing up the music room. She half-hoped Lord Peyton would stride into view, but he did not. Instead, her aunt arrived with her sketchbook in hand.

"Lord Warwick and his brother have gone."

Melanie swallowed her disappointment. "I see." She glanced at the sketchbook. "Were you able to draw many of the girls?"

"All of the children, actually. I slipped into the dining hall just as choir practice ended and I persuaded the lads to sit for me."

Genevieve showed Melanie her winsome sketches. As she turned the pages, Melanie shook her head in admiration.

"Aunt Ginny, these are perfect!" She deposited an impulsive kiss on the woman's cheek. "Once Lord Peyton's story has been published, we'll post these portraits wherever we can."

Melanie waited to say anything more of significance until she and her aunt were in their gig and on the way home. Once they had left the orphanage behind, Melanie took a deep breath and said, "I almost burst into tears when the children asked if they could come live with me."

Genevieve nodded. "I did, too. Although I *am* interested in taking in a child, if I had said anything other than what I did, they would have all been begging to be chosen. I just couldn't bear the thought of it."

"Mr. Chastain asked me to marry him."

"What?" Her aunt tightened her grip on the reins, nearly bringing the gig to a halt. "Why didn't you tell me?"

"I didn't say anything because it's difficult to know with Mr. Chastain whether or not he is entirely serious. He did say, however, that he would be willing to take five children if we were wed." Melanie shrugged. "I put him off, of course, but now I'm not so sure it isn't the right thing to do."

"Oh, Melly." Genevieve urged Plaid forward. "Do you care for the gentleman?"

"I like him very much. I'm just not sure I could ever love him in the way I could love...well, someone else."

"I like Mr. Chastain very much as well but he seems to be a trifle young to jump into matrimony."

"I understand." Melanie paused. "Even so, he seems to be smitten with me and after what happened today, I'm not ready to dismiss his proposal completely. I could save five little girls, Aunt Ginny."

"At the cost of your own happiness, dear."

Melanie frowned. "Life with Mr. Chastain would be a lark, don't you imagine? I don't believe he would make me unhappy."

Genevieve gave her a level glance. "Even in the marriage bed?"

"I-I don't know anything about that so I couldn't say."

"Neither do I, but I think you know exactly what I mean."

Melanie lowered her gaze to her lap. "I have no assurance I will ever experience that sort of — " she cast about for the right word, "— *romance*, Aunt Ginny. Mr. Chastain's offer to take so many orphans is a very generous one."

"Yes, it is."

"I've just been wondering if I shouldn't encourage him."

"If you are asking for my opinion, I would say you should develop your friendship with the man and see where it leads. We have a little while until the orphanage closes its doors forever and the children might all be placed by then."

Melanie felt her shoulders relax. "All right." She gave her aunt a curious glance. "Do you intend to encourage Lord Warwick?"

"I'm inclined to wait until Lord Warwick's ball before I decide whether or not to pursue him."

"You are referring to Blanche."

"Just so. A girl of eighteen is quite capable of bearing him children whereas my own situation is far less certain. I must see for myself what interests Lord Warwick most."

Melanie's mood turned dour. "Whatever happened to 'dazzling spinsters'?"

Her aunt sighed. "The Peyton brothers."

••••

The following morning at breakfast, Newman brought the post into the conservatory. As it turned out, one of the envelopes was an invitation to dine at Prospero's Retreat on Saturday night.

"How delightful!" Genevieve's eyes sparkled with enthusiasm. "I will wear my crimson foulard. No, crimson isn't quite right for summer." She stared off into space. "The peach silk with the tulle underskirt is perfect. It's both youthful and fetching. What about you?"

"I-I don't know." Truth be told, the thought of spending an evening with Lord Peyton was sending Melanie into a panic. "It really doesn't matter what I wear."

"Of course it matters! You don't know who else has been invited."

"That's true." Melanie shrugged. "I shall wear something with a high neckline."

Her aunt looked at her askance. "Why a high neckline?"

Melanie allowed herself to smile. "There may be vampires about."

Genevieve laughed. "We've been reading too many gothic novels, I think."

"I'm not sure that's possible." Melanie reached for the morning paper. "Let me see if Lord Peyton's article has been published yet."

To her pleasant surprise, the article appeared on the second page. Her aunt rose from her chair and came around the table to read over Melanie's shoulder.

"He writes very well, I must say." Genevieve finally returned to her chair. "I do hope people will be moved."

"I wonder if Lord Warwick managed to discover relatives when searching through children's files yesterday?"

"I don't know." Genevieve reached up to smooth her hair. "Perhaps I'll go with you again today...to lend a hand."

Melanie gave her an amused glance. "I'm sure Lord Warwick will welcome your assistance."

"I should think he would." Genevieve winked.

"Why don't you paint this morning while I go for a walk?" Melanie's gaze flickered toward the view of the garden. "I've been neglecting my exercise lately."

"I wish I could join you, but I really *would* like to work."

"I thought as much." Melanie pushed back her chair. "I'll fetch a hat and be off before it gets too hot outside."

Once she had donned a broad-brimmed straw hat, she left the house and made her way to the gooseberry shrub. She was pleased to discover it had taken root, apparently, and was thriving in the sun. Her next destination was the weeping willow where she and Lord Peyton had eaten their picnic. She sat down, rested her back against the tree trunk, and closed her eyes. The vivid memory of him whispering, "At least I provoke you, Miss Starhope. Anton could never say as much," sent a delicious shiver down her spine. Her aunt had suggested his teasing was a form of courtship, but Melanie believed that to be wishful thinking.

She got to her feet and began walking downhill. When she drew closer to the road, she was surprised to hear a child calling, "Miss Starhope! Miss Starhope!" Melanie glanced around until she discovered young Josie standing near the cherry grove, waving madly with both her arms. Melanie waved back before jumping over a small hedgerow, crossing the road, and fording a ditch to join her.

The child came at a run. "Good morning!"

"Good morning!" Melanie gave the grove a curious glance. "Where is your nanny?"

"She's giving Sterling a bath. I'm supposed to be walking the grounds, getting fresh air." Josie pointed at the grove. "Can you pick some cherries for me? I can't reach."

"Let's see if any of the cherries are ready to pick."

Melanie peered at the trees, where the fruit was just starting to ripen. A few cherries were nearly ready, so she picked one for Josie.

"Here you go. Mind you don't swallow the pit."

The girl popped the cherry into her mouth, chewed for a moment, and then spit it out. "Eew!" Josie stuck out her tongue in distaste. "Sour!"

Melanie laughed. "I think the cherries might need another week or so before they are sweet and juicy. Would you like to try some gooseberries?"

She beckoned Josie over to the gooseberry, where the plump, delicious fruit was begging to be picked. After the child had eaten her fill, she smiled.

"Gooseberries are better than marmalade."

"I quite agree." Melanie edged back. "I should be going, but it was lovely speaking with you."

Josie caught her sleeve. "Would you like to see my mama? There's a large portrait of her in the entrance hall."

The prospect of seeing the woman who had captivated Lord Peyton's heart so thoroughly was tempting, but what if the gentleman caught her?

"I wouldn't dream of disturbing anyone's privacy — especially not your Papa or your uncle."

"Uncle Ceddy is driving Papa to the train station. Papa won't be home until tomorrow."

"Oh?" If that was the case, perhaps she could slip inside for a quick peek. "I would love to see your mama, but only if we hurry."

"Let's go!"

Josie took off at a run, shrieking with joy, and Melanie followed, glad for the opportunity to act like a child for a little while. When they darted through the opening in a tall hedge, the house came into view. The elegant residence was Georgian in style and quite old.

"Your home is lovely."

Josie grabbed her hand and tugged. "You can come inside."

The child led her to the front door and opened it. As Melanie escorted Josie into the entrance hall, which was flanked by two rising staircases, a butler came hastening over with a frown on his face.

"May I help you, miss? It's customary to knock and wait to be admitted."

Josie tossed her head. "I invited her, Williams. Miss Starhope is our neighbor."

Melanie nodded. "That's true. My aunt is Mrs. Hornsby, across the road."

The butler did not seem impressed. "You may wait in the drawing room, if you wish. Lord Peyton will return shortly."

"I haven't come to call. Miss Josephine merely wished to show me her mama's portrait."

Josie pointed to a large, imposing oil painting centered in between the staircases. "There she is. That's Mama."

Melanie's lips parted as she gazed on the late marchioness. Lady Warwick had possessed fair golden hair with a hint of copper, large expressive eyes, and regular features. She had indeed been a stunning woman and Melanie no longer wondered why Lord Peyton and his brother had both fallen irrevocably in love with her.

She swallowed hard. "Miss Josephine, your mama reminds me of a beautiful angel."

The little girl sighed. "I can't remember her face, exactly, but I remember she used to smell like flowers."

"That's a wonderful memory and I'm glad you have her portrait." Melanie gave Josie a kind smile. "You'll never forget her that way."

The butler was still glowering, so Melanie squeezed Josie's hand one last time before releasing it. "I expect your nanny will be looking for you, so you'd best run along. Thank you for introducing me to your mama."

Josie curtsied. "You're welcome."

The child skipped toward one of the staircases and began to climb upward as the butler opened the front door. "Good day, miss."

Melanie left, suppressing the impulse to stick her tongue out at the man. As she headed down the long driveway, she sorely wished she hadn't come. So long as she didn't know what Lady Warwick had looked like, she could conjure any image she wished. Now that she'd gazed upon the woman's beauty for herself, she knew she could never hope to earn Lord Peyton's admiration. It was little wonder he could not escape his affection for the lady.

The sound of carriage wheels on gravel brought Melanie up short. Her eyes darted toward the break in the hedge up ahead, but she knew she could never make it through before Lord Peyton saw her. She was caught in an awkward situation and would just have to make the best of it. A scant few seconds later, the gig appeared with Lord Peyton at the reins. His eyebrows lifted when he recognized the woman walking along his driveway.

He reined in his horse, set the brake, and jumped down with his hat in hand. "Did you come to pay me a visit, Miss Starhope?"

"No. I walked Miss Josephine back to her house just now and she wished to show me the portrait of her mama."

"Ah, yes. So, you've seen Audrey."

"Indeed, I did. She was absolutely stunning, in my opinion. In fact, she's *almost* the most beautiful woman I've ever seen."

Lord Peyton cocked his head. "Almost?"

"My aunt is extraordinarily handsome, so I must rank her a trifle higher." Melanie averted her gaze. "And then there is my younger sister, Blanche."

"Your sister is a famous beauty, is she?"

"She's the most beautiful girl in Bromley, by far. Furthermore, I never saw her equal during my time in London."

"Her looks surpass those of my late sister-in-law, you say?" He frowned. "I'm intrigued."

Melanie forced a smile to her lips. "I thought you might be, sir. Blanche will be visiting us in

August, so you'll have the opportunity to meet her then." She curtsied. "Good morning."

She continued walking, even as a wave of emotion threatened her composure. She'd piqued Lord Peyton's interest in her sister, to be sure, and when Blanche arrived, Melanie's daydreams would be crushed forever.

As they should be.

••••

Once Melanie told Genevieve that Lord Warwick would likely be in London for the day, the woman begged off accompanying her to the orphanage.

"I'm working on a difficult watercolor, and I can't seem to get the colors right."

"Don't feel as if you have to make excuses, Aunt Ginny. Not to me."

As Melanie drove away from Asphodel that afternoon, she felt a sharp pang of loneliness. Although she'd become dispirited before, she hadn't suffered from genuine melancholy until now. It was almost as if she'd been wrapped in a wet bag and couldn't move. The horrid feelings she'd tried to leave behind in Bromley had returned with a vengeance and all she could see was despair.

When she arrived at the orphanage, she was obliged to take a few moments to regain her poise. On her way to the music room, she imagined Mr. Chastain was by her side, dancing a jig every few yards to make her laugh. The hugs she exchanged with the girls outside the dining hall helped cheer her a trifle, but she still felt as if a dark cloud was hanging over her head.

Melanie's piano lessons gave her a brief respite, but as soon as her last pupil left, the clouds returned. Hadn't Lord Peyton said when God closes a door, He opens a window? She closed the windows with a mirthless laugh, knowing she was completely boxed in, nevertheless.

As she reached for her hat, however, the door popped open, and Lord Peyton appeared in the doorway with his hands behind his back.

"I've brought something for you, Miss Starhope." He produced a rosebud and crossed over to press it into her hands. "Have a seat. There's more." He strode from the room.

Baffled, she sank onto the piano bench and waited. Very shortly thereafter, the boys from the choir filed into the room, with Lord Peyton leading the way. He turned, lifted his arms as a musical director would, and when he lowered his arms, the boys began to sing, "Three little maids from school are we," from *The Mikado*. They posed and minced and fluttered their lashes like schoolgirls — particularly Frederick, who was the drollest of the lot as he sang the role of Yum-Yum. Melanie screamed with laughter at their antics. Afterward, the choir took a bow and she stood up to applaud.

"I don't know when I've ever seen anything so entertaining," she said. "Thank you for your wonderful performance!"

The lads come over to give her hugs before running from the room, whooping and hollering. Lord Peyton stayed behind — an uncharacteristically kind expression on his face.

"I can't tell you how much I enjoyed that," she said. "It came at the perfect time."

"I'm glad. I've never seen you so dispirited as you were this morning." He took the rose from her hands and tucked it behind her left ear. "Is anything amiss?"

"Oh, well, I..." Melanie's voice trailed off. "Have you ever solved a personal problem only to discover you've merely turned it inside out and are back where you started?"

"Hmm. That's a rather philosophical question, Miss Starhope." Lord Peyton sat down on the piano bench alongside her. "I suppose it's a little like traveling to a foreign country and bringing luggage with you."

"Yes. No matter where you go, the luggage stays the same." She sighed. "If there is a way to leave the luggage behind, I have not discovered it yet."

"Maybe you ought not attempt to leave it behind. Your luggage is part of you, after all." He rubbed his chin. "Perhaps you should allow a porter to carry it for you from time to time?"

The image made her giggle. "You're humoring me."

"A little." He gave her a tiny smile. "It may surprise you to know this, but I don't like to see you sad."

"That does surprise me." Melanie studied him for a moment. "In that case, I take it back. You're not a vampire after all."

"I'm glad we've put that allegation to rest." His grin spread. "Please say I still get to be a pirate."

"Lord Peyton, you're still a pirate."

"Excellent." He stood. "Captain Gooseberry, at your service. Shall we set sail for home?"

She nodded. "Let us weigh anchor."

••••

Lord Peyton tethered Matador to the back of Melanie's gig, slid into the seat next to her, and took the reins.

She stared at him. "What are you doing?"

The man shrugged. "Just think of me as your porter this afternoon." He clucked his tongue at Paint, who started forward.

His presence, which ordinarily would have set off all her senses in forbidden ways, filled her with warmth instead.

"Thank you for being so considerate, Lord Peyton."

"I'm glad for the rare opportunity to show a less curmudgeonly side of myself."

She allowed herself to relax and enjoy the passing scenery, but her thoughts returned to the orphanage sooner than she might have liked.

"Did your brother manage to find any relatives during his search of Mrs. Wheeler's files?"

"Back to business, is it?" He chuckled. "Edmund found only one. Jonah Braithwaite has a cousin by the name of Rudolph Braithwaite. The man lives in London."

"I hope the man can be persuaded to take Jonah in." She pictured the lad as he had monkeyed about in the music room. "I like Jonah very much. He's a natural leader, I think."

"He's natural troublemaker, more like it." Lord Peyton laughed. "Reminds me of myself. During my younger days, the headmaster of my school broke no fewer than five rulers across my backside."

Melanie examined his profile. "Were you really that fractious?"

"I tended to engage in fisticuffs." He gave her a crooked grin. "I didn't like being bullied."

Her eyes widened. "I can't imagine anyone attempting to bully *you*."

"My appearance seemed to invite smart remarks."

"Oh." She glanced away. "I can well imagine."

"Anyway, Edmund has traveled to London, hoping to convince the cousin to take responsibility for Jonah. He'll return tomorrow, to report on what he found."

"Given Lord Warwick's initial indifference to the orphans' plight, I'm impressed that he's going to so much trouble on their behalf."

Lord Peyton grinned. "Apparently, I beat some sense into him and he's now sufficiently motivated to court a particular lady with whom you are intimately acquainted."

"You're referring to my aunt, of course. I'm glad you are supportive of the match."

"My niece and nephew need a mother. If it isn't to be *you*, then Mrs. Hornsby fits the role admirably."

The response served as a painful reminder that Lord Peyton had originally thought Melanie suitable to be his brother's wife. Clearly, he would never have done so if he'd found her attractive himself. Her wounded pride was already too battered to ache overmuch, so she decided to smile instead.

"So, if my aunt and your brother wed, he will be my Uncle Edmund. Would that make you my uncle as well?"

He frowned. "I've never been much good at family trees, but that doesn't sound right. I definitely wouldn't want you to address me as Uncle Cedric."

"No, you will forevermore be Captain Gooseberry."

Lord Peyton made a comical face. "Not that, either. I imagine you would just call me Cedric."

"I have something to look forward to, then."

"Speaking of which, I hope Edmund and I will have the pleasure of your company at our dinner party this Saturday? Your aunt as well, of course."

"We wouldn't miss it."

His expression turned playful, and he launched into a rhythmic sea shanty. Melanie began to nod along with the beat and after a short while she was singing counterpoint during the chorus. Without much effort, the smile returned to her face, and she was dispirited no longer. If she couldn't have Lord Peyton as a lover, she would at least have him as a friend. It was far better than nothing at all and freed her to consider Mr. Chastain's offer more seriously.

A half hour later, Lord Peyton drove Melanie's gig to Asphodel's courtyard, where a horse was tethered to one of the posts.

He frowned. "Your aunt has a male visitor, it seems."

Melanie tossed her head. "I take umbrage at your assumption, sir. The visitor could be waiting for me."

He chuckled. "You are perfectly right."

Lord Peyton continued on to the stables, where he freed Matador from the gig and climbed into his saddle. "Good afternoon, Miss Starhope."

She smiled and lifted her hand in farewell as he cantered off.

When Melanie entered the house a few moments later, Newman was there to take her things. "You have a visitor waiting with Mrs. Hornsby in the drawing room, Miss Starhope. Mr. Chastain has come to call."

"Thank you."

Melanie glanced in the mirror hanging next to the front door. After she smoothed her hair, pinched her cheeks, and went to join the man who would most likely be her husband one day.

Chapter Thirteen
Just Cedric

Late morning the following day, Melanie stood shoulder to shoulder with Mr. Chastain in Aunt Ginny's library. As they surveyed the eighteen sketches and accompanying profile cards laid out on the oriental carpet at their feet, Melanie took Mr. Chastain's left arm and gave it an affectionate squeeze. "I couldn't have done it without you, sir."

"I have always heard my penmanship is beyond reproach." He blew on the fingernails of his right hand and pretended to buff his manicure on his lapel. "I can confirm the rumors were correct."

"Indeed, they were. Now, we must persuade the good shopkeepers of Ledbury to post Aunt Ginny's sketches and your cards." She crossed over to the table to retrieve a pad of paper and a pencil. "Have you any suggestions who we should approach?"

Mr. Chastain's expression became thoughtful. "It would be best to approach those merchants with whom we have business."

"I frequent the fabric shop and the bookshop." She scribbled those down on the paper. "Oh, and the music shop, but that one is Aunt Ginny's."

"I patronize the tailor, the hat shop, the barber, and the stationery shop."

She shook her head. "The only one of those that would work is the stationery shop. You must think about those places a great many women patronize."

"Have you ever been to the Ledbury Tea Shop? I took Cousin Heloise there for tea last week but they serve luncheon as well." He stuck his thumb in the direction of the courtyard. "I drove my gig here this morning. Why don't we drive to Ledbury, approach merchants, and take a break for lunch afterward?"

She smiled and nodded. "I would enjoy that very much but I must be back before one o'clock so I may still drive to the orphanage for my piano lessons."

"Bring your things with you and I'll take you to the orphanage myself."

"But my lessons last two hours!"

"I'll find a way to amuse myself." He gave her a sidelong glance. "Don't forget, we must pick out our children together."

"Mr. Chastain, don't talk such nonsense." Melanie bent to pick up portraits and profile cards from the carpet. "I would have to know you far better to even contemplate marriage."

He bent to help. "You know me sufficiently well, Miss Starhope. I'm rather like orange marmalade in that regard — never changing and always the same."

"Never changing and always the same." Melanie paused. "Aren't those the same things?"

"You're right! I'm quite mistaken." He chuckled. "Just take what I said and reverse it. Oh, and I left off sweet. I'm so terribly, terribly sweet you can never have enough of me."

"You *are* sweet, I'll give you that. Consider, however, that you might meet someone else who will turn your head. What would I do then?"

He caught her hand and gave it a kiss. "I'm devoted to you, Miss Starhope. I will never meet another lady who is as witty as I am or as attractive. We're made for one another."

Melanie laughed. She might not be in love with Mr. Chastain, but she was having a tremendous time with him. Despite the gentleman's protestations of devotion, she suspected he was not deeply in love with her either. Even so, they would have scant few weeks to make up their minds before the orphanage began placing children elsewhere.

••••

"I cannot believe we managed to post so many portraits around town." Melanie gave Mr. Chastain a smile as they drove away from their luncheon at the tea shop and left the town behind. "It was all due to your charm."

"With my charm and your beauty, we shall conquer the world!" He lifted a finger in the air. "Well, we shall conquer Ledbury, at least."

"Ledbury will have to do." She sorted through the remaining portraits. "I have only five remaining."

"If that isn't divine intervention, I don't know what is. Those five will be our new family."

She jostled him with her elbow. "Be serious."

"Ow!"

Melanie ignored him. "I held back Jonah Braithwaite's portrait on purpose until I hear whether or not his cousin will agree to take him. I also have Frederick Anderson's portrait because I'm secretly hoping my aunt will agree to be his guardian. Then, there's Willa Bains. The vicar's wife expressed some interest in her."

"I remember quite well." Mr. Chastain gave an emotional sigh and wailed in falsetto, "'It breaks my heart to think Willa shall be sent off to an institution where she doesn't know a soul.'"

Melanie bit back a smile. "It's not very nice to poke fun at Mrs. Oglethorpe, sir. She's married to a man of the cloth."

"Forgive me, but you may have noticed I can often be irreverent."

"Heavens, yes! I'm not insensible."

His smile slipped. "My late father encouraged me to join the clergy, believe it or not. In point of fact, he insisted upon it."

"You had other ideas, evidently."

"I wished to study music, but he thought it frivolous." He swallowed. "My father was quite severe upon me my entire life, I'm afraid. Cousin Heloise used to intervene regularly on my behalf, so I'm exceedingly obliged to her. I owe her my life."

"Lady Dellingpole, you mean?"

"That's right."

"What about your mama? Was she severe as well?"

"I was raised by a series of governesses and tutors. After my father passed away, my mother remarried. She lives in London, but I'm not sure where."

Melanie leaned over to deposit a kiss on his cheek. "I'm very sorry."

Mr. Chastain turned his head to give her a long, lingering glance. "Cousin Heloise knows my history, of course, but I've never told another living soul."

"I shall keep your confidence, I promise."

"I never had any doubt." He took a deep breath and the merriment returned to his eyes. "At any rate, I always try my level best to be as lighthearted and occasionally irreverent as possible."

"Mr. Chastain, you are a ray of sunshine wherever you go, and I consider myself fortunate to have made your acquaintance."

"That means everything to me, Miss Starhope."

As the orphanage drew closer, Melanie had to acknowledge she had experienced a momentary tug of attraction to the gentleman at her side. Perhaps, if she nurtured that spark, it might yet grow into a flame.

When Melanie and Mr. Chastain reached their destination, two carriages were parked in the driveway while Matador was in his usual spot under the tree.

Mr. Chastain chuckled. "Is the facility usually this busy in the afternoon?"

"No, but perhaps members of the Ladies' Sewing Circle are delivering the boys' uniforms a day early."

Mr. Chastain directed his gig onto the grass on the far side of Matador's shady tree and they entered the main building shortly thereafter. The sound of choir practice filled the corridors. Unfortunately, the sound of a heated argument was emanating from Mrs. Wheeler's office as well.

Melanie's eyes widened as she met Mr. Chastain's gaze. "What in the world?"

He grimaced. "The new uniforms must be dreadfully ugly to have caused such a row."

They hastened over to the open doorway, where a harried Mrs. Wheeler was apparently attempting to calm a shouting match between Mrs. Oglethorpe and Mrs. Steed.

"I've been telling everyone I intended to take Willa!" Mrs. Oglethorpe's face was red. "You knew that, Isabelle!"

Mrs. Steed's complexion was more mottled than red. "Telling people doesn't mean anything, Louella! Every year my husband says he intends to take me on holiday to France and it hasn't come to anything yet. *I* spoke to Mrs. Wheeler about Willa this past Sunday, so I am the first one to actually claim her!"

Melanie's heart sank to discover her worst fears had come true. Two prominent women were in danger of losing their friendship over the same orphaned child and no doubt the rift would spread throughout the community.

She raised her voice to be heard. "Ladies, please! Let's step back from the acrimony and discuss this like civilized people. In the end, we must put the child's welfare over every other consideration."

Both women glared at her, looking for all the world like angry hens but Mrs. Wheeler wore an expression of relief. "That's just what I've been saying, Miss Starhope, but emotions are running a trifle high."

Mr. Chastain cleared his throat. "I'm no King Solomon, of course, but here is what I propose; since each of you would make extraordinarily fine guardians, I suggest you arrange for the child to visit your homes. After you've had the opportunity to speak with Willa, I think it would be prudent to let the child decide which home suits her best."

Mrs. Oglethorpe and Mrs. Steed scowled at one another for several long moments. Finally, the vicar's wife nodded. "I suppose that would work."

Mrs. Steed spoke more grudgingly. "I agree."

"Excellent." Mrs. Wheeler gave Mr. Chastain a smile of gratitude. "And who are you, sir?"

"Mrs. Wheeler, allow me to introduce Mr. Chastain. Mr. Chastain, Mrs. Wheeler is the matron of the orphanage. I believe you already know Mrs. Oglethorpe and Mrs. Steed."

He sketched a bow. "May I say, I admire the passion with which you are approaching a difficult situation. You are not so much adversaries, I think, as advocates for Willa. If you work together, I believe the situation will be resolved amicably."

Mrs. Steed's demeanor softened. "That's what I think as well, Mr. Chastain." She offered a tiny smile to the vicar's wife. "I apologize for shouting just now, Louella."

"I may have allowed my emotions to get the best of me, Isabelle, and I regret it." Mrs. Oglethorpe took a deep breath and let it out in a gust. "We shall both schedule visits with Willa and let her decide."

Mr. Chastain beamed. "What a beautiful thing, to have two friends agree on a good deed." He laid a hand over his heart. "I confess, I'm deeply touched."

The two women actually smiled.

"Perhaps I should mention that Willa is best friends with Anne Leighton." Melanie spread her hands wide. "It would be lovely if the girls went to two wonderful families who are already close. They could continue to grow up together that way."

"I remember Anne Leighton." Mrs. Oglethorpe gave Mrs. Steed an excited glance. "She's the one with the curly red hair."

"Oh, yes! Now that you mention it, she's an adorable child, too." Mrs. Steed's eyes widened.

"What would you say if we arranged visits with both girls separately, to see where they might fit best?"

As the women began discussing details with Mrs. Wheeler, Melanie excused herself to continue down the hall to the music room with Mr. Chastain.

She slid the man an affectionate glance. "Well done, sir. For a moment there, I thought the ladies would come to blows."

He made a sound of disappointment. "If I had thought that was likely, I never would have intervened!"

Melanie laughed. Not only had Mr. Chastain made a bad situation better but two girls now had a good chance of finding homes. Things were looking up. Unfortunately, her joy was blunted somewhat shortly thereafter. Outside the dining hall, the girls surrounded her for hugs as usual, but each of them scowled at her escort.

She knelt to whisper, "Girls, this is Mr. Chastain. He is a very good friend to the orphanage."

Grudging curtsies ensued. Melanie sighed and escorted Mr. Chastain into the music room. "I'm sorry about that. The girls are usually far more polite."

He made a comical expression of alarm. "I haven't been that popular since I switched the salt with the sugar in the kitchen at home. The cook and maids refused to speak with me for weeks."

"When did you do that?"

"I was a tender lad of seven."

"It's nothing to do with you, really." Melanie shut the door and crossed over to open the windows. "The girls think I should marry Lord

Peyton and take all of them in as wards. They likely see you as a threat to their future."

"In that case, they should scowl at Peyton, not me. *I'm* the one who has made you an offer, after all, and *I* would be willing to take in five." He paused. "Besides which, Peyton reminds me unpleasantly of Heathcliff, from *Wuthering Heights*."

"Come now." She looked at him askance. "You and Lord Peyton have more in common than you know."

Mr. Chastain tossed his head. "I can't believe anyone would like that chap more than me. If I were capable of taking umbrage, I most certainly would."

"Once the children get to know you, I'm certain their opinion will change."

His frown deepened. "It's your opinion that concerns me most."

"You needn't worry about that." She glanced at her timepiece. "My first pupil arrives momentarily. Do you have a way to amuse yourself until four o'clock?"

"I shall walk the grounds, singing to myself like a madman."

Melanie giggled. "Thank you again for settling the argument between Mrs. Oglethorpe and Mrs. Steed. You were brilliant."

He gave her a slow smile and a wink before he let himself out of the room. Once again Melanie felt the same tug of attraction as before. Mr. Chastain really was a wonderful man. Whether or not he would become her fiancé remained to be seen but her affection for him was definitely increasing, day by day.

••••

Shortly after Melanie's last pupil had waved good-bye, Lord Peyton appeared. "Good afternoon, Miss Starhope. I don't see your gig outside."

"I didn't drive myself here today." She finished closing the windows. "Mr. Chastain and I managed to post most of the portraits and profile cards in town this morning and he brought me here afterward."

"What?" Lord Peyton's expression darkened. "I thought you and I would visit shops together."

She gathered up her music. "Mr. Chastain volunteered, so it's done now. Did your brother have good news regarding Jonah Braithwaite's cousin?"

"No. Apparently Rudolph Braithwaite is a hopeless drunk who lives in Spitalfields. He consorts with reprobates and would not be a suitable guardian at all."

"If that's so, my aunt and I will take Jonah's portrait along with the remaining four to Mr. Abernathy tomorrow." Melanie reached for her valise. "Let me give you the profile cards for the newspaper. Mr. Chastain and I made copies."

He stuffed the cards into a pocket. "You and Mr. Chastain are spending a lot of time together." His tone was somewhat clipped.

"Yes." Melanie gave Lord Peyton a puzzled glance along with the cards. "He's a very pleasant man and I think you'd like him if you would just give him a chance."

"Stop saying that."

Anger shot down her spine. "Forgive me, sir. I forgot that you don't like anyone."

Lord Peyton advanced. "I like many people but I have nothing positive to say about a man who monopolizes your time and goes behind my back to undermine my efforts."

"You do not own my time, sir. Furthermore, just because Mr. Chastain has contributed to the cause doesn't mean he went behind your back or undermined your efforts." She shook her head. "You've gotten this all wrong and I can't help but think it's deliberate."

"Well, I think you are deliberately trying to annoy me by cultivating that court jester!"

Melanie gasped. "That court jester, as you put it, is a decent gentleman. He has offered to take five children if I accept his proposal and I've almost made up my mind to—"

"Accept him? Ha!"

"Yes!"

As they glowered at one another, the air seemed to crackle with tension. Out of the corner of Melanie's eye she saw movement at the door.

"Is everything all right, Miss Starhope?"

Mr. Chastain leaned against the jamb with his arms crossed and his gaze leveled at Lord Peyton. His posture seemed relaxed, but his muscles were coiled at the same time, like an animal in the wild. Melanie was taken aback at the simmering anger on the man's face, and she prayed that Lord Peyton would not continue to provoke him.

"Perfectly so, sir. Lord Peyton and I were having a difference of opinion but I'm sure we will both regret it once our tempers have cooled."

Mr. Chastain straightened. "Lord Peyton, I do not know who you are to raise your voice to a lady, and I must say your actions don't do you credit."

Lord Peyton's eyes narrowed. "Nobody asked you to weigh in, Mr. Chastain. Furthermore, I don't think much of a fellow who uses children to make his marriage proposal attractive."

"At least I made her a proposal, which is more than I can say for you." Mr. Chastain smiled. "Shall we go, Miss Starhope?"

"Gladly."

Melanie grabbed Mr. Chastain's arm and practically yanked him from the room. As they headed down the corridor, she struggled to draw breath. She and Lord Peyton had been congenial of late, so why had his mood become mercurial? Furthermore, why had he taken such a dislike to Mr. Chastain, who had done nothing to him — either in word or deed?

By the time she and Mr. Chastain reached his gig, her eyes were brimming with emotion. He pressed a handkerchief into her hands and patted her back until she regained her poise.

"Thank you." Melanie dried her tears. "I dislike arguments and that one was ghastly."

"Let's get you home." He helped her into the gig and they drove off at a fast clip.

She bit her lip. "If you overheard any part of the discussion I had with Lord Peyton, I'm mortified."

"His insults are nothing I haven't heard before." Mr. Chastain gave her a searching glance. "Is there something between you and Peyton of which I should be aware?"

"Of course not." She took a deep, calming breath. "We had a bad beginning at first, but I thought we'd become friends."

"Friends?" Mr. Chastain stared straight ahead. "I think the fellow is exceedingly confused about his feelings for you."

Melanie shook her head. "That can't be true. He is irrevocably in love with his late fiancée."

"Is that so? I can't believe he ever convinced anyone to accept his proposal." Mr. Chastain met her gaze. "Speaking of which, did you say you'd made up your mind to accept me?"

"I-I said *almost*. I'm not quite there but I *am* becoming more comfortable with the idea."

"I suppose that's better than you deciding the notion is repugnant."

Melanie managed to smile. "Really, you say the most outrageous things."

"That's part of my charm." He paused. "I hate to admit it, but Lord Peyton did make one good point. I hope you don't think I'm using children to induce you into marriage. Truly, it was the furthest thing from my mind."

She gave his arm a squeeze. "I know."

As Mr. Chastain drove her the rest of the way home, Melanie resisted the urge to look over her shoulder. Lord Peyton was likely following behind and she didn't want to give him the satisfaction of knowing he made her uncomfortable. Something had upset him, but she could not figure out what it could have been — unless he simply could not bear the thought of her being happy with Mr. Chastain. Their contretemps, along with the earlier argument between Mrs. Oglethorpe and Mrs. Steed, had thoroughly jangled her nerves.

After Mr. Chastain had seen Melanie home, she joined her aunt in the conservatory.

Genevieve glanced up when she entered the room. "Would you like a cup of tea, dear?"

"No." Melanie collapsed into a chair and heaved a great sigh. "Truth be told, Aunt Ginny, I would very much prefer a snifter of brandy."

••••

Melanie went through the motions at dinner that night. Since Genevieve had received a visit from Lord Warwick that afternoon, however, Melanie did not wish to spoil her good mood.

"His housekeeper prepared a list of dishes to be served at the break and since the guest list is ready, Lord Warwick will order the invitations tomorrow." Genevieve gave a happy sigh. "The ball will be a lovely affair."

"Yes, I imagine so." Melanie felt her aunt's eyes on her and glanced up. "What?"

"Your mind is elsewhere."

"Oh...er, I'm just hoping that Mrs. Oglethorpe and Mrs. Steed will continue to work things out amicably. Mr. Chastain did a splendid job smoothing out their hurt feelings."

"That can't be all there is to it, Melly. One does not yearn for brandy over the hurt feelings of acquaintances." Genevieve returned to her pot pie. "I don't wish to press, of course, but you know you can tell me anything."

Melanie gritted her teeth. "Lord Peyton and I had another argument. He has nothing pleasant to say about Mr. Chastain and it's horribly unfair."

"Hmm." Her aunt picked up a bite of carrot with her fork. "I can't help but recollect "The Dog in the Manger" fable."

"Surely Lord Peyton would not be so spiteful."

"The gentleman may not know his own mind. Perhaps his friendship with you makes him feel disloyal to the memory of his former fiancée."

"If our tenuous friendship confuses Lord Peyton, I cannot wait until he meets Blanche." Melanie stared at her pot pie with no appetite at all. "He will likely forget his own name."

Genevieve laughed. "I daresay a great many things have come easily to Lord Peyton. This may be the first time in his life a woman has been indifferent to his looks."

Melanie met her gaze. "I'm not indifferent."

"He doesn't know that. Furthermore, he may not know how to woo a lady properly."

"Lord Peyton should take his cues from Mr. Chastain."

"Mr. Chastain is not as handsome as Lord Peyton. He may feel he must try harder to compensate."

"I understand trying harder to compensate quite well." Melanie managed to smile. "It's little wonder I like Mr. Chastain so much."

Her aunt sat back. "I have an idea to cheer you up. We've finished *Blodwen and the Bloodless*, but I have a few other gothic novels in reserve. Shall we read aloud tonight?"

"Yes, but I would prefer something more lighthearted. I noticed you have a great many Jane Austen novels. Would one of them suit you?"

"*Pride and Prejudice* or *Emma*. Your choice."

"I prefer Mr. Darcy's journey from glowering lout to golden hero, I think. Emma always annoys me with her meddlesome ways."

"Mr. Darcy it is." Genevieve gave Melanie's dinner a pointed glance. "You've not been eating enough, dearest, and your figure is one of your best assets. If you lose any more weight, we shall have to fill your corset with padding."

Alarmed, Melanie raised a hand to her bodice. "Am I too thin?" She picked up her fork and set about polishing off her pot pie. If she lost her looks, she might also lose Mr. Chastain's admiration. Where would she be then?

••••

Melanie paused to take a sip of water before reading the remaining part of *Pride and Prejudice*, Chapter Three:

> "*...Lizzy does not lose much by not suiting his fancy; for he is a most disagreeable, horrid man, not at all worth pleasing. So high and so conceited that there was no enduring him!*'"

As Melanie drew breath to continue, however a knock came on the front door of the house. She glanced at her aunt. "Who could that be at this hour?"

Genevieve sat up straight. "I haven't a clue."

Melanie heard a murmur of voices in the entrance hall, but she could not make out the words. Very shortly thereafter, Newman entered the drawing room.

"Lord Peyton has come to call, Mrs. Hornsby. Are you at home?"

Genevieve's eyebrows drew together. "Yes, of course." After the butler left, she gave Melanie a wide-eyed glance. "I do hope nothing is wrong."

Melanie's tone was level. "Perhaps the gentleman wishes to borrow a cup of sugar."

When Lord Peyton strode into the room, Melanie put down her book and rose along with her aunt. The man carried a basket covered with a napkin.

Genevieve's smile was gracious. "Good evening, sir. I hope everyone at Prospero's Retreat is well?"

"Yes, we are all in perfect health. Forgive me for calling this late, but I came to offer Miss Starhope an apology for the way I behaved this afternoon." He crossed over to thrust the basket into Melanie's hands. "I thought you might like to have this."

She gasped when she heard a mewing sound. "What is it?"

He pulled off the napkin to reveal a wee black kitten. Melanie gasped with delight, set the basket on the sofa, and picked up the adorable creature. As she cuddled the squirming kitten in her arms, she was overcome with joy.

Lord Peyton's shoulders moved up and down in a sort of embarrassed shrug. "Our groundskeeper's cat had a litter of kittens about three months ago."

Melanie gave her aunt a pleading glance. "Aunt Ginny, may I keep her?"

"Of course." Genevieve crossed the room to pick up the basket. "Put the kitten in here and I'll carry her to the kitchen. Cook and I will find her something to eat." She winked. "It may take some time."

Moments later, Melanie and Lord Peyton were alone. Her eyes grew moist with tears of happiness and relief that he had chosen their friendship over enmity.

"Thank you for the apology...and the kitten."

She gave him an impulsive hug. Although she expected him to freeze up, his arms tightened around her, and he rested his cheek against her hair.

"It's good to know you're not afraid of me any longer," he murmured.

"I never was." Melanie closed her eyes and breathed in the man's fragrance. "I'm glad we're friends again."

"I behaved abominably toward you — and Mr. Chastain. I shall call on him tomorrow to apologize."

Melanie pulled back enough for a mischievous glance. "Will he get a kitten too?"

"No." Lord Peyton chuckled. "Most definitely not."

His smile faded as his gaze flickered to her lips. Her heart began to pound as he bent his head toward hers...but he merely brushed a kiss against her cheek before releasing her.

"I'm glad you like the cat."

"Yes." She swallowed her disappointment. "I like her very much, Lord Peyton."

"Just call me Cedric, if you wish. We are very likely to be brother and sister one day." He cleared his throat. "Good night, then. Please give my regards to your aunt." He strode out.

Once Melanie heard the front door close, she collapsed onto the sofa.

Genevieve hastened into the drawing room with a questioning smile. "Well?"

"We are on good terms again but nothing more." Melanie averted her gaze. "All things considered, I can live with that."

Chapter Fourteen
Short-Sighted

The following morning, Melanie received a letter from her father along with her allowance and a short note to say the family was looking forward to visiting Ledbury in a few weeks' time. After Melanie read the note to her aunt, she smiled.

"I've enjoyed my time away from Bromley, but it will be lovely to see my parents and sister again." She set the letter and money aside. "Once everyone in Ledbury has had the opportunity to meet Blanche, I'm sure she'll be very popular."

"What about you?" Genevieve gave her a pointed glance. "You've been spending far too much of your time volunteering at the orphanage. Much of Ledbury society is still in London for the Season, but you could visit Miss Oglethorpe. You are both the same age, so perhaps the two of you could become better friends."

"That's true. I suppose I have been rather a hermit since I arrived." Melanie glanced over toward her new kitten, who was gamboling around the conservatory, batting at ferns. "If I rearrange my schedule, however, I'm afraid the girls will feel as I'm abandoning them."

"You might be surprised to learn the children would be happy to have some time off. It may be their last summer in Ledbury, and they are entitled to enjoy themselves."

"I-I hadn't thought of that." Melanie stared at her, stricken. "Perhaps I've been short-sighted."

After breakfast, Melanie brought a blanket out to the weeping willow tree and sat down to think. She could see a man atop of a ladder in the cherry grove across the way, but he was too far off for her to make out his features. When he glanced in her direction, however, and lifted his hand in greeting, she knew him instantly. Cedric was a strange sort of aristocrat to involve himself in physical labor and teaching orphaned boys how to sing, she mused. Then again, perhaps he enjoyed making himself useful, as did she.

Melanie lay back on the blanket, closed her eyes, and let her mind wander. For some reason, her aunt's observations bothered her. She originally intended to spend only a few afternoons giving lessons but had quickly expanded her commitment to five. Outside of Ethan, only a handful of girls had demonstrated any talent for the piano, and the remainder seldom practiced on their own. Indeed, the girls were so thirsty for attention, they probably would have been delighted if she'd taught them how to polish shoes. She enjoyed the feeling of being needed — but had she been using the children to lift her battered self-esteem?

Now, against all odds, she had promised to help them find homes. Unfortunately, Lord Warwick could very well be right about the likely outcome. She must possess a great deal of hubris to think she could work miracles. How could anyone make people care about children with whom they shared no bonds? A handful of families might take in a few orphans, but the remaining children would be cruelly disappointed. Had she just made a dire situation worse by raising their hopes?

"Hullo!" A deep, masculine voice floated across the lawn. "May I join you, Miss Starhope?"

When Melanie sat up, she spotted Cedric in her aunt's driveway. A broad smile spread across her lips as she beckoned to him. The sky overhead was hazy with clouds, so how could the man have the uncanny ability to fill her with sunshine?

When Cedric arrived, he lowered himself to the blanket with athletic grace. Although he was clad in rough breeches and a coarsely woven work shirt, he looked for all the world as if he belonged in the finest drawing rooms in Europe.

His expression was mischievous. "I brought you a gift."

She laughed. "Don't tell me you have a puppy in your pocket?"

"I think you could tell if I had." He deposited a handkerchief on the blanket and unfolded it, revealing two ripe cherries. "Those are the only ones I found that are ready to eat."

"I'm honored you chose to share one with me." Melanie bit into the sweet, delectable cherry, enjoying the explosion of juice on her tongue. When only the pit was left, she turned her head to spit it out before tossing the stem aside. "Delicious."

Cedric's eyes widened. "Did you just spit out that cherry pit?"

"I did." Her smile turned into a giggle. "Don't tell the etiquette police."

"You lobbed it nearly ten feet, I'd say." He stared at her, clearly incredulous. "Who taught you to do that?"

"There's always a neighborhood ruffian from whom you can learn all manner of bad habits." She shrugged. "In my case, it was the farrier's son."

"I've been accused of being a ruffian upon occasion. Let's see if I can do any better."

He chewed the second cherry and spit the pit at least a dozen feet.

"I concede, sir." Melanie saluted. "You are more of a ruffian than I am. Oops..." She spied a bit of red juice on his mouth and leaned closer to blot it away with his handkerchief. "We must get rid of the evidence." She held his gaze for a long, unnerving moment before dropping the linen square to the blanket. "Now you're perfect once more."

"It seems I'm frequently in need of looking after." He picked up the handkerchief and returned it to his pocket." Thank you for your kind attentions, Miss Starhope."

"Melanie." She shrugged. "There's no reason to be formal when no one else is around."

"No, indeed." Cedric lowered himself to an elbow. "How is the kitten settling in?"

"I've named her Mozart because it sounds like music when she purrs." Melanie lay down on her back. "She's lovely."

"If that's the case, why do you seem worried?"

"Sometimes I think you can see right through me." She took a deep breath. "Cedric I'm beginning to think I've been exceedingly foolish as far as the orphanage is concerned. I ingratiated myself with the children and they are counting on me for help." She turned her head to meet his gaze. "Despite my good intentions, I suspect I will fail the vast majority."

"When you stood up to ask Mr. Fletcher if the orphanage could be saved, you were inspiring — like Joan of Arc." He reached out to move a strand of her hair away from her face. "I've never seen a woman act so fierce."

"It's one thing to believe in a worthy cause and quite another to affect a solution. In the end, I'm merely a girl without the fortune or status to do anything for anyone."

"I beg to differ. I've not said anything until now, but the purpose of my brother's journey to London was two-fold. He also met with his solicitor regarding the acquisition of property in Ledbury which would be suitable for farming."

Melanie shook her head. "That's lovely, but I don't see how it can have anything to do with me."

"Any orphan who does not find a family of his or her own could be transferred to the farm, which will be known as Prospero's Home for Children."

"How wonderful!" She bolted upright. "Where is the property?"

"Edmund is considering his options, so I don't know." He shrugged. "It will be a working farm, of course, so the children will be expected to contribute according to their abilities.

"Even so, they will stay together." A wellspring of emotion filled Melanie with joy. "I-I don't know what to say."

"Miss Melanie Starhope, rendered speechless?" He sat up. "That is a first. Since nothing has been finalized yet, you ought not say anything to anyone."

"Not even Aunt Ginny?"

"Naturally, you may confide in her. In fact, I insist you do." He chuckled. "Edmund is eager to have her opinion."

"As admirable as your brother's actions have been, he will be very fortunate to win my aunt's heart. She is a rare jewel worth having."

"I quite agree." He averted his gaze. "By the way, I sent Anton a note of apology this morning and I will call on him after choir practice this afternoon."

Cedric stood and helped Melanie to her feet. As she gazed into his eyes, she felt the overwhelming need to tell him how she felt.

She gulped. "I want you to know something."

He gave her an expectant smile. "Yes?"

"Well, it's just that I..." as she cast about for the proper words, her courage failed her. "I plan to reduce the afternoons I spend at the orphanage from now on. I've been working the girls too hard, and they should be able to enjoy their summer without feeling obliged to me."

A peculiar expression crossed his face, even as he nodded. "That's good, I think. You'll have more free time with Anton and I'm sure you both will be very happy."

With one final smile, Cedric strode across the lawn back toward the driveway. The man had at once made her overjoyed on behalf of the children and yet wistful he did not return her affections. Even so, she was relieved he intended to cultivate Mr. Chastain as a friend. It would be best if they could all get along.

As she bent to retrieve the blanket, she noticed Cedric's handkerchief had fallen out of his pocket and he'd left it behind. She picked it up and held it to her lips before tucking the handkerchief into the bodice of her gown. Hopefully, he would not ask for its return because she planned to keep the token under her pillow.

•••

Although Melanie's aunt said little over lunch, her mood was ebullient once she learned of Lord Warwick's efforts on behalf of the orphans. Although Melanie was no less thrilled to hope the children would be taken care of, she was somewhat pensive at the same time. In a moment of weakness, she'd nearly blurted out her feelings to Cedric. Would he have laughed off her confession as a joke or would he have merely felt a sense of pity for her unrequited affections? Whenever she was thus tempted in the future, she must shed all her garments and find an anthill to sit on. Surely the pain in her backside would remind her why she should never speak what was in her heart.

Melanie folded her napkin and tucked it under the side of her plate. "When do you wish to visit the music shop, Aunt Ginny? I really must post the last five portraits."

Genevieve blinked. "Since Lord Warwick is going to provide for the children, is that strictly necessary?"

"Cedric told me the property has not yet been acquired and even when it has, the children ought to have every opportunity to find families."

"*Cedric?*" Her aunt gave her a curious glance. "You and Lord Peyton are on intimate terms, then."

"We are on friendly terms — for now." Melanie sighed. "Don't worry about the music shop. I'll stop by on my way to the orphanage and persuade Mr. Abernathy to post the portraits myself. If he refuses, I'll take them to the post office, and we can plan on purchasing a piano in London."

"I hope you don't mind if I stay here." Genevieve pointed to her lap, where the kitten was curled up in a ball. "Mozart has taken a liking to me, and I wish to sketch her."

Melanie suspected her aunt wished to be at home should a particular gentleman pay her a visit, but she saw no need to tease her. "I don't mind at all, but you must promise to give me one of the sketches when you are through."

"Of course!"

"Oh, and I'll be home late. I plan to stop by the vicarage and call on Miss Oglethorpe."

"I'm glad you are taking my advice to socialize more." Genevieve chucked Mozart under her chin and she began to purr. "Have a lovely time and give my regards to Miss Oglethorpe."

"I shall."

••••

Melanie gave the music shop proprietor a friendly smile. "Mr. Abernathy, you may have read that recent newspaper article about the orphanage?"

"I did, indeed."

She produced the final five portraits, spread them out on the counter "Would you be willing to post these portraits and profile cards in your window? We are hoping to interest people into becoming guardians for some of the children."

He removed his spectacles and began to polish them with his handkerchief. "You're wasting your time, Miss Starhope."

The abrupt reply set her back on her heels. "What?"

He returned the spectacles to his face. "I don't mean to offend you, but I've not spoken to a single soul who is interested in taking in a strange orphan."

Although Melanie disliked hearing the children described in such a callous fashion, she held her tongue.

"I can very well understand that sentiment, but I believe if the residents of Ledbury could just see the children, they would not seem so strange. My aunt, Mrs. Hornsby, is a very talented artist and these sketches are her work." She pointed at a portrait. "This is Jonah Braithwaite, who is ten years of age. He likes music but he's a trifle mischievous." Melanie pointed at the next one. "This is Willa Bains, who is a very sweet little girl of nine. Several ladies have already expressed an interest in her but nothing is final yet."

She pointed at the third sketch, but Mr. Abernathy held up a quelling hand. "Please, Miss Starhope, that's enough. Because you've been a good customer, I'll put the portraits up only until the end of the month. If my wife objects, however, they'll come down immediately."

Melanie mulled over whether or not she ought to take the sketches to the post office, but since she would have to turn the gig around, it would make her late for her lessons.

"I'll leave them with you, then. I feel certain that when Mrs. Abernathy sees these sketches, she'll be moved to assist us in our cause." She stepped back. "Good afternoon."

She left the shop, concealing her pique as best she could. None of the other shopkeepers she and Mr. Chastain approached the other day had objected to posting portraits. Whenever she'd been in the music shop before today, Mr. Abernathy had been gracious and generous with his time. As Melanie climbed into her gig, she made a sound of frustration. Perhaps the fellow was cross for some other, unfathomable reason.

Before Melanie released the brake, she spied the bookshop across the way. With her allowance burning a hole in her pocket, she decided to pop in and purchase a few gothic novels for her and Genevieve to enjoy. On her way into the shop, she paused to admire the shop window where three of her aunt's portraits were displayed. The smiling faces of those children tugged at her heartstrings. Surely, they must be creating a stir.

Melanie hastened toward the shelf of gothic novels and picked up two new titles by the same author of *Blodwen and the Bloodless*. Since she and her aunt had enjoyed the story, she anticipated the novels would also be filled with the same satisfying excitement.

As she paid for her purchases, she gestured toward the shop window display. "Has anyone said anything about the orphans yet?"

The clerk shook her head. "Not to me, Miss Starhope." She rested her hand on a ball of twine. "Would you like your books wrapped up?"

"No, thank you. I'll drop them in my carryall."

Melanie made her way to the door just as a young woman entered the shop. "Hello, Miss Oglethorpe!"

The vicar's daughter smiled. "Good afternoon, Miss Starhope."

"I was planning to call on you later this afternoon, if you will be at home."

Miss Oglethorpe's expression reflected pleasure. "I'm going to return to the vicarage after two o'clock."

Melanie smiled. "I should finish my duties at the orphanage by four o'clock, so I'll drive to your residence directly thereafter."

"Plan on staying for tea, won't you?"

"I look forward to it."

Melanie left the bookshop and practically ran across the street to her gig. She would have liked to inquire about Mrs. Oglethorpe and Mrs. Steed, but since she was late, that would have to wait until tea.

On her drive to the orphanage, Melanie had mixed emotions about her day. Her encounter with Cedric that morning had been bittersweet but at least she had gained fresh hope for the children unable to find homes. She had managed to post the last five portraits, which was wonderful, but she did not know how long they would remain in Mr. Abernathy's window. Sadly, neither he nor the bookshop clerk had given her any reason to believe the sketches were exciting any interest. At least she would have the opportunity to deepen her acquaintance with Miss Oglethorpe. Until their chance encounter just now, she hadn't realized how much she had longed for the company of female friends.

•••

As Melanie passed Mrs. Wheeler's office, she noticed Mr. Fletcher had come and was conferring with the matron. His arrival explained the presence of the carriage parked outside and she wondered if the fellow had brought more bad news.

When she reached the dining hall, the girls watching the choir rehearsal rushed to envelop her in hugs. Afterward, she beckoned them to follow her into the music room and shut the door.

"The boys are wearing their new uniforms today!" Denise's face glowed. "The sewing circle ladies brought them this morning after breakfast."

Melanie's eyebrows rose. "Do the boys look handsome?"

The girls giggled as they exchanged glances with one another.

Catherine beamed. "They're not as handsome as Lord Peyton."

"Few could boast that honor, I'm afraid." Melanie sat down on the piano bench. "I wanted to ask your opinions about something, and I hope you will be as honest as you can." She paused. "Although I hadn't considered this before today, my aunt suggested that you are missing a great deal of summer by taking piano lessons so often."

Some of the girls stared down at their shoes and others put their hands behind their back.

"I like taking lessons," Elizabeth murmured.

Melanie nodded. "If you were offered the chance to continue, however, would you?"

One of Elizabeth's shoulders lifted, and she frowned. "I don't know."

After a bit of gentle probing, Melanie learned none of the girls were genuinely enthusiastic about the piano. Although she was disappointed, she was also relieved to hear the truth.

Melanie smiled. "I am so glad we are close enough friends that you can tell me how you feel."

Anne threw her arms around Melanie. "Don't be angry!"

All the girls pressed in, in a tearful display of emotion.

"I could never be angry with you." Melanie became misty. "Not any of you."

Denise's mouth turned down at the edges. "If we don't take lessons, does that mean you won't come visit us?"

"No. I volunteered to share my talents with you, but piano is not the only talent I possess." Melanie shrugged. "I like to sew." None of the girls responded and she bit back a smile. "If that doesn't appeal to you, I also like to read."

Their eyes brightened and the room was suddenly filled with excited conversation. Melanie had to raise her voice to be heard. "Girls!"

Once they were quiet, Melanie gave them a sidelong glance. "As it so happens, I have a gothic novel with me. Would you like me to read a chapter or two aloud?"

Catherine gaped. "My teacher at school says books like that are decadent!"

Willa and Anne exchanged a puzzled glance. "What's that?"

"Hmm..." Melanie wondered how best to define the concept. "I think what she means is that people who are stodgy won't enjoy them."

Denise jumped up and down." I'm not stodgy!"

Melanie spread her arms wide. "All right then, I think we should all go outside and find a shady spot to sit."

Willa straightened. "There's a weeping willow next to the girls' dormitory."

"Weeping willows are perfect for reading gothic novels." Melanie gave her a decisive nod. "I'll fetch a lap rug from the boot of my gig and meet you there directly."

Elizabeth's eyebrows drew together." What about the piano lessons?"

"If you decide you wish to resume, let me know. In the meantime, I'll plan to come every Wednesday afternoon to read — just so long as you enjoy it."

••••

Melanie's eyes were glued to the page as she came to the end of Chapter Two:

"Jonquil hurtled into the house and threw the bolt just as a loud thud came on the other side. Her heart was hammering in her chest as she backed away in horror. Relief at her escape flowed through her and she tried to calm herself.

"I'm safe." Her whisper echoed in the dark, cavernous entry hall. "I'm safe."

She stepped back once more — and bumped into something cold.

"Are you looking for me, Miss Jonquil?"

The vampire's voice made her nearly jump out of her skin as she turned. Moonlight streaming through the windows fell upon Mr. Hellebore's glittering black eyes and without warning, he bared his fangs."

The girls burst into giggles, and she gave them a puzzled glance. They pointed to one side of the weeping willow, and she glanced over to discover Cedric had appeared. He stood there with both hands raised like claws and he'd opened his mouth as if he possessed fangs the size of a walrus's.

Melanie gave him a sidelong glance as she closed the novel. "Lord Peyton, you've spoiled the suspense!"

He dropped his pose in favor of a pout. "I'm sorry, but I just couldn't help myself. What on earth are you reading?"

"Jonquil and the Ebony Shadow." Melanie held up the book. "It's a gothic novel."

Cedric peered at the cover, which featured a lovely maiden in a flowing gown. "What ever happened to piano lessons?"

"These young ladies and I have thrown off the yoke of convention and decided to have a bit of decadent fun instead." Melanie stood. "Speaking of which, girls, why don't you run along and play?"

After hugs were exchanged, the girls joined hands and skipped off toward the field nearby. Melanie waved good-bye and bent to retrieve her lap robe.

Cedric stretched his head. "So…no more piano lessons?"

She shrugged. "I asked the girls if they wished to continue, and they were unsure. Until they decide, every Wednesday afternoon I'm to read literature to them — preferably, novels of which their schoolteachers would not approve."

He laughed. "Would it be too much trouble if you attended my choir practice Friday afternoon? The lads are to perform this Sunday and they must get used to singing with a musical accompaniment."

"I'm happy to help." Melanie smiled. "I hope the girls won't be jealous."

"They can watch our practice, if they wish. The choir should get used to singing for an audience as well." Cedric leaned against the trunk of the willow tree. "I'll pick you up in a gig at one o'clock and we'll drive together."

She gave him a searching glance. "Are you certain that's a good idea? Tongues will wag if people see us out for a drive together."

"The only one who matters is Anton and I'll tell him of our plans when I see him." Cedric stuck his thumb toward the road. "I'm leaving for his residence now."

"I'm on my way to call on Miss Oglethorpe."

He cocked his head. "Do you have anything in common with the vicar's daughter?"

"I hope so." She paused. "By the way, I noticed Mr. Fletcher was huddled with Mrs. Wheeler in her office."

"So did I. Perhaps it's true love."

Melanie scowled at him. "This is serious, Cedric. What if he plans to transfer children, forthwith?"

"On that, I can set your mind at ease. Mrs. Wheeler and Mr. Fletcher are drawing up an application for prospective guardians and planning when the Board of Governors should review them."

"How do you know all this?"

"Eavesdropping, of course."

Melanie gaped at him. "You're awful."

He grinned. "That's not what I've heard."

••••

As Melanie sat in the parlor of the vicarage, she felt almost as if she'd gone back in time. The Tudor cottage resembled something out of a storybook from a prior age and she could almost picture characters from *The Merry Wives of Windsor* making themselves at home. An upright piano sat against one wall, and Melanie gave it a curious glance.

"Do you play, Miss Oglethorpe?"

"A little." The young woman poured steaming amber liquid into two teacups and handed one to Melanie. "Please help yourself to sugar and lemon." She gestured toward the silver tray on which a porcelain bowl of sugar and one of lemon slices sat.

"Thank you." Melanie dropped a half teaspoon of sugar into her cup and stirred. "It was lovely to see you in town earlier today and quite the coincidence. I had already planned to call on you this afternoon."

Miss Oglethorpe beamed. "I'm glad. We really didn't have the opportunity to chat with one another at your aunt's home."

"Unfortunately, we did not." Melanie cast about for a topic of conversation. "Since you were on your way into the bookshop, I must assume you like to read?"

The young woman laughed. "Yes, but I'm sure you wouldn't approve of my reading materials. I love gothic novels."

Melanie's eyebrows rose. "We have that in common, then." She reached into the carryall by her chair and produced her two new novels. "Have you read either of these?"

Miss Oglethorpe peered at them. "No, but I see they were written by the same author of *Bronwen and the Bloodless*. Are they just as good?"

For a quarter hour, Melanie enjoyed talking with the vicar's daughter about vampire novels and their favorite characters.

Finally, Miss Oglethorpe smiled. "I'm so glad to discover you're not a prig. I think everyone assumes that of me because of my father, but I'm actually rather independent, with opinions of my own. Occasionally, I imagine Mama might wish otherwise."

"Do you think your mama will really take Willa Bains or Anne Leighton as a ward?"

"I hope so." Miss Oglethorpe frowned. "If Mama is busy with a new child in the house, I might have more freedom. I would wish to visit relatives, or perhaps sail across the ocean."

"You're intrepid, then."

"I would certainly like to be more adventuresome." Miss Oglethorpe shrugged. "The orphans have created a stir amongst the Ladies' Sewing Circle, I must say, but I cannot promise it is anything more than talk."

Despite Melanie's best efforts, her shoulders slumped. "I seem to be having difficulty generating genuine interest, even among Ledbury merchants. For example, Mr. Abernathy at the music shop took my last few portraits for his window display, but he did so grudgingly at best."

"Oh, dear. I'm surprised he took them at all." Miss Oglethorpe grimaced. "He and his wife lost two children to a fever about ten years ago and they have never been the same. Mrs. Abernathy was so prostrate with grief, we were afraid we would lose her as well."

Melanie closed her eyes in horror. "Merciful heavens. If I had known as much, I never would have approached him at all." She shook her head. "I seem to have a knack for gaucherie."

"Don't be hard on yourself." Miss Oglethorpe offered her a plate of shortbread biscuits. "Few young women care about much of anything except for dances and parties. I admire you very much."

"Thank you. To be perfectly honest, I care about dances, parties, and all manner of things just as much as lost causes. Perhaps you and I could do something silly and shallow, just to be different."

Miss Oglethorpe laughed. "There *is* something silly and shallow you could help me with. Your clothes are so stylish, perhaps you could help me with choosing fabric and a pattern for a new gown."

"I would love to help, and I don't think it's wrong to be happy with your clothes."

"Mama and Papa would surely say vanity is a sin, but I'm tired of being overlooked and taken for granted."

Melanie bit back a smile. "I understand exactly how you feel." She cocked her head. "Perhaps there is a particular gentleman whose interest you would like to attract?"

"Perhaps." Miss Oglethorpe averted her gaze. "Lord Shearling has been in London for the Season, but I feel certain he will return for Lord Warwick's ball. I would love to catch his eye."

Melanie gave the young woman an appraising glance. Miss Oglethorpe was not a classic beauty by any stretch of the imagination, but she was reasonably pretty. Furthermore, her abundant dark gold tresses could be stunning if styled in a flattering manner. Hair ornaments would draw attention to her best feature and an appropriate neckline would accentuate her feminine curves.

"Yes, I expect if you wore the proper gown, all of Ledbury would be taken aback by the vicar's daughter."

"*Taken Aback by the Vicar's Daughter,*" Miss Oglethorpe mused. "That sounds like the title of a right proper romance novel."

Melanie giggled. "A right proper romance novel with a happy ending."

Suzanne G. Rogers

Chapter Fifteen
Grain of Sand

When Melanie returned to Asphodel that afternoon, twilight had not yet fallen, but the hour was quite late. After she gave her things to Daisy, she joined her aunt in the drawing room. Genevieve had a length of red ribbon in her hand and she was playing with Mozart.

"There you are!" She picked up the kitten and sank down on the sofa. "I was beginning to worry you wouldn't make it home before dark."

"Sorry. Miss Oglethorpe and I were talking and didn't pay enough attention to the time." Melanie sat. "We're to meet in town tomorrow afternoon at the fabric shop."

Her aunt blinked. "What about your piano lessons?"

"They are suspended until further notice." Melanie shrugged. "As you suspected, the girls are not certain they wish to continue. Therefore, I spent the afternoon reading to them from *Jonquil and the Darkest Shadow*."

"Well, you must be a trifle disappointed."

"Not really. The whole point was to be kind and I can do that in other ways. I'll be reading to them every Wednesday, as a matter of fact." Melanie's gaze dropped to the bundle of fur in Genevieve's lap. "I can't wait to see your sketches of Mozart."

Her aunt slid her a guilty smile. "You'll have to wait a trifle longer, I'm afraid. Lord Warwick came to call and we toured Asphodel on foot."

"I guessed he would come to visit. He would be a fool to let you slip from his fingers."

Mozart jumped down from Genevieve's lap and made her way over to Melanie. She lifted the little creature into her arms and nuzzled her fur with her cheek.

Her aunt's expression turned dreamy. "I'm in a fair way to fall in love with that man."

"Has he proposed?"

"Not yet, but it cannot be much longer. When you are slightly more mature, I think you know your mind more quickly."

Melanie lowered the kitten to her lap. "I'm afraid I have little choice but to put my faith in Lord Warwick in other ways as well. It's beginning to look as if few people in Ledbury wish to become guardians."

"There are plenty of farms in the county. I'm sure he will find someone willing to sell."

••••

On Thursday morning, Melanie was pleased to discover the newspaper had printed the orphan's profiles she and Mr. Chastain had laboriously composed. Melanie had included where the child had been born, their age, and some details she hoped would be engaging. For example, she mentioned how much Denise loved to skip rope and that young Frederick never met a stranger. Henry loved to whistle through his teeth like a locomotive and Anne enjoyed braiding her friends' hair. Jonah was strong enough to walk on his hands, and Elizabeth liked to memorize passages from Shakespeare. Each child had a personality quirk of their own, and Melanie prayed that the good people of Ledbury would be a little intrigued. Then again, she refused to get her hopes up.

In the early afternoon, Melanie met Miss Oglethorpe at the fabric stop. They spent a pleasant hour poring over fashion plates, patterns, fabrics, and trim for a new ball gown. To the best of her ability, Melanie guided the vicar's daughter toward those styles and colors that would be most flattering to her. As the clerk measured out yards of silk and tulle at a cutting table nearby, Miss Oglethorpe gave Melanie a grateful smile.

"I haven't been so excited about a project in a long while. If it weren't for you, I would have chosen the most boring style and the wrong colors."

"You will look lovely no matter what you wear, Miss Oglethorpe."

"You are kind to say so, even though that isn't true." She shook her head. "Since you arrived in Ledbury, everyone has remarked on what a striking beauty you are. What is it like to be admired wherever you go?"

A flush of pleasure accompanied Miss Oglethorpe's words.

"Since I've always been overshadowed by my younger sister, I wouldn't know what that's like at all." Melanie shook her head. "The notion that anyone considers me a striking beauty, however, buoys my spirits more than you could ever understand." She reached out to squeeze Miss Oglethorpe's hand. "Thank you."

"I cannot imagine your sister overshadows you. Her looks must indeed be extraordinary."

Melanie nodded. "You'll have the opportunity to meet Blanche at the ball. As a result, many a lady will discover whether or not the object of her affection returns her regard or whether they are distracted by a fresh, pretty face."

Miss Oglethorpe frowned. "I confess, if Lord Shearling is taken with her looks, I will be disappointed in him." She shrugged. "Even so, I will enjoy myself at the ball and have a wonderful time with my friends and neighbors."

"I admire your attitude."

As Melanie selected buttons for Miss Oglethorpe's ball gown, she pictured Cedric bending low over Blanche's hand and pressing his lips against her glove. *If I am unfortunate enough to witness his newfound devotion, I can only hope I will remain as sanguine.*

••••

Cedric drove his gig down Asphodel's driveway with Melanie by his side. As he turned left onto the road, his shoulder touched Melanie's for a brief period of time. Although she pretended not to notice, the warmth of his touch filled her with longing.

He gave her a sidelong glance. "I visited Chastain and we managed to have a civil discussion."

"Oh? What was your impression?"

"He's too young for you." Cedric shrugged. "I'm not sure if he has anything on his chin to shave."

Melanie made a dismissive motion with her hand. "You must work harder than that to get a rise out of me, sir."

"Hmm." He frowned. "Everyone will mistake you for his governess?"

She lifted her chin and shook her head.

"His carriage is a pram?"

She made a sound of exasperation. "Cedric, surely you and Mr. Chastain exchanged views and chatted about things you have in common?"

The gentleman stared straight ahead. "I suppose we found some similarities. For example, we both wear trousers."

"That's a good beginning."

"If you want me to admit he's an affable fellow, you have me there. Anton is ingratiating, witty, and talented." Cedric gave her a pained glance. "Must I go on?"

"No, but I hope you continue to cultivate him. Your personalities are exceedingly different, admittedly, but you complement one another well."

"You'll be happy to learn I invited him to dine on Saturday night and he has accepted."

Melanie was oddly disappointed. "We shall be a merry party, then."

"Just so." He paused. "Of course, his addition has thrown off the number. Have you any spare women you could bring?"

"Like a sack of potatoes?" Melanie bit back a laugh. "How about Mrs. Wheeler?"

He sighed. "Preferable someone under the age of infirmity."

"Miss Oglethorpe." She gave a decisive nod. "I like her very much."

"In that case, will you extend the young woman an invitation to dine with us? We will sit down at seven o'clock."

"Let's call on her on the way home, shall we? I feel certain she would rather hear the invitation from your lips."

"If you wish." He paused. "I have made another sacrifice on your behalf, for which I demand credit."

She laughed. "I cannot guess to what you may be referring but the suspense is unbearable."

"I rode Matador into town this morning to purchase *Jonquil and the Dark Shadow*."

"You are making fun of me."

He cleared his throat. "'*Jonquil could not tear her gaze away from the man, try as she might. Mr. Hellebore was the most exquisite creature she had ever beheld and yet danger surrounded him just as completely as the woolen cloak draped around his shoulders.*'" Cedric grinned. "That's from Chapter One."

Melanie clapped a hand over her mouth and her eyes grew wide.

"I can see I've shocked you." Cedric chuckled. "Excellent."

She dropped her hand to her lap. "Why?"

"I like to shock you."

"No, why would you bother reading a silly gothic novel? I enjoy such things, but you are a gentleman. Wouldn't you prefer to shoot quail or menace trespassers?"

"Oh, I enjoy both those activities, admittedly, but I also possess a curious mind. I wished to discover for myself why you are so greatly entertained by gothic novels. Call it a scientific experiment, if you like."

She could not stop a smile from spreading across her face. "I enjoy gothic novels because they usually involve a young woman who gets into a dangerous situation with unnatural creatures, and she finds a way to survive."

Cedric gave her a sidelong glance. "I think you wish to live vicariously through the heroine."

"I think that's the entire point, don't you?"

For the remainder of the drive, they debated gothic novels in general and *Jonquil and the Dark Shadow* specifically. She'd had many such discussions with women, but never with a man, and she found his perspective fascinating. Furthermore, she was more than a little flattered he had purchased literature just so he could discuss it with her. Cedric may not have Mr. Chastain's finesse when it came to wooing a woman, but he had unwittingly touched her deeply.

As they were arriving at the orphanage, Melanie met Cedric's gaze. "Thank you for the conversation, sir. I enjoyed it thoroughly."

His expression was more light-hearted than she'd ever seen before. "As did I."

••••

The choir practice was held in the music room where the piano was located. The girls were more than delighted to sit on the floor to watch as Cedric directed the boys in, "It Is Well with My Soul." As Melanie played, she glanced over to admire the boys' uniforms. The children all seemed to have more confidence now that they had new clothes, although Jonah had already managed to knot his kerchief wrong, and Frederick's cowlick was sticking up in back. Although she knew she was prejudiced on the subject, she thought the choir's rendition was very touching, especially since the lads managed to muster the proper pious expressions.

After the choir had run through the hymn four times, Cedric nodded. "I believe you are ready, so let's end practice here. I will see all of you Sunday morning...and thank you for your hard work."

The boys let out a cheer and tore from the room, although Cedric snagged Jonah as he ran past and retied his kerchief properly. The girls jumped to their feet and clustered around Melanie.

Willa jumped up and down. "Anne and I are visiting the vicarage tomorrow and Mr. and Mrs. Steed thereafter."

"How exciting!" Melanie's smile slipped as she noticed the other girls' enthusiasm was muted. "As for the rest of you, someone very smart recently reminded me that when God closes a door, he opens a window somewhere." She patted their cheeks. "Have faith that something good will happen."

Denise touched Melanie's sleeve. "Will you come read to us on Monday? I can't wait to hear if Jonquil makes it out of that old house alive!"

A chorus of pleading ensued, whereupon she nodded. "I'm very happy to read the next two chapters on Monday."

Cedric glanced over. "May I come?"

She peered at him. "What about choir practice?"

"We are done for the summer." He shrugged. "I decided to follow your lead and let the boys play."

Melanie gave the girls a mischievous smile. "What is your opinion? Shall we allow a gentleman into our midst?"

"Yes!" The girls all shouted at once.

Her glance flickered toward Cedric. "In that case, His Lordship and I will see you Monday, at two o'clock."

After the children sped from the room, Melanie cocked her head. "That was very kind of you. I believe the girls enjoy your company as much as mine."

"I think they enjoy imagining me as Mr. Hellebore." He bared his non-existent fangs and bore down on Melanie. "Bwahahahaha!"

She shrieked with laughter and darted away but he chased her into a corner.

"You've made a fatal mistake, Miss Starhope." His voice had grown husky. "You've no means of escape."

As Melanie gazed up at him, escape was the furthest thing from her mind. "My only hope is to appeal to your sense of pity, I suppose."

He clutched his chest and staggered backward. "There it is! A stake to the heart. I am undone."

"It's a very good thing you don't make your living on the stage, sir." Melanie gave him a level glance. "You would soon starve."

••••

Miss Oglethorpe blinked in surprise. "A dinner party at Prospero's Retreat tomorrow night?" She glanced from Melanie to Cedric and back again. "I would love to attend."

Melanie had an inspired thought. "Why don't you pack your things and I'll pick you up tomorrow morning at eleven. You can spend the night at Asphodel and Aunt Ginny will drive us to church on Sunday."

Miss Oglethorpe's smile slipped. "Mama is to have the girls come visit tomorrow afternoon."

"That's right." Melanie nodded. "I can pick you up at four, if you prefer."

"How delightful. I've not spent a night away from the vicarage since I was a little girl."

"I'll have a room prepared for you." Melanie rose. "I'll see you tomorrow."

Cedric stood. "My brother and I look forward to your company, Miss Oglethorpe."

The young woman curtsied. "I'm honored by the invitation."

Melanie and Cedric took their leave and began the drive home.

Cedric glanced at her. "Miss Oglethorpe is a trifle more animated then when she and I were first introduced."

"I think once you get past her reserve, she becomes more vivacious."

"Perhaps you've been a good influence."

"Thank you, but I don't flatter myself that I'm a good influence on anyone."

"No? I beg to differ." He laughed. "In my case, you've been a grain of sand in my oyster."

She peered at him. "I've irritated you into producing a pearl?"

"Don't be offended. Some people take more prodding than others."

Before she could respond, he launched into another sea shanty. It was one she hadn't heard before, so she listened to the chorus twice before attempting to join in. As they sang together, she thought about what Cedric had said. She hadn't set out to annoy him, but she'd never had any intention of appeasing him, either. If an independent woman had induced him to soften his hard edges, so much the better. Truth be told, he'd softened her edges as well, and in ways she could never have anticipated.

As soon as they had left Ledbury behind and were away from prying eyes, Melanie slid her hand around his arm. The movement caused him to break off his song with a puzzled smile.

"I would like us to remain friends, Cedric — no matter where life takes you."

"I'm not going anywhere."

She did not say so, of course, but she knew once he met Blanche, he would be smitten in the blink of an eye. "Just promise you'll never forget me."

"I can safely promise you that much." He paused. "Miss Scrumper."

"Lord Gooseberry."

He held her gaze for several long heartbeats before glancing away. As he began the sea shanty once more, she sang harmony...and reveled in the experience all the way home.

••••

When Melanie arrived at the vicarage the following afternoon, a carriage was just pulling away from the curb. Willa and Anne stuck their arms through the window and waved at her madly. She waved back just as madly before parking her trap out in front.

A housekeeper let her in, just as Miss Oglethorpe hastened down the stairs. "Hello, Miss Starhope! You just missed Mama. She is taking Willa and Anne over to Mr. and Mrs. Steed's residence."

"I saw them drive off just now. How was the visit?"

Miss Oglethorpe frowned. "Mama is enchanted with the idea of having a little girl in the house, but Papa is still unconvinced. He's at church right now, practicing his sermon for tomorrow."

The response was not what Melanie had hoped for, unfortunately. If the vicar could not be moved to take in a ward, what chance did the children have with his congregation?

"Let us pray your papa receives some divine inspiration." She glanced around. "Where is your luggage?"

"Our manservant is bringing it down right now." Miss Oglethorpe beamed. "I can't wait to see Asphodel."

"Tea will be waiting for us in the conservatory when we arrive."

A few minutes later, Miss Oglethorpe's bags were strapped into the boot and the two young women set off.

"I'm usually invited to parties and gatherings because my papa's the vicar and no one wishes to offend him. Even so, I cannot remember looking forward to an occasion more than I am tonight." Miss Oglethorpe touched Melanie's sleeve. "I know the invitation was your doing, so I'm very grateful."

"You are included tonight on your own merits." Melanie shook her head. "In my opinion, you ought to be valued for yourself alone and not merely to please your papa."

"That's the problem, isn't it? Even if I manage to catch Lord Shearling's eye, I'm not sure he will ever see me as anything other than the vicar's daughter."

"Since I left Bromley for much the same reason, I understand how you feel. I was always Miss Blanche Starhope's elder sister and received no attention from young men unless they wished to court her."

"I suppose it's no different for daughters of wealthy aristocrats. It would be very difficult for such women to know if a gentleman wishes to cultivate them for honorable reasons or what he can gain."

"That's yet another reason to keep gentlemen at bay until they've proven themselves." Melanie sighed. "Admittedly, it's awfully difficult to do that once the heart becomes involved."

Miss Oglethorpe gave a decisive nod. "I've made up my mind, then. I shall wait until after Lord Warwick's ball and then I shall set off for parts as yet unknown. I can never be valued in my own right until I leave Ledbury."

"If things go badly for me, I might just join you." Melanie forced a smile to her lips. "Mr. Chastain will be at dinner tonight. He's spent time in Italy and Lord Peyton has spent time in Spain. Perhaps they could tell us something about living abroad."

"What a wonderful topic of discussion!"

Melanie rolled her eyes. "Yes. I learned my lesson the hard way not to broach anything controversial."

Miss Oglethorpe giggled. "Mama says gentlemen always prefer to talk about themselves anyway, so we shall accommodate them."

The young woman's mirth was catching. "Just so." Melanie laughed. "That's it exactly."

••••

As Daisy stood to one side, Melanie examined her reflection in the floor-length mirror. She had several lovely dinner gowns from which to choose, but she finally decided on a dramatic, off-the-shoulder dinner dress in sapphire silk.

"Thank you, Daisy. Why don't you help Miss Oglethorpe dress? I'm certain she will need help with her hair."

The maid curtsied and hastened from the room, leaving Melanie to admire her reflection once more. The demi-train in back made her feel extraordinarily fashionable, and the netting trim around her shoulders was accented with seed pearls. Her ebony hair, by contrast, was simply arranged, with a pearl ornament to give it interest. Rarely could she compete with Blanche in looks, but she was satisfied with her appearance tonight. Would Cedric notice her daring neckline and come to his senses? Melanie gave an unladylike snort. Perhaps not, but at least he would have a glimpse of her feminine charms.

She left her room and went to see if she could assist Miss Oglethorpe. She tapped on the door, which was half-open.

"It's Melanie. May I come in?"

"Yes, of course. I can't move at the moment."

Melanie stepped inside. Miss Oglethorpe was seated at her vanity, clad in a cotton wrapper, and Daisy was arranging the woman's tresses.

"I wish I had your hair." Melanie came to stand where Miss Oglethorpe could see her without turning her head. "The color and texture are truly outstanding."

The young woman's green eyes riveted on Melanie's gown, and she grew pale. "Oh, no! Your dress is stunning and mine is..." she gestured toward the gown laid out on the bed, "...ghastly. I'm going to look exactly like a vicar's daughter, and everyone will laugh behind my back."

Melanie went over to examine the dress, which was exceedingly ordinary. It was not ghastly by any stretch of the imagination, but she found nothing redeeming about it. Ecru had always been one of her least favorite colors and the muslin fabric was not suitable for dinner with a marquess. Not even the addition of a silk shawl or a brooch would help. Worse, the style served to hide a woman's figure, not enhance it.

Melanie wracked her brain for a solution. "No one would dare laugh at you, Miss Oglethorpe, but I do have a dinner gown I brought from Bromley that nobody in Ledbury has seen. We are about the same size, and I think it would suit your coloring, if you'd care to take a risk."

"Miss Starhope, if you rescue me from my fate, I will be your friend forever."

"Have a look at the dress before you make such promises." Melanie smiled. "I'll be back in a moment."

She returned to her room, pulled the gown from her closet, and retrieved a mother-of-pearl comb for Miss Oglethorpe's hair. Ever since Melanie acquired a whole new wardrobe in London, she had planned to give the dress to Blanche. Her sister had plenty of things to wear, however, and Miss Oglethorpe's need was greater. What did it matter if her friend wore the dinner gown once?

Melanie shrugged. "Besides which, what Blanche doesn't know won't hurt her."

She brought the gown into Miss Oglethorpe's room and held the garment up where the woman could see it. "The fabric is a very elegant silk brocade, and the pink color would suit your complexion magnificently."

Daisy gasped in admiration. "Ooh, yes, that would be lovely on you, Miss Oglethorpe."

"I've never worn pink before, but it's so much prettier than anything else I own." Miss Oglethorpe smiled. "If you don't mind, I would love to borrow it."

"I don't mind at all." Melanie draped the gown next to the one Miss Oglethorpe had brought. "I usually wear this comb with it." She deposited the mother-of-pearl ornament on the vanity. "I'll leave you to get ready, then."

Miss Oglethorpe caught Melanie's hand. "Thank you, from the bottom of my heart."

"I'm just glad I could help."

••••

When Melanie stepped into the entrance hall of Prospero's Retreat, her eyes went immediately to Audrey Peyton's portrait. Although Melanie was still a trifle intimidated by the woman's untouchable beauty, she also felt a wave of pity. How dreadful it must have been for her on her deathbed, knowing she was leaving two adorable children motherless. For them, if for no other reason, Melanie hoped Genevieve and Lord Warwick would cement their relationship sooner rather than later.

As the butler took Melanie's evening wrap, she could see a glint of recognition in his eyes. Even so, his expression reflected no embarrassment or regret at all for treating her like a vagabond that morning with Josie. The man seemed to possess no warmth whatsoever, so she hoped he was unmarried. No woman deserved to be wed to a fellow like that.

Genevieve handed Williams her wrap, revealing her dinner gown of warm peach silk and an underskirt of blush tulle. The square neckline dipped down low enough to accentuate her feminine curves, and the clever darts in the bodice made her waistline appear incredibly tiny. Once more, Melanie was struck by her aunt's beauty. Genevieve would never find the late marchioness's portrait intimidating and Melanie vowed to take her lead.

Miss Oglethorpe's appearance had been well-served by the loan of Melanie's gown. The fit of the keyhole bodice, although not perfect, had been enhanced by the use of bust improvers. The pink color was at once feminine and flattering and it was clear from the young woman's confident posture that she felt very pretty indeed.

Melanie had every expectation the evening would be one to remember

Suzanne G. Rogers

Chapter Sixteen

Dinner With the Marquess

After a ten-course meal filled with convivial conversation about life in Italy, Spain, and — in Lord Warwick's case — France, the ladies withdrew to the drawing room while the gentlemen stayed behind for their obligatory brandy and cigars. Melanie waited to speak until the doors were closed before letting out a great sigh.

"I'm so glad you warned us about eating as lightly as possible, Aunt Ginny, because I couldn't hold another bite. The most formal dinner I ever attended before had six courses." She sank down onto a sofa, wishing she could loosen her stays.

"That's me as well." Miss Oglethorpe shook her head. "Honestly, where do gentlemen put it all?"

Genevieve laughed. "To be fair, they don't have to wear corsets."

Miss Oglethorpe wandered over to the baby grand piano in the corner. "What a beautiful instrument!" She sat down and began to play, "La donne è mobile" from Rigoletto. Melanie was taken aback by the deft performance and closed her eyes to listen.

After the last triumphant note, she gave her friend an admiring glance. "When you told me you play 'a little,' I didn't realize that meant you play a little magnificently!"

"Yes, *Brava!*" echoed Genevieve. "You are a woman of many talents, Miss Oglethorpe. My niece informs me that you also sew."

"Thank you for your compliments." Miss Oglethorpe lowered the fall on the keyboard and came to join them. "My sewing ability is limited to technical competency, I'm afraid. If it wasn't for Miss Starhope, the ball gown I'm sewing would have been rather ordinary. I'm not sure a sense of style can be learned."

"I don't think you're being fair to yourself." Melanie smiled. "My sense of style, as you put it, was greatly enhanced when I was shopping in London. I've had the benefit of seeing in person the finest gowns worn by the most fashionable women. That's all due to my aunt."

"In that case, I thank you both." Miss Oglethorpe gestured toward Melanie. "I'd love to hear you play."

"Certainly." She rose. "Have you ever heard a sea shanty?"

Genevieve laughed. "I can't say that I have."

"Neither have I." Miss Oglethorpe's expression brightened. "What fun!"

The last sea shanty Lord Peyton had sung to Melanie had remained in her mind, largely due to its rhythm and repetition. She played it from memory, albeit not faithfully, and even sang the lyrics as best she could. Miss Oglethorpe and Genevieve came over to listen and clapped along. At length, they began to dance together in a reel, laughing as they spun around on the oriental carpet.

Out of the corner of Melanie's eye, she noticed the drawing room doors open and she broke off playing before the gentlemen could witness her aunt and Miss Oglethorpe acting silly. When the three fellows appeared, however, they had evidently heard the music as they approached.

Lord Warwick raised his eyebrows. "For a moment, I imagined myself in some sort of Irish tavern."

Mr. Chastain bounded over to the piano. "I for one, would love to imagine myself in an Irish tavern."

"New Zealand. The whaling song hails from New Zealand." A smile played on Lord Peyton's lips. "You have a good memory, Miss Starhope."

Mr. Chastain's gaze flickered from Lord Peyton to Melanie. "I thought I could hear *Rigoletto* earlier," Mr. Chastain gave her an approving nod. "As much as I enjoy ale-drenched music, I confess I prefer Italian opera."

She blinked. "There's nothing wrong with your hearing, sir, but the credit for *Rigoletto* belongs to Miss Oglethorpe."

Mr. Chastain gave the young woman a startled glance. "The vicar's daughter is well-acquainted with opera?"

"Yes, and I even speak a little Italian." Miss Oglethorpe's expression was carefully polite. "I am far more than my father's daughter, you see, just as I'm certain you are more than merely your father's son."

His color rose. "You're quite right, Miss Oglethorpe. I meant no offense."

Lord Warwick cleared his throat. "Mrs. Hornsby, you look as if you might enjoy some fresh air. Will you take a turn in the garden with me?"

"I'd be delighted sir."

Genevieve glanced at Melanie as she crossed the room and the gesture spoke volumes. Unless

Melanie missed her guess, her aunt was about to receive a proposal. How could she bridge the gap in her absence?

She rose from the piano bench. "I would love to hear Mr. Chastain on the piano while Lord Peyton plays his guitar."

Melanie could see from the lack of enthusiasm that the ice between the two had not completely thawed.

She bit her lip. "Er...I don't mean that you must play a duet, of course. Perhaps, Lord Peyton, you should go first, with Mr. Chastain to follow?"

He bowed. "As you wish."

Mr. Chastain seemed relieved as he took a seat in a wing chair and Melanie sank down next to Miss Oglethorpe on the sofa. Lord Peyton retrieved his guitar from a cabinet and took a few moments to make sure it was in tune. As he perched on a chair with the guitar across his lap, he glanced around. "This is a piece by the renowned Spanish guitarist, Fernando Sor, called *Introduction and Variations on Mozart's "Das klinget so herrlich,"* Opus Nine."

As Lord Peyton began to play, Melanie did not need to know much about the guitar to realize the man was a brilliant musician. When she exchanged a glance with Miss Oglethorpe, the young woman shook her head in awe. Although Melanie tried to catch Mr. Chastain's eye, the gentleman was seemingly transported by the music and peered at the instrument with avid interest.

When Lord Peyton was done, Mr. Chastain rose from his chair. "Peyton, we've had our differences, but I am humbled by your virtuosity. Thank you for that performance."

Lord Peyton peered at him, as if trying to determine whether or not he was joking. Finally, he accepted the accolade with a nod. "Coming from a musician of your caliber, I consider that a rare compliment indeed."

Melanie's heart was warmed by the moment of cordiality. "Indeed, I think we are all impressed, Lord Peyton."

"I cannot say I've ever heard anyone play the guitar with such masterful delicacy." Miss Oglethorpe's gaze settled on Mr. Chastain. "Your reaction, sir, informed my opinion."

Melanie's sigh was a happy one. "This is simply the most delightful evening. Mr. Chastain, would you care to play or perhaps sing?"

"I shall sing, I think." He grinned. "Will you accompany me in "La donne è mobile," Miss Oglethorpe?"

Her eyebrows rose. "Oh...certainly."

Melanie wriggled with excitement as Miss Oglethorpe crossed over to the piano. Mr. Chastain stood nearby as she began to play the music and when he opened his mouth, he filled the room with his exquisite tenor. Just as he reached, "*E di pensier!*" the drawing room doors burst open, and Genevieve appeared. The paleness of her complexion was in stark contrast to the red smudges on her cheekbones and her eyes snapped with fury. Mr. Chastain and Miss Oglethorpe broke off and stared at her, wide-eyed.

"Forgive me for interrupting. Melanie and Miss Oglethorpe, we have stayed far too long." She curtsied to the gentlemen. "Thank you for a lovely evening, but we must go."

Genevieve turned on her heel and disappeared into the entrance hall, leaving confusion in her wake. Melanie tried to hide her alarm as she took her leave, but from the expression on Lord Peyton and Mr. Chastain's faces, she could tell they were stunned by the abrupt ending to what had been an enjoyable occasion. She and Miss Oglethorpe hastened into the entrance hall, collected their evening wraps from the butler, and left the house. Genevieve had already climbed into their carriage when they reached the courtyard and was staring out the window.

As they drove away from Prospero's Retreat, Melanie dared not say a word. Fortunately, Miss Oglethorpe was sensitive enough to remain silent as well. Fortunately, the journey home was mercifully short. Although Melanie might have supposed her aunt would take her into her confidence, Genevieve merely said good night and began to climb the stairs before the butler could help her with her things. She paused after a moment and glanced back.

"Newman, please tell Cook I will take breakfast in my room tomorrow morning. I will not be attending church, unfortunately, because I will be indisposed." She continued upward with her head held high.

Melanie and Miss Oglethorpe gave their things to the butler and went into the drawing room to talk.

"What on earth could have happened between your aunt and Lord Warwick?" Miss Oglethorpe's voice was low.

"I cannot guess." Melanie sank down into a chair. "I had assumed he took Aunt Ginny aside to propose."

"Things must have gone very badly indeed."
Miss Oglethorpe sat.

"I'm quite devastated." Melanie frowned. "The
evening went so swimmingly, too."

"Yes." Miss Oglethorpe averted her gaze. "Mr.
Chastain managed to improve my opinion of him,
actually. I'd thought him rather silly before
tonight, but he seems to have matured in the short
while I've known him. Furthermore, his tenor sent
a delicious shiver down my spine."

Melanie managed to laugh. "Mine, too."

"It must be difficult for you to choose."

"Choose?"

"Between Lord Peyton and Mr. Chastain, I
mean." Miss Oglethorpe gave her a searching
glance. "They are both in love with you."

Melanie blurted out, "I wish that were so"
before she thought too much about it. "What I
mean to say is, both Lord Peyton and Mr. Chastain
are friends of mine. I have no expectations or
aspirations where Lord Peyton is concerned, I
assure you. As for Mr. Chastain, I'm well on my way
to loving him dearly — but as a brother more than
anything romantic."

"Really?" A ghost of a smile lifted the corners
of Miss Oglethorpe's lips. "I-I wouldn't mind
knowing him better, but he will never see me as
anything more than the vicar's daughter."

"I'm not so sure. You certainly surprised Mr.
Chastain with your talent tonight."

"Did I?" Miss Oglethorpe stifled a yawn. "I
suppose we should turn in. Your aunt may not
attend church tomorrow, but I have no choice."

"Nor do I. Lord Peyton's boys' choir is singing
a hymn tomorrow and I wouldn't miss it for the
world." Melanie rose. "I'm glad you came with us

tonight, Miss Oglethorpe. You added something indispensable to the mix."

"Call me Priscilla." She came over to give Melanie a hug. "You're almost like the sister I never had."

"My name is Melanie, although Blanche calls me Melly. You may use either, as you wish."

As they walked upstairs, Melanie wished she knew what had happened between Genevieve and Lord Warwick. Unfortunately, her aunt's door was closed, and Melanie would never dream of disturbing her privacy.

As she shed her gown and got ready to retire, she thought about what Priscilla had said. *It must be difficult to choose between Lord Peyton and Mr. Chastain.* Unfortunately, her choice had already been made the day she'd been caught scrumping, for all the good it did.

Melanie slid under the counterpane, where Mozart was curled up in a ball. She stroked the kitten's fur and sighed. "If the stupid man would only open his eyes, maybe — just maybe — he might love me back."

••••

True to Genevieve's word, she did not come down for breakfast Sunday morning. Melanie and Priscilla ate quickly and left for the vicarage so they could drop off her luggage before heading to church.

Outside St. Michael's, Priscilla squeezed Melanie's hand in farewell. "I must go sit with Mama, I'm afraid. Thank you for inviting me over last night. Up until the end, it was wonderful."

"Let us hope the quarrel is sorted out soon."

Priscilla hastened off. Melanie lingered in the back for a short while as she searched for a place to sit. Lord Peyton and his brother sat in the front pew with other luminaries — including Lord and Lady Dellingpole and Mr. Chastain. The orphan girls, Mrs. Wheeler, and the staff sat near the front as well, presumable so they could have a view of the service. The boys, clad in their new sailor suit uniforms, sat with the choir. Although they were fidgeting with their kerchiefs and glancing around, they were mainly well-behaved. Melanie found a seat as far forward as possible.

The service proceeded as usual until after the homily, when Mr. Oglethorpe introduced the Ledbury Country Home for Children boys' choir. The lads sang, "It Is Well with My Soul," as the collection plate was passed among the congregation. Melanie was so engrossed in their performance, she dropped her coin into the plate and passed it along without being aware she had done so. Her heart swelled with pride as the lads raised their voices to the rafters.

Afterward, Mr. Oglethorpe returned to his pulpit and took a moment to wipe his spectacles with a handkerchief — as if he were trying to regain his composure. He cleared his throat a few times before addressing the congregation.

"I found myself greatly moved by these children as they lifted up their faith to the Lord in song. I had the opportunity to visit with these fine boys this morning and I was reminded what it was like to be a lad in need of a firm, guiding hand."

Melanie swallowed the lump in her throat.

Mr. Oglethorpe continued. "Jonah Braithwaite, will you stand?"

The boy got to his feet, wide-eyed, as if he'd been caught getting up to some sort of mischief.

The vicar gazed out from his pulpit. "A shepherd must set a good example for his flock." He glanced at Jonah. "Young man, we have room for you in our home, as soon as may be."

Melanie gaped. As happy as she was for Jonah, what would become of Willa Bains and Anne Leighton? Had Mr. Oglethorpe even consulted his wife?

A deep voice shouted from the back of the church. "Child snatcher! You can't have my Jonah!"

Melanie turned to stare along with the rest of the congregation. An unkempt, ill-dressed man stood in the aisle, shaking his fist. "My name is Rudolph Braithwaite. Jonah is my blood relative, so he is, and I've come to take him to London where he belongs!"

As the church erupted in a cacophony of noise, Melanie groaned and shook her head. Lord Warwick's visit to Rudolph Braithwaite had only managed to stir up trouble, apparently, and this was the result. When the man continued to shout insults and demands, he was dragged outside by the arms. Mr. Oglethorpe nodded at the organist, who began to play the recessional, and the service came to an ignominious and undignified end.

Although Melanie tried to make her way forward to comfort the children, she was swept from the church by a wave of people and was obliged to wait outside for them to emerge. A constable had arrived to detain Mr. Braithwaite, who looked as if he wished to crawl into the inside of a gin flask. Lord Warwick crossed over to the constable and after a terse conversation, the cousin was bustled into a wagon and hauled away.

Mrs. Wheeler led the orphans from the church in two lines, but as soon as they caught sight of

Melanie, any pretense of order disappeared. The children ran over for hugs and Melanie could not help but notice Anne and Willa's faces were tearstained.

She gave them all a reassuring smile. "Now *that* was the most exciting church service I've ever attended!" Her mild joke broke the tension a trifle. "You boys performed exceptionally well and I was terribly proud."

Catherine frowned. "Who was that strange man?"

"A fellow who claims some distant kinship with Jonah. The constable is dealing with him now."

Mrs. Wheeler beckoned. "Come along, children!"

Melanie raised her hand in farewell. "I'll see you tomorrow for our book club, girls."

As she watched them climb into their wagon, Mr. Chastain, Lord Warwick, and Cedric emerged from church. Although Mr. Chastain and Cedric took note of her, Lord Warwick's gaze flickered away.

"I'll ride on ahead, Cedric." The marquess strode off, but not before Melanie saw the grey pallor of his complexion and black circles under his eyes.

She offered Cedric a smile as he and Mr. Chastain came to join her. "The choir was brilliant today and it was all due to you, sir."

A muscle worked in his jaw. "It's a pity the boys' efforts were overshadowed by that drunkard. I suspect Rudolph Braithwaite came with his hand out, hoping to be paid for his absence."

"I don't think the boys' choir was overshadowed, Peyton." Mr. Chastain frowned. "I, for one, was very impressed."

Melanie lowered her voice. "I still have no idea what transpired between Aunt Ginny and Lord Warwick last night."

Mr. Chastain shook his head. "I left immediately after you did, so I haven't a clue."

"My brother refuses to speak of it." Cedric gave Melanie a worried glance. "Has Mrs. Hornsby been taken ill?"

"She was too indisposed to attend church today, I'm afraid. More than that, I cannot say." She glanced around at members of the congregation, who were clustered together in excited conversation. "I confess, I don't know what possessed Mr. Oglethorpe to make such an announcement, especially since he knew his wife yearned for a little girl."

"Mrs. Oglethorpe was in tears just now." Lord Peyton grimaced. "I hated to see it."

Mr. Chastain pointed his thumb toward the church. "My cousins are attempting to broker some sort of peace, but Sunday dinner at the vicarage will likely be served with a side of cold shoulder."

"It's always darkest before dawn, as the saying goes." Melanie averted her gaze. "Let us hope that there is light just around the corner."

• • • •

When Melanie walked into the entrance hall at Asphodel, Mozart came scampering over, begging for attention.

Newman appeared. "May I take your things, Miss Starhope?"

"Yes." She surrendered her hat, gloves, and shawl. "Is my aunt still in her room?"

"Mrs. Hornsby is in the conservatory, I believe."

Melanie scooped Mozart up in her arms and went to join Genevieve. Her aunt sat on a chaise longue, clad in a silk wrapper, with her hair loose about her shoulders. Although she gave Melanie a wan smile, the skin under Genevieve's eyes was marred with shadows and her face was blotchy. Melanie had never seen her aunt look so unwell before.

"How was the church service?" The woman sounded tired.

"It was eventful." Melanie studied her a moment. "Before I say anything more, however, I've half a mind to summon a physician."

Genevieve waved a dismissive hand. "No doctor has a remedy for a broken heart, I'm afraid."

Melanie put the kitten down on the floor and he jumped into Genevieve's lap. "Did you eat breakfast this morning?"

Her aunt shook her head. "I've had no appetite." She stroked Mozart's fur.

Melanie reached for the brass bell sitting on a table and rang for a servant. When Daisy appeared, she ordered a tray with tea and toast. "Oh, and hot cross buns if we have any."

The maid wore a worried expression. "Yes, Miss Starhope." Her gaze flickered toward Genevieve before she hastened off.

Her aunt sighed. "I'm really not hungry, Melly."

Melanie's tone was firm. "You'll eat something, if only to keep me happy." She sat down to describe what had happened at St. Michael's that morning. "Everything is so topsy-turvy; I cannot predict how things will end."

"I can tell you for a certainty that I will not be marrying Lord Warwick." Genevieve was almost limp as she spoke.

"He did not propose?"

"Oh, yes. Edmund proposed and I accepted...until I discovered he had designs on my property." Genevieve averted her gaze. "After we were married, he intended to turn Asphodel into a farm and house the orphans here."

Melanie peered at her. "What?"

"The man refused to understand why I might object to losing everything I'd created — even if it was for a worthy cause." Genevieve shook her head. "He was dismissive of my feelings, and I realized we weren't compatible at all. Once again, I would rather remain a dazzling spinster than to marry a selfish man."

"Lord Warwick could buy any farm in Ledbury. Why would he want to take Asphodel from you?"

"A man who is used to getting what he wants is always surprised to discover anyone objects." Genevieve's lips flattened. "May the devil take Edmund because I certainly don't want him."

Mozart jumped down and went to explore the sunspots streaming in through the glass.

"This is worse than I thought." Melanie's shoulders slumped. "I'm so very sorry."

A tear slid down her aunt's cheek and Melanie wished she could do something more helpful than merely remain quiet. When the tray came, she poured Genevieve's tea and pressed her to eat a piece of toast. As the woman dutifully brought the bread to her lips, her hand was shaking.

Melanie grabbed a hot cross bun, pulled off a piece, and chewed without tasting. Her aunt was exceedingly proud of Asphodel and what it represented. Melanie understood full well the neglect her aunt had endured at the hands of her late husband and undoubtedly Genevieve viewed Asphodel as a testament to her survival. Had Lord Warwick been too blind to realize he could not simply sweep that away in such an insensitive fashion? The situation might have been different if Genevieve had offered him the property, but she had not, and Melanie did not blame her.

"Drink your tea and I think you'll start to feel a little better." She gave her aunt a pained glance. "Perhaps in a few days, you'd like to visit Bath or maybe—"

A commotion in the entrance hall reached Melanie's ears. Newman seemed to be arguing with someone, but she could not make it out.

Genevieve groaned. "Are the servants having a row? I cannot deal with this today."

Melanie rose. "Wait here, Aunt Ginny and I'll see what's going on."

She hastened from the conservatory, but her footsteps slowed when she spied Lord Warwick brush past Newman and start up the stairs.

"Genevieve," he bellowed. "Genevieve!"

Melanie darted forward. "Lord Warwick, what is this about?"

The marquess stopped. "I must speak with Genevieve."

Newman scowled. "Miss Starhope, shall I summon the footmen to see His Lordship out?"

"No, let me speak with him."

Newman moved off down the hallway, but not before giving Lord Warwick a level glance. The marquess practically leaped down the stairs and bounded over to Melanie. The agitation was clear from his expression, and he seemed desperate.

"Where is she?"

"Forgive me for speaking plainly, but you've done enough damage already, sir. Aunt Ginny doesn't wish to speak with you."

"Don't you think I know that?" He raked his hair back from his forehead with his fingers in a gesture of frustration. "Stand aside and I'll find her myself."

"Lord Warwick, I beg you to calm yourself. Perhaps if you wrote her a letter—"

"Gah!" The marquess darted toward the conservatory. "Genevieve!"

Melanie's jaw dropped. "Sir, I protest!"

She picked up her skirts and ran, determined to get between Lord Warwick and her aunt by any means necessary. Unfortunately, the marquess outpaced her with his longer legs and she could not catch up. When she reached the conservatory, however, Lord Warwick and Genevieve were engaged in an embrace. It was clear from the passionate way her aunt's arms were wrapped around the man's body that she was perfectly happy with his presence. Melanie backed away as quietly as humanly possible and pulled the conservatory doors closed. When she returned to the corridor, a glowering Newman was lurking with two of the brawnier male servants.

Melanie lowered her voice to a whisper. "Intervention won't be necessary. My aunt has agreed to speak with Lord Warwick, and she has asked for privacy. Don't disturb them for any reason unless my aunt rings for a servant."

Somewhat shaken by the incident — if not bewildered — she went to her room to change out of her Sunday dress and into a looser-fitting cotton gown of dotted Swiss. She donned a large straw hat, retrieved a blanket and brought a gothic novel to the weeping willow for some solitude.

Melanie sprawled out on her back and stared up at nothing as she tried to make sense of the morning's tumultuous events. Based on what she had witnessed in the conservatory, it seemed likely that her aunt and Lord Warwick would set aside their quarrel and come to some sort of amicable agreement as to Asphodel. Although she was glad and relieved for Genevieve, she was still worried about the orphanage. If Mr. Oglethorpe became Jonah's guardian, Mrs. Steed could offer Willa home. Anna would be heartbroken, of course, unless someone else in Ledbury took her in. After the ugly outburst in church, would the community be less likely to consider taking in a ward?

She rolled over on her stomach and tried to read *Castle on the Cliff*, but her mind kept wandering. Only when she noticed Lord Warwick making his way down the driveway on foot did she pack up her things and return to the house. Genevieve was still in the conservatory, but the kitten was in her lap and her demeanor had become ebullient.

"There you are!" She scratched Mozart under her chin. "I went upstairs but you were not in your room."

"I brought a book outside to read." Melanie sank down into a chair. "May I presume you and Lord Warwick are on good terms?"

Her aunt's laughter was full of joy. "Indeed, we are. He has agreed to let me keep Asphodel as it is and will look for another property in the neighborhood."

Melanie's focus was drawn by a glint on Genevieve's left hand. She was now wearing a ring Melanie had never seen before — a lovely opal set amid sparkling diamonds.

"You're engaged." Melanie's throat swelled with emotion. "Thank heavens."

Her aunt beamed. "Edmund will make a formal announcement at the ball. Until then, we will keep it private."

Melanie nodded. "Since I must tell Priscilla Oglethorpe something, I will just say the quarrel between you has been mended."

"That's perfect." Genevieve sat back on her chaise and let out a pleasurable sigh. "Edmund will take out a special license and we will be married mid-August."

Melanie's eyes widened. "So soon?"

"I'm not getting any younger, Melly."

"Yes, but what about your wedding clothes and the like?"

"I plan to visit Madame Montagna's showroom later this week to order my wedding gown." Her expression brightened even further. "In fact, why don't I open the London townhouse and we'll plan on spending several days there? You could even invite Miss Oglethorpe, if you wish. We'll attend the theater and go shopping for my trousseau."

"If we invite Priscilla, she will know you are planning a wedding."

"We'll swear her to secrecy." Genevieve lowered Mozart to the floor and rose. "We'll have the wedding breakfast here, of course, and I must order that piano. Oh, there's so much to be done that I must begin making lists!"

She rushed from the conservatory, leaving Melanie alone with the kitten.

"Mozart, when God closes a door, he indeed opens a window somewhere." She took a deep breath and let it out slowly. "I pray the good Lord will also work a miracle for a very special group of orphans."

Suzanne G. Rogers

Chapter Seventeen
Mysterious Ways

Monday afternoon, Cedric arrived in a gig to take Melanie to the orphanage. After he helped her climb into the carriage, he sat on the bench next to her and picked up the reins. "I brought a large blanket. Did you remember to bring *Jonquil and the Darkest Shadow?*"

She patted her carryall. "Indeed, I did, and it was all I could do not to read ahead."

"That would have been cheating."

Melanie laughed. "Only a little." As they drove down the driveway, she gave him a sidelong glance. "It seems we are to be related by marriage after all."

"Yes, we got there in the end, didn't we?" He chuckled. "I think Edmund paced all Saturday night after your aunt left the dinner party. Then, when she didn't attend church, I wondered whether or not he would expire from the strain of pretending he didn't care."

"Please don't tell him I said so, but after your brother barged into Asphodel yesterday, our butler assembled the footmen to toss him out. They would have done it, too, except I told them to stop."

Cedric gaped. "Edmund barged into your house?"

"Didn't he tell you?" Melanie shook her head. "It was startlingly out of character for a marquess but also exceedingly romantic. I daresay his passion was what won Aunt Ginny over."

"Did you ever find out why they quarreled?"

Melanie had no intention of betraying a confidence, even to Cedric. "Let's just say your brother discovered he was dealing with a thoroughbred mare."

"Ah." He shrugged. "I daresay I'll winkle it out of him eventually."

"Knowing you, it's a certainty."

"You might like to know that I rode over to the jail this morning and had a word with the constable about Mr. Rudolph Braithwaite. I convinced the authorities to let the fellow go, provided he leaves Ledbury, forthwith."

"Do you think Mr. Braithwaite will comply?"

Cedric gave her a crooked smile. "I gave him a sovereign and threatened to break his fingers if I ever saw his face in Ledbury again."

Melanie shuddered. "For Jonah's sake, I hope his cousin stays in Spitalfields." She suddenly remembered the errand Genevieve had given her. "Do you mind if we stop at the music shop on the way to the orphanage? I promised my aunt I would order her a piano."

"It's no trouble at all."

When Cedric pulled his gig up to Abernathy's Fine Instruments, however, Melanie was surprised to see a CLOSED sign in the window.

"Why would the shop be closed on a Monday?" She gave Cedric a puzzled glance. "I hope Mr. Abernathy isn't ill."

"I don't know, but the portraits are gone."

Her eyes widened as she realized Cedric was right. "Blazes! I wish the man had had the grace to notify me that he meant to take them down." She made a sound of frustration. "His wife must have objected after all."

"We can stop back again on our way home, if you wish."

"I'm not sure I'm inclined to purchase a piano from Mr. Abernathy now. Perhaps my aunt and I will order one when we are next in London."

As they continued on their way, Melanie peered at the window of the bookshop with dismay. "Cedric, all of the portraits are missing from Amity Books." She shook her head. "In one fell swoop, Rudolph Braithwaite managed to dissuade everyone from helping."

A muscle worked in Cedric's jaw. Although he made no response, his countenance darkened. Her mood deflated further when she noticed all the portraits had been removed from Ledbury Tea Shop, too.

"I can't look anymore or I will go mad." She stared straight ahead. "I shall focus on having a delightful afternoon with you, Jonquil, and the girls. Everything else is out of my hands."

"I agree." Cedric's knuckles showed white as he tightened his grip on the reins. "We've done the best we can, Melanie."

Despite her dour mood, the sound of her name on his lips gave her a pleasurable sense of warmth. "You called me Melanie."

His shoulders moved up and down in a slight shrug. "We're to be family soon, so it seems appropriate."

The warmth faded. "Yes."

When the orphanage became visible, Melanie was shocked to see all manner of carriages filling the driveway and parked along the side of the road.

"What on earth is going on?" She gave Cedric a panicked glance. "You don't suppose the Board of Governors have come to take the children away so soon, do you?"

"I doubt it. Mrs. Wheeler would have informed us."

Melanie's mind was reeling. "Unless she didn't know."

Cedric was obliged to drive past the orphanage to find a place to park. They made their way into the main building, which was abuzz with activity. Several people were queued up outside Mrs. Wheeler's office, even though the matron was standing in the hallway. As Melanie and Cedric watched, a couple left the office and she waved them down the corridor.

"You're to go to the dining hall now, my dears. A member of the staff will help arrange your interview."

As the couple headed down the hall, Melanie glimpsed a sketch clutched in the woman's hand. Although she couldn't see the face clearly, she knew it was a child's portrait.

"Mrs. Wheeler, what is happening?"

The woman was fluttering with nerves. "People began arriving this morning, to see the children. So many showed up that I was obliged to send Mr. Fletcher a telegram. He arrived just a short time ago and began handing out applications."

Melanie stared at her, dumfounded. "Applications to become guardians?"

The matron nodded. "Mr. Fletcher and I worked out the procedure the last time he was here, but we didn't expect to implement it to this scale." She made a sound of frustration. "It's been bedlam!"

Cedric glanced down the hallway. "So the applicants have been meeting with children in the dining hall?"

"Some children have met with several prospects." Mrs. Wheeler produced a handkerchief and mopped her brow. "All our activities for the day have been canceled, I'm afraid."

An older woman emerged from the office with a portrait in her hand.

Mrs. Wheeler pointed. "Walk along the hallway and make a right turn at the end, my dear, and you'll have the opportunity to meet..." Her gaze flickered to the portrait, "...Denise Farmer."

The woman's eyes seemed to shimmer with emotion as she hurried off.

"Has every child been shown interest?" Melanie studied Mrs. Wheeler. "I'm concerned for Anne Leighton in particular."

"Oh, you needn't worry about her. Mrs. Steed showed up first thing to apply for both Willa Bains and Anne Leighton. I think all the girls will find homes."

Melanie nearly went limp with relief. "Thank heavens."

Cedric cocked his head. "And the boys?"

Mrs. Wheeler's smile faded. "Poor Frederick is the only child who has not been applied for. He waited all morning in the dining hall, hoping to be chosen, but nobody came. He's behind the boys' dormitory right now, crying his eyes out."

"I cannot believe that. Frederick is a bright light who is full of charm and life." Melanie felt tears sting the backs of her eyelids. "He'd be an asset to any family."

"Mrs. Wheeler, please find Frederick and tell him he's wanted for an interview." Cedric glanced at Melanie. "I'm sure Miss Starhope will be happy to fill in while you are away."

The matron peered at him. "I'm not understanding you. Nobody has come for the lad."

A faint smile lifted the corners of Cedric's lip. "They have now."

The woman's eyes widened as she caught his meaning. "Oh, my. Oh, my. Yes, I'll fetch Frederick right away and you can submit your application later." She hastened off.

Melanie gave Cedric a searching glance. "Are you absolutely sure this is what you want?"

"Did you not say yourself that the lad is a bright light, full of charm, and would be an asset to any family?"

"Yes, I adore Frederick, but *you* are the one who would be taking on a ward."

"If you approve of the lad, that's good enough for me. I've come to realize that your opinion is unerringly correct where people are concerned." He reached up to straighten his neckpiece. "Wish me luck." He sauntered off down the hall.

Melanie murmured, "Good luck," but what she really wanted to say is that she'd never loved him more than she did at that very moment. *When God closes a door, He opens a miraculous window somewhere. And sometimes, He creates heroes out of the most unlikely people.*

Although her eyes filled with tears, she had no time to dwell on her feelings. Another couple had just come into the building with a child's portrait in hand. The man held his wife's hand, which was clearly trembling. In her other hand, she held the portrait of Frederick Ingram.

She gasped, "Mr. Abernathy!"

"Good afternoon, Miss Starhope." The man was clearly overcome with emotion as he led his wife over. "This is my wife."

The woman held up the portrait. "We're here about this boy."

"Bless you for coming, Mrs. Abernathy." Melanie gestured toward the queue. "If you'll join this line for an application, it's moving quickly. It shouldn't be too long until you are able to meet Frederick. He's..." her throat swelled up with emotion. "...he's truly an exceptional lad."

Mr. Abernathy put his arm around his wife's waist and escorted her to the end of the line. At that very moment, Mrs. Wheeler ushered Frederick through the front door. The boy's face was pink, as if the matron had scrubbed it with a washcloth, and Melanie guessed his cowlick had been barely restrained by a wet comb.

When Frederick saw Melanie, he rushed over for a hug. "Somebody wants me, Miss Starhope."

She failed to restrain her tears. "I think you'll find more than one guardian wants you, Frederick." Melanie patted his cheek. "Better late than never, hmm?"

His laugh was full of joy. As Mrs. Wheeler escorted him down the hall, Melanie met Mrs. Abernathy's gaze and gave the woman a nod. Mrs. Abernathy stared at Frederick as he passed by with such a nakedly vulnerable expression that Melanie had to avert her eyes. Would the Board of Governors approve their application over Cedric's? Either way, someone was bound to be disappointed.

•••

As Cedric drove away from the orphanage, Melanie gave him a worried glance. "Are you going to be all right?"

"I suppose. Yes, definitely." His smile seemed wistful. "I'm certain Mr. and Mrs. Abernathy will be excellent guardians."

"I'm not completely certain the Board will award Frederick's guardianship to them."

"Mr. Fletcher accepted my application, but he made it clear that the only way a single man would be allowed to take a child is if no suitable married couples apply." He inhaled deeply. "Besides which, Mr. and Mrs. Abernathy's need is greater than mine."

"I cannot argue with you." Melanie bit her lip. "Was Frederick surprised when he realized you'd come for him?"

"He was surprised and delighted. The lad threw his arms around me and wouldn't let go." Cedric swallowed hard. "In that moment, all my uncertainties disappeared."

"I'm so sorry." She paused. "Please allow me to say that I respect you immensely for offering Frederick a home." Of course, the word *respect* did not begin to convey how she really felt. "You will make a wonderful father someday."

"Thank you." He chuckled. "I would like to think so."

They drove the rest of the way home in companionable silence. Earlier that day, Melanie had intended on stopping by the vicarage to invite Priscilla to London. All things considered, however, she decided to send her friend a note instead. Undoubtedly, the Oglethorpes would not welcome outsiders until the family had made peace with one another.

When they passed Abernathy's Fine Instruments, the shop was still closed. Even if it had been open, however, she would have declined to stop. Ordering a piano could certainly wait a day or two and she wouldn't dream of bringing Cedric along. Undoubtedly his feelings about Frederick would be raw for some time to come and the last thing he needed would be to meet Mr. Abernathy face to face.

As Cedric turned into the driveway leading to Asphodel, he gave her a smile. "Since we are home early, why don't you don your gardening gown and come over to pick cherries? I'm sure Josie would love to see you."

"I would adore picking cherries." She beamed. "That will be perfectly wonderful."

••••

Friday

Melanie, Priscilla, and Genevieve stepped down from the cab and onto the pavement in front of the showroom belonging to Madame Montagna.

Priscilla's eyes widened as she gazed at the awning. "I cannot believe I'm actually going to see Madame Montagna's showroom." She glanced at Genevieve. "Thank you so much for getting married!"

Genevieve laughed. "Believe me, no one is more surprised than I am."

"We should go in, Aunt Ginny. We're already a few minutes late for our appointment."

They entered the establishment, the interior of which was a feast for the senses. Melanie inhaled the lightly scented air and let out a sigh of pleasure. "I love the smell of luxury."

Priscilla lowered her voice. "I would love it more if it weren't so expensive."

The shop manager approached. "Good morning, Mrs. Hornsby and Miss Starhope. I see you have brought a friend?"

"Good morning, Miss White." Genevieve gestured toward Priscilla. "This is Miss Oglethorpe."

"Welcome to our showroom, Miss Oglethorpe." Miss White's red hair gleamed in the light from a chandelier overhead. "We are ready for your showing, Mrs. Hornsby." She beckoned them over to a sitting area which was situated near a raised dais. "Excuse me while I summon Madame."

From her seated position, Melanie glanced around the shop as best she could. Several new items were on display from the last time she had come, and she yearned to see them more closely. Even so, she reminded herself that she had very little money of her own to purchase anything and the focus should remain on her aunt anyway. Priscilla seemed to be no less interested in the display items than Melanie was as her head swiveled to and fro.

Finally, she reached over to touch Melanie's arm. "Now I know where you get your style!"

Before she could respond, an older woman emerged from a curtained doorway in back with the showroom manager.

Melanie caught Priscilla's eye long enough to whisper, "That's Madame Montagna."

Although the modiste was clad in a simple black gown, the fabric was exquisite, and the tailoring was impossibly chic.

She glided over. "*Bon matin*, Madame Hornsby, Mademoiselle Starhope, and Mademoiselle Oglethorpe."

Genevieve stood. "*Bon matin*, Madame!"

The two women kissed each other on both cheeks.

"I have arranged a showing of wedding clothes and trousseau gowns, Madame Hornsby. As our mannequin, Mademoiselle Liberté, displays each ensemble, Mademoiselle White will record your impressions." She gestured toward the shop manager, who wielded a pad of paper and a pencil. "Shall we begin?"

For the next hour, Melanie was agog as the lovely mannequin stepped onto the dais clad in beautiful gowns and accessories fit for a marchioness. While the mannequin changed into her next ensemble, Genevieve spoke with Madame and Miss White about what she liked or didn't like about the gowns and accessories. Although Melanie tried to remain poised, she couldn't help but gasp with admiration now and again. After every gown, she glanced at Priscilla to gauge her reaction. The vicar's daughter was spellbound for the most part, although she occasionally posed questions to Madame in flawless French.

At the end of the showing, Miss Liberty emerged from the curtained doorway, clad in a dramatic wedding gown of satin and gossamer tulle. Genevieve sat up straight as the mannequin stepped onto the dais and turned a slow pirouette.

"*C'est magnifique.*" Priscilla's eyes were glued to the mannequin. "*Incroyable.*"

Melanie couldn't hold her tongue. "Aunt Ginny, you would look stunning in that gown."

"It's so different from the one I wore to marry Reginald." Genevieve's smile was slow and dreamy. "You have outdone yourself, Madame."

"*Merci.*"

Madame clapped her hands and Miss Liberty stepped down from the dais and disappeared behind the curtain.

"Madame Hornsby, if you will try on the gown, we shall discuss any alterations you would like to have." The modiste gestured toward her manager. "Please be so kind as to follow Mademoiselle White and she will assist you."

As Genevieve crossed the showroom on her way to be fitted, Madame gave Melanie and Priscilla an appraising glance. "Mademoiselles, I have two sample gowns I think would suit you very well."

Priscilla's lips parted. "I'm so sorry, Madame, but I don't believe I could afford so much as a sachet from your showroom."

"Nor could I," Melanie said. "My aunt has already spent too much money on my clothes as it is and I—"

"Did I say anything about payment?" The older woman smiled, looking for all the world like a satisfied cat. "For you, mademoiselles, the gowns are a gift. Wait here a moment so my staff can arrange a dressing room for you." She glided off.

Priscilla stared at Melanie. "Is this a joke? Surely Madame Montagna doesn't mean to give away gowns out of the goodness of her heart!"

"She doesn't. Don't you realize how much money my aunt just spent today?" Melanie laughed. "It's just good business to make the two of us happy." She paused. "Besides which, I think Madame was impressed with your ability to speak French. How did you learn?"

"When I was eight, Mama and I traveled with Papa to Algeria. He was a missionary at the time."

Melanie bit back a smile. "Well...I suppose God works in mysterious ways."

••••

August 3, 1886

Melanie held Mozart in her arms as she waited by the drawing room window. Genevieve glanced up from her latest gothic novel with an amused expression.

"They won't arrive any faster with you standing there."

"I know, but I couldn't sleep a wink last night knowing they were coming today." Melanie deposited a kiss on Mozart's head. "It's been over two months since I left Bromley."

"Are you glad you came?"

"Oh, yes!" Melanie studied her aunt a moment. "Have you and Lord Warwick decided where you are to live?"

"He's given you permission to call him Edmund."

Melanie frowned. "I know, but I'm having trouble with that. I've never socialized with a marquess before, much less been on intimate terms."

"To answer your question, Edmund has agreed to reside at Asphodel. There is plenty of room for the children and their nanny, after all."

Melanie averted her gaze. "My room would be perfect for Josie."

Genevieve blinked. "Yes, but where would you go?"

"I shall return to Bromley after the wedding." Melanie put the squirming kitten down on the carpet and the creature scampered under the sofa. "As much as I love it here, you and Lord Warwick

— Edmund — really deserve to begin your new life together with a modicum of privacy."

Her aunt set her book aside and rose. "He doesn't mind you living here. We've discussed it at length."

Melanie smiled. "I love Asphodel, to be sure, but perhaps it is more accurate to say that I wouldn't feel comfortable residing here with Lord, er, *Edmund*, after you are married. Perhaps I could come for a visit next year, after you've had the opportunity to settle in."

Genevieve frowned. "I understand, but I will miss you dreadfully until you return."

"You won't miss me as much as you might think." Melanie gave her a teasing glance. "Your new husband will be distraction enough." She winked.

Her aunt laughed. "I confess, I'm quite ready for a little *distraction*. I feel as if I've been waiting my entire adult life."

The two women embraced until the sound of carriage wheels reached their ears.

"They're here!" Melanie beamed. "I'm going outside to greet them."

Genevieve crossed toward the bell pull. "Let me alert the servants and I'll join you directly."

Blanche was the first to descend from the carriage. She squealed with delight when she saw her sister. "It's so good to see you, Melly!"

Melanie wrapped Blanche in her arms and gave her a squeeze. "I've missed you."

She moved on to her parents, who wore beaming smiles. "Mama and Papa, it seems like ages since I left Bromley."

Her father kissed her on the cheek. "It hasn't been the same without you."

Genevieve arrived with a phalanx of servants and a flurry of greetings ensued. Finally, after the footmen began unloading the luggage, she waved everyone inside.

"The maids will show you to your rooms. We're to have lunch in the conservatory at one o'clock."

Blanche grabbed Melanie by the hand and gave it a tug. "Let's go to my room so we can get caught up on our news!"

They ascended the stairs, side by side. As they passed Melanie's bedroom, Blanche stopped long enough to dart inside.

"Isn't this my room? It's gorgeous."

"It's my room, actually." Melanie stuck her thumb toward the door. "Yours is just down the hall."

Blanche unpinned her hat, shed her travel cape, and jumped onto the bed. "How glorious!"

Melanie laughed as she picked up her sister's discarded hat and cape and set them on a chair. "I think I said something quite like that when I first arrived." She perched on the bed next to her sister.

Blanche propped herself up on an elbow. "Isn't it marvelous? We're to be related to a marquess. Do you know how that will elevate our status on the marriage market?"

"I haven't thought about it, really."

"Nonsense! Of course you have." She pulled the pillow over and sank onto it. "Lord Warwick has a brother, you said. What's he like?"

Melanie felt wistful as she pictured the man in her mind. "Lord Peyton is as handsome as a pirate. I'm sure you'll find him very appealing."

Blanche's blue eyes widened. "I like the sound of that!" She giggled. "I can't wait to meet all your friends at the ball."

"They can't wait to meet you either, I'm sure."

Her sister sat up then and gave Melanie a piercing glance. "You look different."

"It's the gown." Melanie smoothed her lavender-striped skirt. "Aunt Ginny bought it for me in London."

"No, it's not that. The gown is lovely, to be sure, but you look prettier than I remember." Blanche frowned. "I confess, I'm a trifle jealous. I'm supposed to be the prettier sister."

Melanie thought her sister was speaking in jest at first, but her expression said otherwise. "I think we are both attractive after our own fashion."

"Yes, but..." Blanche gasped. "Are you in love? I've heard women who are in love are ten times prettier than before! Tell me his name, Melly. I want to know all about him. Will he be at the ball?"

"No, no, it's nothing like that."

Blanche's eyes narrowed. "If he's at the ball, I'll spot him right away."

"Don't be silly. You'll be far too busy with your own suitors to invent any for me." Melanie rose. "Come along and let me show you your bedroom. After luncheon, if you wish, we can walk around the grounds."

Blanche jumped off the bed. "I want to hear all about the orphans!"

Melanie smiled. "I'll tell you everything about the orphans, too."

Chapter Eighteen
The Ball

Melanie, Blanche, Mrs. Starhope, and Genevieve settled into the carriage as best they could considering the voluminous nature of their skirts, while Mr. Starhope was obliged to ride alongside the driver.

"Poor Papa." Melanie shook her head. "Not only is he outnumbered by four women, but he must suffer the indignity of riding out in the open."

"Hmph." Blanche tossed her head. "I think gentlemen ought to make sacrifices for ladies."

Mrs. Starhope smiled. "I'm sure your Papa is perfectly all right. Genevieve, didn't you say Prospero's Retreat is a very short drive?"

"It's a short walk, actually." Genevieve glanced out the window. "It would be inappropriate, however, to arrive at a ball on foot."

"I would force a servant to carry me, if it came to that." Blanche reached up to smooth her tresses. "Oh, why can't the horses walk faster?"

"That is probably because they are not used to carrying six people, Blanche." Melanie chuckled. "Have pity on the poor beasts."

Very shortly thereafter, they arrived in Prospero Retreat's courtyard, stepped out of the carriage, and made their way into the entrance hall. Three musicians clustered in one corner, playing delicately understated music, and the room was decorated in an abundant quantity of flowers.

As Melanie gave her wrap to a footman, movement from the gallery level caught her eye.

Young Josie was crouched down behind the balusters, watching the guests arrive. Melanie gave her a surreptitious wave and the child's face lit up with a smile.

After Melanie joined the receiving queue along with her family, she took the opportunity to straighten the tulle trim around her shoulders.

Blanche nudged her. "How do I look?"

Her sister was a vision in a white silk gown with blue grosgrain ribbon trim the color of her eyes. Her glossy fair hair was beautifully arranged, with a cascade of corkscrew curls in back, and a single white rosebud was tucked into the mass at her crown.

"You look like a fairy-tale princess." Melanie patted her cheek. "I'm very proud of you."

Blanche giggled. "I hope all the gentlemen fall in love with me...especially the ones with titles. It would be ever so nice to be addressed as Lady So-and-So."

Melanie pretended to misunderstand. "I don't think any aristocrats with the name of So-and-So will be in attendance tonight, I'm afraid."

"Oh, you!"

Genevieve, who was standing in front of Melanie, wore an off-the-shoulder satin creation in champagne silk. The woman looked radiant, with several jeweled combs drawing attention to her sable tresses.

As for Melanie, she'd chosen a stunning silk masterpiece of pewter satin. The daringly low-cut bodice was studded with tiny crystals and the skirt flared out from her tiny waistline. Her father's countenance had darkened when he had seen the provocative way her feminine curves were displayed, but fortunately her mother had shushed him before he said anything. Melanie would have ignored his criticism anyway because she could ill afford to hide her light under a bushel. Tonight, if Cedric preferred Blanche, Melanie would at least know there was nothing more she could have done.

When the queue moved forward, Melanie caught her first glimpse of Cedric. She suddenly felt as if her body was filled with sunshine and pure joy. He looked handsome in his evening clothes, naturally, but it was his mere presence that brought her happiness. And yet...she was moments away from possibly losing him forever. Melanie tried to prepare herself for the inevitable, but she knew her bravery was merely a facade.

As Genevieve presented each member of her family to Edmund and his brother, Melanie took the opportunity to give Cedric a smile. He gave her a tiny wink in return before his features returned to a polite reserve. Although she tried to gauge his reaction to Blanche, his expression gave nothing away. She, on the other hand, dipped into a low graceful curtsy before fluttering her lashes.

Once Melanie and Blanche were through the receiving line, her sister tugged her down the corridor and stopped behind a potted palm tree.

"When you said Lord Peyton was handsome, I didn't know what to expect. I'm completely and totally smitten!"

Melanie swallowed. "Yes...that's not an uncommon reaction. The girls at the orphanage could barely be nudged aside whenever they were watching Lord Peyton's choir practice."

Blanche glanced up and down the corridor, where guests were chatting in groups of two and three. "Who else are you acquainted with? I want to be introduced to every handsome gentleman here."

"I haven't seen my closest friends yet but then we haven't gone into the ballroom."

"Melanie?" Genevieve approached. "Your parents are waiting for us in the ballroom. Since Edmund will be welcoming his guests for a while longer, I'm going to introduce them to everyone I know. You and Blanche should come as well."

Melanie nodded and steered her sister toward the open double doors. As she and her family circulated around the room with Genevieve, they were finally introduced to someone Melanie had not yet met.

"Lord Shearling, may I present my brother and his wife, Mr. and Mrs. Starhope, and my two nieces, Miss Melanie Starhope and Miss Blanche Starhope."

Since Priscilla had mentioned the man's name before, Melanie wished to know him better. The fellow was boyishly attractive more than handsome, but he did have a winsome manner. Unfortunately, his attention riveted instantly onto Blanche and Melanie's heart sank. When Priscilla arrived, she would be sorely disappointed.

Melanie glanced around and spotted Mr. Chastain across the room, chatting with Mr. Steed. She waited until Lord Shearling paused to take a breath before she could extricate herself from the conversation. "Forgive me, but I see one of my friends. Please excuse me." She hastened off.

As she approached, Mr. Chastain broke off his conversation with Mr. Steed and gaped.

"Merciful heavens." He clutched his chest. "Miss Starhope, you are the loveliest creature I ever beheld."

Melanie laughed as he made a ritual of bringing her hand to his lips. "Mr. Chastain, you have a way of ingratiating yourself into my heart." She glanced at Mr. Steed. "How are you and Mrs. Steed settling in with your new wards?"

He beamed. "Thank you for asking, Miss Starhope. The house has come alive again, it seems."

"I couldn't be more delighted."

Mr. Steed bowed. "If you don't mind, I was just on my way to the smoking room." He ambled off, leaving Mr. Chastain and Melanie alone.

He gave her a sidelong glance. "All of Ledbury has absconded with our children like the Pied Piper and we are left to cling to one another. We shall just have to pour balm into each other's wounded bosoms." His gaze flickered to her bodice, and he lifted one eyebrow. "Some bosoms are less wounded than others."

"Oh, stop it!" She laughed. "Don't let Papa catch you joking around in that fashion. He is apt to take you more seriously than you wish."

In the next moment, Mr. Chastain's gaze slid past Melanie and his expression turned to one of awestruck admiration. His lips parted and he murmured, "She's *beautiful*."

Something twisted in Melanie's midsection. She had known Blanche would be admired, but she hadn't thought Mr. Chastain would be so obviously transported by her looks as he seemed to be. She might not be in love with him, but his unexpected defection disappointed her, nevertheless.

Melanie swallowed the lump in her throat. "Please allow me to introduce you to my sister, sir. I'm sure she would be delighted to meet you."

Mr. Chastain appeared not to have heard her. As he continued to stare, Melanie turned to follow his gaze. Priscilla had entered the ballroom, clad in the ball gown Madame Montagna had given her. The low-cut satin dress was white with a pattern of red roses, and the underskirt was fashioned of lettuce-edged tulle. Priscilla's golden tresses were arranged in a lovely twist, with a quantity of curls pulled forward over one shoulder.

Melanie gave Mr. Chastain a knowing glance. "If you like what you see, woo her before some other gentleman has the chance."

When he finally tore his gaze away from Priscilla, a wave of guilt passed over his countenance. "I...well, that is to say...you'll always be my first love, Miss Starhope."

"We shall always remain the very best of friends, Mr. Chastain. Nothing can ever change that."

A sweet smile accompanied the twinkle in his eye, and he hurried off toward the object of his affection. As Melanie turned to watch his progress, she noticed Lord Shearling was striding toward Priscilla at the same time. Blanche was also following Lord Shearling's progress with a frown.

Time seemed to slow as Cedric entered the ballroom and crossed toward her sister. He reached for her dance card with the wicked smile that had always weakened Melanie's knees. After he scribbled his name on her dance card several times, he bent closer to whisper something in her ear and then he and Blanche left the ballroom together.

They made a striking couple.

Time sped up again. The orchestra was setting up in the corner, tuning their instruments and making a cacophony of noise. The ballroom had grown crowded and she couldn't breathe. She fixed a pleasant smile on her face, left the ballroom, and strode down the corridor. Moments later, she burst through the doors and found herself on the empty patio overlooking the garden.

She gripped the railing, closed her eyes, and drew in night air as deeply as she could. Over and over again, she filled her lungs with air until she finally grew calm. She'd tried to anticipate the inevitable but however much she had prepared herself for the moment Cedric chose Blanche, she could not have imagined the unbearable pain. All the other times she'd been overlooked or dismissed by lesser mortals meant nothing when compared to watching that splendid gentleman be captivated by her sister.

Melanie opened her eyes and stared at the rising crescent moon, which blurred and swam as the tears stung the backs of her eyelids. When she heard someone walk out onto the patio, she fought to regain her poise. It wouldn't do for anyone to see her crying, or they might leap to exactly the right conclusion.

"Are you all right?"

She nearly jumped out of her skin at the sound of Cedric's voice. Although she responded, "Yes, of course," she didn't trust herself to turn around. He would know instantly she was upset and wonder why. "I'm just getting a little fresh air."

Cedric came to lean against the railing. "I'm sorry."

Her laughter sounded hollow, even to her own ears. "I can't imagine why. You haven't done anything to be sorry for — at least not lately."

"I'm talking about Chastain and Miss Oglethorpe. I imagine that was a bit of a blow."

"You're quite wrong if you imagine I'm upset about that. In fact, I'm delighted."

"Liar." Cedric pulled her into his warm embrace and cradled her in his arms. "Perhaps it's just a passing fancy and Chastain will be back by your side soon."

His tone was soothing, but it had the opposite effect. How could the man be so dense?

Melanie pushed him away. "If he and Priscilla fall in love, I will be overjoyed."

"If that's the case, why are your eyes so red?"

She turned away. "I'm happy, that's all."

"Oh." Cedric frowned. "I find that hard to believe."

Melanie finally met his gaze. "You've *always* had the wrong idea about Mr. Chastain and me. I love him quite dearly, to be sure, but as the brother I never had."

A peculiar expression crossed his countenance. "I see." He paused. "Your sister is very pretty, I must say."

"Yes. She is the jewel in our family crown." Melanie swallowed. "We are all very proud of her."

"She's not the only jewel in the Starhope family, nor the brightest."

"Yes, my aunt is an incredible beauty as well."

"I'm talking about you, Melanie." Cedric peered at her. "You're physically beautiful, to be sure, but there's so much more to you than that. Your strength of character is the stuff of legends, and your passion is magnetic. I suppose that's why I was drawn to you from the very beginning."

Melanie shook her head in confusion. "What are you talking about? You *despised* me from the very beginning."

"I believe I was merely shocked that you found me repulsive."

"I never found you repulsive!"

He bore down on her. "Admit it! Your insults were legion!"

"That's because you're the most attractive man I've ever met!" As soon as the words left her lips, Melanie felt like clapping her hands over her mouth. The most she could do is try to recover some of her wounded pride. "N-Not that it matters."

Cedric stepped toward her with a gleam in his eye. "You're in love with me."

She retreated. "Don't be silly."

He continued to move toward her, as graceful as a panther. "You've been in love with me all along."

"Not at all." Melanie stumbled backward until the railing on the balcony arrested her progress. "Your vanity wishes it to be so."

Cedric rested his hands on the railing on either side of her body. "I wish it to be so because I'm hopelessly in love with you."

The angular planes of his face were illuminated by the crescent moon overhead and her body trembled with emotion.

"Show me."

Her whisper hung in the air for several heartbeats before her drew her into his arms. His tender kisses traveled from her lips, down the tender skin of her neck, and across her décolletage. Her breath caught in her throat as her blood turned molten and she met his ardor with unbridled passion of her own.

Finally, he pulled back long enough to murmur, "Do you believe me now or must I go on?"

"Cedric..." The temptation was too great. "I-I'm not quite convinced, I'm afraid."

"Excellent."

His kisses grew deeper and more intense until she felt as if she would be burned to a crisp. Only the sound of the orchestra playing the opening Promenade brought her to her senses.

"I'm convinced."

"That's too bad." Cedric stepped back and straightened his clothes. "I hope I've compromised you sufficiently."

Melanie peered at him. "Not nearly enough. Why do you ask?"

"So that your father won't refuse his permission for us to marry."

"Oh, Cedric." She threw her arms around him, buoyed by more joy than she thought humanly possible. "I love you so very completely that I would elope with you this very moment."

His embrace tightened. "Don't give me any ideas, Melanie. I'm barely holding myself in check as it is."

Suddenly, she pushed him back. "Wait a moment...why were you flirting with Blanche in the ballroom a few minutes ago?"

His expression grew puzzled and then he threw back his head and laughed. "Flirting, do you call it? I happened to notice Lord Shearling throwing her over for Miss Oglethorpe. She looked so forlorn, I signed her dance card and offered to introduce her to an old friend of mine who just arrived from Spain."

Melanie felt foolish. "Oh."

He caressed her cheek. "As much as I respect your sister, I'm not attracted to her looks. I made that mistake once before and I bitterly regret wasting all these years in resentment. Fortunately, you knocked some sense into my head."

Her eyes narrowed. "All right, but why were you so harsh toward me that day at tea?"

Cedric grinned. "I do apologize for that, but I didn't trust my brother the marquess not to compete with me for your affections."

Melanie looked at him askance. "As much as I respect your brother, I'm not attracted to his title."

"I'm glad we've come to an understanding, then." He offered her his arm. "Shall we join the ball?"

Her spine straightened. "Blazes! I was so upset, I forgot to get anyone to sign my dance card."

"It won't stay blank for long. You're the most beautiful young woman in the room."

Melanie glanced up at him. "My sister said women who are in love are ten times prettier than before." She squeezed his arm. "I'm so completely in love with you, Cedric, I must look like an angel."

"You do." His expression became humble. "And that makes me the luckiest man on Earth."

••••

Very shortly after midnight, many of the older guests took their leave — including Mr. and Mrs. Starhope. As Melanie's father shook Cedric's hand, he gave him an approving nod. "I've always had an interest in the guitar, sir. Perhaps, one day, you might give me a lesson or two."

Cedric beamed. "All things considered, I'll be happy to give you as many lessons as you wish."

Mr. Starhope chuckled. "I look forward to having you as a son-in-law." He glanced at Genevieve. "I'll send the carriage back for you and the girls."

Edmund shook his head. "That's not necessary, Mr. Starhope. Your family will have the use of our carriage anytime they wish to depart."

Melanie gave her parents a hug and they made their way from the house. Dawn was glimmering over the horizon when she, Genevieve, Blanche, and Priscilla climbed into the Peyton family carriage, waved good-bye to Edmund, Cedric, and Mr. Chastain, and began the short drive home.

"Thank you for allowing me to spend the night, Mrs. Hornsby." Priscilla gave her a tired smile. "Otherwise, I would have had to leave far too early."

"It's my pleasure." Genevieve stifled a yawn. "Our housekeeper will furnish you a spare toothbrush."

"And I'll lend you a nightgown." Melanie bit back a yawn of her own. "Only you'll have to share my room. Between Blanche and my parents, we have a full house."

"I believe we have a spare cot somewhere." Genevieve's eyes slid closed. "We'll manage."

"I'm so tired, I could sleep on the floor." Priscilla laughed.

Blanche stared out the window, uncharacteristically quiet.

Melanie nudged her sister with her foot. "Did you have a good time?"

"Oh, yes, it was splendid." Her expression was animated. "I shall be able to tell all my friends that I danced until dawn. Only..." her voice trailed off.

Priscilla cocked her head. "Only what?"

"For the first time in my life, I wasn't the center of attention."

Genevieve opened her eyes.

Blanche continued. "The three of you are pretty, accomplished, and well-read, whereas I'm merely beautiful. No gentleman tonight sought out my company for more than a few minutes." She gestured with her hands. "I bored them silly."

Genevieve leaned forward. "I don't know that that's true, but if it is, what do you intend to do about it?"

"I will improve myself." Blanche shrugged. "I'll read books and resume my piano lessons. Perhaps I'll even devote myself to a good cause." Her lips flattened. "I refuse to be overlooked!"

Melanie, Genevieve, and Priscilla exchanged a knowing glance.

"Hear, hear." Melanie took Blanche's hand and gave it a squeeze. "All women deserve to be dazzling."

Blanche rested her head on Melanie's shoulder. "Yes," she yawned, "...they do."

••••

September

Everybody in the county had been invited to the wedding breakfast, it seemed. In stark contrast to the sophisticated wedding breakfast held in honor of the Marquess and Marchioness of Warwick, both Melanie and Cedric had invited every former orphan and their guardians, Mrs. Wheeler, the former staff at Ledbury Country Home for Children, and every merchant who had helped display children's portraits. Even Ethan and Mrs. Pendergast were there. As guests ate food at tables set up in the conservatory, children ran to and fro across the grounds, playing with pinwheels and other small toys the newlyweds had provided for their entertainment. Priscilla and Mr. Chastain had stopped by the day before, to set up a game of horseshoes and a game of croquet.

After the cake had been served, Melanie and Cedric took a stroll through the garden, hand in hand. They passed Blanche and Lord Shearling on another path, walking together arm in arm. Blanche's voice carried as she carried on a conversation.

"I understand a German chap by the name of Benz has been granted a patent for a horseless carriage. Do you think such things will ever become popular in England?"

Lord Shearling chuckled. "Not unless Her Majesty approves of them."

"You'd look awfully smart behind the wheel, I think."

Melanie and Cedric exchanged an amused glance.

"How did your sister learn about horseless carriages?" he murmured.

"She's taken to reading the newspaper these days. Blanche is determined to improve herself."

"I imagine she's trying compete with her brilliant elder sister." He gave her a beaming grin. "Let's go visit our gooseberry shrub."

"Oh, yes. Let's."

They headed across the lawn, where Mr. and Mrs. Abernathy were playing horseshoes with Frederick. Melanie waved to the new family.

"It's wonderful to see the Abernathys so happy." Melanie squeezed Cedric's hand. "I don't know how Mrs. Abernathy did it, but she finally tamed Frederick's cowlick."

"She strikes me as a woman who is not to be gainsaid by a tuft of wayward hair."

When Melanie spotted the gooseberry shrub, she let out a gasp of pleasure. "Look how it's thriving!"

"This is our first collaboration." Cedric reached out to touch one of the leaves. "I expect the shrub will even bear fruit the year after next."

"I'm looking forward to many more collaborations with you." Melanie gave her husband a slow smile. "Beginning with our wedding night."

His face was suddenly suffused with crimson. "Lady Peyton, you've made me blush."

"Excellent." Melanie slipped her arms around his waist and drew him into an endless, passionate kiss.

THE END

Note From the Author

Although *The Prettier Sister* is not in the Mannequin Series, it has a shared world. That is to say, there are crossover characters that appear in both *The Prettier Sister* and the Mannequin Series — particularly *The Star-Crossed Seamstress*.

If you have not already read the Mannequin Series, here are the titles published as of this writing:

The Mannequin (Book One)
Grace Unmasked (Book Two)
The Star-Crossed Seamstress (Book Three)
A Chance of Rayne (Book Four)
The Substitute (Book Five)

A Personal Request
From the Author

I love to write, but I can't do it without *you*. If you enjoyed *The Prettier Sister*, would you consider leaving a review? Not only would I like to hear your thoughts, but also your review is very helpful to other readers. Thank you in advance!

Suzanne G. Rogers

About the Author

Originally from Southern California, Suzanne G. Rogers currently resides in beautiful Savannah, Georgia on an island populated by exotic birds, deer, turtles, otters, and gators.

For notification of freebies, sales, and new releases, sign up here:
https://tinyurl.com/y4nya7pb

Visit her historical romance blog:
http://suzannegrogers.com

Visit her fantasy blog:
https://childofyden.wordpress.com

Find her on Facebook at:
https://www.facebook.com/SuzanneGRogers

Follow her on Gab:
https://gab.com/Suzanne_G_Rogers

Historical Romance Titles

*Available in audiobook format

Fantasy Titles

<u>The Yden Series</u>
The Last Great Wizard of Yden (Book One)
Dragon Clan of Yden (Book Two)
Secrets of Yden (Book Three)
Kira (Prequel to the Yden Trilogy)

<u>Standalone Titles</u>
Dani & the Immortals
The Dragon Rider's Daughter*
Clash of Wills
Tournament of Chance: Dragon Rebel
Magical Misperception
Whimsical Tendencies*
Something Wicked in L.A.
Royal Promenade

*Available in audiobook format

Printed in Great Britain
by Amazon

12909955R00200